# GENETIC IMPERFECTIONS
## A Novel

by

Steve Hadden

TELEMACHUS PRESS

Cover Designed by Telemachus Press, LLC

Cover Art:
Copyright © Thinkstock/104710851/Cancer Cell/iStockphoto
Copyright © Thinkstock/108511342/DNA blue background with formulas/iStockphoto
Copyright © Thinkstock/133985128/rear view one lovers couple walking holding hands/iStockphoto

Edited by Winslow Eliot
http://www.winsloweliot.com

Published by Telemachus Press, LLC
http://www.telemachuspress.com

Visit the author website
http://www.stevehadden.com

ISBN 978-1-938135-06-4 (eBook)
ISBN 978-1-938135-07-1 (paperback)

Version 2021.07.20

# Acknowledgements

This book would not be possible without the support and hard work of my wife, CJ. She reads every page and keeps me going on the days when pages are hard to come by. Special thanks to the team at Telemachus Press for another great job, especially Steve Himes, Steve Jackson and Johnny, who brings my covers to life. Thanks to Winslow Eliot, again, for her wonderful editing, advice and perspective. I also appreciate the great work by Doug Wagner of The Editorial Department who edited the updated version of this book.

# Also by Steve Hadden

# GENETIC IMPERFECTIONS
## A Novel

# PROLOGUE

*November 8, 1996*

CONNOR XAVIER WELLINGTON'S young life wasn't supposed to end this way. There was supposed to be a breakthrough—a dramatic-last minute cure produced by his father's heroic three-year effort at Rexsen Labs. But David Wellington knew he'd failed. There would be no cure, no last-minute miracle, only suffering and guilt.

The decision to move Connor into Saint Michael's Hospice in Irvine was his first admission of failure to his son. David sat anchored next to his wife in the dim glow of the single fluorescent light above the bed. Although they'd been at their eight-year-old son's bedside every minute for the past week, he could barely recognize him. Pale and melting into the white sheets, Connor's blue eyes peeked from underneath his eyelids as the morphine drip did its work and masked the pain of the multiple infections and failing organs, courtesy of the genetic imperfection that prevented his stem cells from developing into healthy blood. His thick brown hair was gone and replaced with a Dodger's bandanna. He hugged his baseball glove while his mother, Linda, stroked the bony outline of his legs. David forced a smile and did his best to hide what they all knew was about to happen. Connor's eyes lifted for a moment.

"Daddy, are you still working on my medicine?"

i

The question cut through David's heart. He glanced at the green numbers on the monitor counting down his son's last heartbeats and reached deep for another smile. He rested his hand on his son's head.

"Yes, sport. We are still working on it."

David looked at Linda and detected no evidence of blame. He'd quit his job at the investment bank in New York, moved the family to Newport Beach and dumped his seven-figure bonus into a fledgling biotech firm in hopes of finding a cure. But the director of research had delivered the bad news a week earlier. Without detailed mapping of the human genome, it was like looking for a needle in a haystack. Despite three years of research, testing and prayer, David could do nothing to stop his young son's killer. He'd failed, and God didn't care.

Connor sucked in a deep breath and sighed. "That's good, Daddy."

Connor closed his eyes and David heard the rhythm of the monitor slow. He reached for his son's hand. Connor's skin was still soft, but the warmth was fading. David heard Linda sob and she rose next to David, leaned in and kissed her son's forehead. David squinted to force the tears back into his eyes. "No, no, *no!*" he begged through his clenched teeth. The monitor stopped and then warbled a continuous tone that David would never forget. Connor Xavier Wellington, the boy who was going to play third base for the Dodgers, was gone. The nurse quietly slipped in and shut down the monitor. Linda hugged her son and wailed. David wiped his eyes, stood and stared at Connor's limp body, and then grabbed the glove at his son's side and dropped it into the trash can on his way out the door.

# CHAPTER 1

*Fifteen years later*

DAVID WELLINGTON FOUND it hard to believe an imperfection could be so profitable. He didn't tolerate them in his minions, hated them in his women and acted as if he had none himself. After fifteen years of excelling at corporate politics, and pretending he cared about his diseased and dying customers, the payoff of his life was at hand.

He celebrated, sipping his Hennessy X.O from a Waterford crystal glass. His Gulfstream V, Rexsen Lab's newest corporate jet, streaked southeast from San Francisco to Newport Beach twenty-nine thousand feet above the chilly Pacific. Equipped with soft leather chairs, inlaid wood cabinetry, and state-of-the-art LCD screens, it surrounded him with the luxury he expected.

The forty-five-year-old CEO had just completed the last of the road shows promoting the most talked-about initial public offering Wall Street would launch this year. The FDA was on the verge of approving his company's first gene therapy treatment for leukemia. The institutional investors had been duly impressed with Wellington's plans and the solid backing of the company's seventy-five-year-old founder, Adam Rexsen, who slept peacefully in the seat across the aisle.

Rexsen Labs would go public within two weeks, and David Wellington would become Newport Beach's newest billionaire.

As Wellington tilted the glass and anticipated the warm burn of the last sip of liquor, he felt the plane shudder and dive to the left. The crystal snifter was ripped from his hand as a blast roared through the cabin. Instinctively, he grabbed the leather armrests, locked his arms and braced himself. A yellow oxygen mask fell from the headliner and bounced wildly in front of his face. Paralyzed, his terror refused to allow him to let go and grab the mask. He pushed back hard on the armrests and fought the invisible force trying to rip him out of the seat.

He assessed the situation instantly, and the conclusion echoed in his head.

*I'm going to die.*

He struggled to get a breath as smoke filled the cabin. The jet's nose plunged steeper into the dive. For the first time since a genetic imperfection took the life of his son, he thought of his soul and its ultimate keeper.

Images flashed through his mind. Hell—Sister Theresa had described it as eternal flames and agony. "Heaven or hell—it's your choice," the nun had said.

For the past fifteen years he'd chosen money. It was how he kept score. Money was his drug of choice, and he was addicted. Suddenly, he understood the nun's warning. He'd already made his choice.

He felt the jet's fuselage start to vibrate. The black smoke thickened. His inner voice summed up the fruits of his time on earth.

*I am selfish, greedy, and alone.*

He knew the voice; it was the one he never listened to. He tried to ignore it, but it was strong and uncontrollable. Expensive leather briefcases and crystal glassware smashed into the bulkhead. He looked to the right at the old man who wagged his head in disbelief.

Adam Rexsen, the founder of Rexsen Labs, was about to die, but *he* had dedicated his life to finding a cure for cancer. *His* life had served a purpose—he'd said so just minutes ago. His wealth was simply a by-product. At the time, Wellington pitied the old man and thought the world had passed him by. Panicking, he now wished he'd listened to his mentor years earlier.

*Purpose! What's my life's purpose? Shit, it's too soon, too soon!*

Wellington had seen no purpose in his life, at least not since he'd stood by helplessly and watched Connor wither away. His son's disease was the reason he'd started with Rexsen. He had left his lucrative future as an investment banker and signed on with Rexsen and a team of scientists who were focused on a genetic cure for cancer. He'd decided he'd dedicate his life to finding the sinister imperfections in the human genome that caused so much pain and heartache. But despite being a brilliant businessman with a Harvard MBA who'd built Rexsen into the leader in genetic oncology research, he could do nothing to stop his son's killer. After three years of research, testing, and prayer, Connor died. God abandoned him in his time of need, he'd concluded, so he'd decided to return the favor. From that point forward, his only purpose in life was to use Rexsen to fill the hole in his heart with money and distract his mind from the pain with self-indulgent behavior.

Now as he faced death, an avalanche of guilt and regret for the life he'd lived engulfed him. He struggled to look aft at Jeff Reese. Minutes ago, Reese had said he was grateful not to have to fly commercially from San Francisco with the peons. Now Wellington could barely see him through the smoke as Reese fumbled with a family photograph taken from his wallet. The most money-hungry man he knew, who'd just presented the medical breakthrough of the century to the most powerful investment bankers and investors in San Francisco, stared at the picture.

Fifteen years ago, Wellington had lost his chance at a happy family. After his son's death, his marriage broke apart. Wellington had given up—sold out. His current wife was the founder's daughter and nothing more than a good career move—a means to more money.

He glanced at Reese again. Reese cried and clutched the picture. Wellington cried for himself.

*I miss my son! God, why did you take my son!*

He hadn't invoked God's help in fifteen years. Now his name was attached to every thought he had. His body was crushed into the seat as the nose of the jet lifted.

"Multiple system failure. Can't make Vandenberg. Prepare to ditch. Prepare to ditch!" the pilot screamed over the cabin's speakers.

*Please, God, it's too soon, too soon!*

He choked as the thick black smoke burned his lungs. He was smothered with the smell of burning oil and rubber.

"Brace for impact! Brace for impact!" the co-pilot squawked.

"Oh, God!" he screamed.

Wellington was driven into the bulkhead face first. His ears throbbed from the roar, and he gagged on several broken teeth. The whole cabin tumbled: the ceiling, the window, the floor and the ceiling, again and again. Still belted in his captain's chair, Wellington's face smashed against a bloody stump of jagged flesh and bone dangling between Adam Rexsen's shoulders.

He felt a sharp pain rip through his chest. Still tumbling, he smelled jet fuel and felt searing heat as the pain and his vision began to fade. Then the crush of seawater overwhelmed him. He tasted blood and salt water and sank in the darkness. He considered surrendering his pointless existence, but something inside him refused to give up. Even *his* life seemed too precious.

*Light—there's light! Swim! Don't breathe! Swim to the light!*

He flailed and fought toward the light. The closer it got the harder he struggled. His lungs were still burning and about to explode. He bobbed to the surface and gasped for breath. Burning jet fuel covered the water behind him. Everything seemed fuzzy, as if in a dream.

A piece of cherrywood floated past. Fabric, liquor bottles, pieces of soundproofing foam, and oil surrounded him. Suddenly he felt cold, freezing cold. The frigid salt water sloshed into his mouth and burned his bleeding gums. He coughed up the water and a few teeth.

A white mist fogged his vision. He couldn't stay conscious much longer. His eyes were swelling shut. He spotted something yellow just off his right shoulder as it surfaced in the rush of bubbles coming from below. He remembered the safety briefing.

*The raft! Reese must have opened the raft before impact.*

His arms burned when he reached for the raft. He felt the slippery, cold rubberized canvas. All his pain faded. There was no noise. The bitter taste of salt water mixed with blood and jet fuel disappeared. Exhausted, he began to give up. There was no point in continuing to fight it; his pointless life wasn't worth it. He surrendered to death's grip, and in a strange way, it warmed him. His vision narrowed to a small hole surrounded by white light, and then nothing but his inner voice's final condemnation.

*Heaven or hell? Probably hell.*

# CHAPTER 2

IT WAS FRIDAY, just before 4 p.m., and Royce Brayton, the self-absorbed thirty-eight-year-old vice president, perched on his throne in his corner office atop the Rexsen Labs headquarters building in Newport Beach. The crown jewel of the Rexsen Labs campus was tucked in among the lush palms and evergreen shrubbery of Newport's most exclusive corporate neighborhood. The four-story structure was covered in imported white Italian marble and overlooked Newport Harbor to the west and the mud flats of Newport's Back Bay to the east.

Inside, marble columns accented the mahogany-paneled walls. Rich hardwood executive desks, imported Persian rugs, upholstered sofas, wingback chairs and antiques adorned the executive suites. A collection of western art, including the works of Remington and Russell, were displayed proudly on the walls. The interior of all of the executive suites subtly reflected the founder's class, warmth, and wealth—all the suites except Royce Brayton's.

He'd personally redecorated his office upon his arrival. The shiny ebony granite floor led to his chrome-and-glass desk centered in the room. The walls were covered with photographs of Brayton with political figures, movie stars, and a parade of the last decade's Wall Street cover boys. He'd intentionally disposed of the side chairs for his desk and insisted on the largest high-back leather chair the Rexsen decorator could find. He was the most important thing in the room, and no one was worthy of sitting in his office and taking up his precious time.

"Mr. Brayton, it's time for the meeting," his silver-haired secretary said as she entered.

Brayton refused to look at her. He rarely did. She turned and quietly retreated to her desk. Once certain she was gone, he checked his watch. The meeting had not been scheduled until that morning, and Brayton knew that meant bad news. No one scheduled a meeting with the vice president Friday afternoon on a beautiful summer day in Newport Beach unless there was bad news to deliver. He was ready to head to Monterey for the board meeting this weekend, and now was not the time for a last-minute problem. Billions of dollars were at stake with the successful initial public offering of Rexsen Laboratories, and he'd do anything to see there was no bad news, especially involving CGT, the company's first-generation customized gene therapy treatment targeted for FDA approval next week. He knew the success of the IPO was riding on its approval—and he'd bet his life on a successful offering.

Brayton stared at the folder on his desk. The latest figures showed his restricted shares would be worth half a billion dollars after the successful IPO and would approach $1 billion with the clandestine backroom deal he had cut with one of the biggest pharmaceutical companies in the world. He'd clear his mountain of debt and have plenty left over. He'd be on the cover of every business periodical in the country. Surely that old bastard of a father rotting in Lompoc Correctional Institution would hear about it. After all, his father had gotten him into this mess. He dropped the folder into a drawer and locked it. Then he walked out of his office, stopped at the secretary's desk, and grabbed the single sheet of paper she held out for him.

"Where's the meeting?" he said, scanning the document.

"It's in the private conference room."

Brayton's jaw stiffened and he poked his finger into the page. "I know Penn, but who is this Tori Clarke?"

"She's a researcher. She's been working in the genetics division for about three years now."

Brayton ignored her and turned away. "Make sure my car is ready to go when I get back. It won't take long." Brayton marched out of the suite.

He wanted to be assured the biggest deal of his career was on track. He knew this deal was a winner, and he needed to win big. Internal estimates for annual earnings from the drug topped $1.7 billion.

After extensive negotiations, Brayton had joined Rexsen Laboratories six months ago. While the company was controlled by Adam Rexsen, his son, Prescott, had persuaded his father to hire Brayton to help take the company public—but only if Brayton remained vice president through the IPO and then cashed out. Adam had made it quite clear he didn't want his life's work to be in the hands of anyone besides David Wellington. The old man frequently lectured Brayton and Prescott that his purpose was to save lives, not make ungodly profits. But Prescott Rexsen and Royce Brayton had other plans for Adam Rexsen's company.

Brayton entered the adjacent conference room and slammed the door. The mahogany sliding panels on the front wall had already been opened and revealed a state-of-the-art projection screen. Benjamin Penn, head of the genetics division, and an attractive young woman with long dark brown hair pulled neatly into a ponytail stood at the front of the room and whispered.

"Afternoon, Benjamin," Brayton said.

Penn abruptly stopped whispering, and his eyes, magnified by his thick glasses, froze on Brayton like prey about to be eaten. The pale, thin man scurried around the table to greet him.

"Good afternoon, Mr. Brayton."

Brayton reluctantly shook Penn's quivering hand, and expecting an introduction, he smiled at the attractive young woman. Penn obliged.

"Mr. Brayton, this is Tori Clarke. I don't think you've met."

The young woman, who appeared to be in her late twenties, stood and shook his hand. She was tall and lanky with the firm grip of a former college athlete, probably basketball. Her blue eyes were partially concealed by a pair of black-rimmed glasses. She lowered her head to avoid Brayton's scowl. Brayton took the opportunity to glance at her breasts.

"Pleased to meet you, Mr. Brayton," she said.

Brayton had no time for either one of them. He viewed Penn as weak. Brayton hated wimps, regardless of how smart they were, and he was only interested in women who slept with him. This one wasn't his type.

"Let's get going," he said as he dropped into the seat closest to the screen. "What's the subject?"

He swiveled in the chair at the front of the conference table, turned his back to the pair, folded his arms and waited for someone to step to the front of the room.

Benjamin Penn stepped forward.

"Mr. Brayton, the CGT team has made another breakthrough." His hands shook and his voice warbled. His eyes never left the papers rattling in his hands.

"Ms. Clarke has developed a new method for genetic profiling using microarrays. It will allow for the rapid pinpointing of genetic flaws that are the precursors to cancers."

So far so good. A new discovery would only enhance the value of the company. He settled back into his leather chair and relaxed a bit. Maybe this wasn't bad news.

Penn explained that the research team, headed by Ms. Clarke, had used the DNA samples from the phase three clinical trials for CGT to test the new procedure. Penn stopped and shuffled the papers in his hands. Brayton impatiently tapped his pen on the conference table. Penn fidgeted, obviously searching for the right words. Brayton leaned forward and scowled in anticipation of bad news. He always knew when it was coming.

Penn looked up from his papers and blurted, "That's when we found the potential problem. Ms. Clarke is here to explain it."

Penn scurried to his seat. It was just like him to leave the bad news to anyone but him. Brayton considered him a wimp, but among his peers, Penn was regarded as a top geneticist.

Tori strode confidently to the front of the room. Brayton eyed her long smooth legs. She picked up the remote control and advanced the Power Point presentation to the first slide. Before the young researcher could speak, Brayton interrupted.

"Ms. Clarke, you can get right to the bottom line here. What's the problem?"

She glanced at Penn, who nodded and immediately returned to fiddling with his papers.

"Well, Mr. Brayton, the process is a great new discovery that will allow the CGT treatment to be even more effective. But we need to make a change. You see, with this technology we can see mutations expressed in the human genome that enable us to predict the development of different forms of cancer well in advance of any symptoms."

Brayton slammed his fist into the table. Tori jumped.

"Damn it! I said what's the problem."

Tori took a deep breath, removed her glasses, and locked eyes with Brayton. "The people from the CGT group showed cancer precursors they didn't have when the trials started."

"Wait a minute," Brayton bellowed, "CGT cures cancer by repairing defective genes. Our trials prove that, and the FDA is approving the treatment on that basis."

"That's still true, sir. But this discovery enhances our ability to identify the genetic expression profiles in each person's DNA with much greater precision. Until now, we couldn't detect the very early precursors to cancer at the molecular level. Now we can, and the microarrays I ran show CGT repairs the damaged proteins within the targeted genes. However, in many of the DNA samples we tested, the treatment also damaged proteins at another chromosomal location, and that expression profile is consistent with the early precursors to pancreatic cancer. We'll have to rerun the trials, using this new detection process, to see how serious and widespread the problem is."

Brayton clenched his jaw. CGT had already been through the pipeline with the FDA. They'd successfully guided CGT through the clinical trials and the New Drug Application process without any hitches. The division director of the FDA had conducted his review and all questions raised had been addressed. The director would sign the approval action letter early next week, allowing Rexsen to market the treatment. Rexsen had invested $300 million to date in CGT, and the IPO launch date was eleven days away. The underwriters and institutional investors had been sufficiently impressed with the road show where he'd personally presented the prospectus with Wellington and old man Rexsen.

He was well aware that the last presentation had been held in San Francisco this afternoon. As far as he was concerned, the train had left the station and there was no turning back. Going back to clinical trials now would destroy the entire IPO. He needed to deal with this quickly but smoothly. He drew in a deep breath and exhaled.

"Wonderful work, Ms. Clarke. Your breakthrough with these new microarrays will add even more value to this company. It's the kind of technical leadership we're looking for." Brayton paused. Clarke seemed to be puzzled but adequately pleased with the praise. After all, Brayton rarely gave it. "Now"—he pointed at Penn—"Benjamin, I want you to get the data and secure it. I'm placing a call to one of the labs we contract with to accelerate this work. Of course, Ms. Clarke, they'll confirm your results, and we'll jump right on the review of CGT."

Penn nodded the whole time Brayton was speaking.

"We'll get right on it, sir," Penn said. He gathered the folders in front of him and ushered Tori out the door.

The door clicked shut, and Brayton shoved himself away from the table.

"Son of a bitch!"

This was a problem, a big one. Less than a week from FDA approval and these assholes were about to screw it up. He wouldn't let that happen. Hell, he couldn't let it happen. The formula was simple: no FDA approval, no IPO; no IPO, no money; no money and those he owed would come to collect. And he was certain he'd pay with his life. He knew he'd have to find a way to make this problem disappear—fast—or *he* would be the one who disappeared.

# CHAPTER 3

IT WAS 4:45 P.M. on Friday and Royce Brayton stormed past his secretary's desk, oblivious to her warning that Prescott Rexsen had just slithered into his office. The meeting with Clarke and Penn sickened him. He understood that to win on Wall Street you need three things: a great product, a great plan, and the ability to beat that plan every quarter. In just one fifteen-minute meeting, he'd heard a problem that could destroy all three.

He knew Rexsen Labs had bet its future on CGT, and with eleven days to the finish line, the biggest genetic breakthrough of the century had an imperfection. In many of the patients it cured of leukemia, it planted another genetic flaw that only Clarke's new technology could see. That flaw in the human genome would direct the molecules in the patient's cells to begin a chain reaction that would end in deadly pancreatic cancer. He was certain that was more than enough for the FDA to deny approval for the treatment. And if CGT failed, the IPO would fail. He'd have no payday, and the collateral for the note coming due was his life.

Brayton slammed his folio on the desk and froze at the sight of Prescott. He was a thin bony man with rounded shoulders, greasy, thin black hair, no chin, and a long nose—a man who thought his family's wealth diminished the need for good hygiene. While only in his early thirties, he looked fifty. Brayton thought he looked like a sewer rat.

"What can I do for you, Prescott?" Brayton groused.

Prescott stared at the view of Newport's Back Bay. When the tide was in, it was a shimmering estuary. But the tide was out and it exposed the mucky mud flats. He twisted around and pointed his craggy finger at Brayton. "I want you to tell me we'll have control within the week. That's what I hired you for."

Brayton ignored the threatening gesture and moved to his chair behind the desk. "Everything is on plan. You have nothing to worry about." Brayton flipped through the stack of messages in front of him.

"I have everything to worry about!" Prescott charged Brayton's desk and leaned in close enough for Brayton to smell his rotten breath. "I've got that jackass of an old man who thinks Wellington is the son he should have had. He also thinks this company is about serving humanity and not making money. He certainly won't drive up the stock price and make us all rich in a merger. And we meet with the board tomorrow in Monterey."

Brayton shot up and his chair slammed into the credenza behind him. Well over six feet tall and two hundred pounds, he knew he could make short work of Prescott.

Prescott jumped back.

"Look, I told you it's under control," Brayton yelled. "So don't come in here like you're the only one with something on the line to lose. I told you I'd deliver and I will."

Brayton understood what was on the line for Prescott. Prescott was the younger of Adam Rexsen's two children and one of two heirs to the Rexsen Family Trust. Brayton had just run the numbers. In eleven days the trust's value would swell to $12 billion through the IPO. And with the backroom deal cut with the pharmaceutical firm, Brayton would flip the shares and drive the trust's total worth to over

$20 billion. The old man wasn't going to live forever, and this little rat he was about to choke would be worth at least $10 billion.

"Okay then," Prescott whined, "just remember who's paying your salary."

Brayton knew who was paying his salary. *All* the shareholders he'd make rich. Not just this little rat. "And you remember you need me to make this deal go. Now, I've got things to do, if you don't mind."

Brayton retrieved his chair from behind him and resumed sorting through his messages. Prescott huffed and slithered out of the room.

Brayton was confident Prescott desperately needed him. That's why he recruited him in the first place. Brayton had taken three other companies public, all smoke-and-mirrors dot-comers. Each time, he cashed out before the inevitable drop came, except the last time. He got caught long with stock on margin, and it nearly bankrupted him. This would be his redemption. He'd be on the covers of *Fortune*, *Business Week*, and *Forbes* at the same time. And one of those copies would mysteriously be mailed to the old man sitting in Lompoc Correctional Institution who'd said his son would never amount to anything.

Brayton was certain he could cover up the problem with CGT. Make it disappear. But he needed help. The kind of help not listed in a Google search. He'd have to rely on help from a contact given to him by the man he had despised most of his life and who'd taught him everything he knew about backstabbing, adultery, manipulation, and stretching the truth and the law to his advantage. He grabbed the phone and punched the numbers he knew by heart. Brayton understood that the methods were wrong by most moral standards, but they got results, at least as he measured results: by sexual pleasure and money. He held the phone to his ear, ignoring what was left of his conscience.

"It's me. We have another problem."

# CHAPTER 4

THE BLACK LINCOLN Town Car darted through the Friday evening traffic, slogging around the perimeter of West Hollywood on the Hollywood Freeway. Joe Pirelli, a fifty-three-year-old muscular, dark-haired Italian-American, nervously checked and rechecked his watch. He knew time could be running out for his boss of fifteen years, if it hadn't already. He raced down the shoulder, giving no thought to the highway patrol eyeing his maneuver from the traffic jam in the opposite lanes, and shot down the exit ramp for Highland Avenue and turned right onto Santa Monica Boulevard. He worked his way through West Hollywood and, using his horn to clear the way, swerved left onto San Vincente at the light. When he turned right on Beverly Boulevard, he dodged a Mercedes, several aluminum light poles and the eclectic mix of pedestrians he expected at the edge of West Hollywood and Beverly Hills.

The Marine veteran-turned-driver-and-bodyguard had been waiting patiently at Cypress Jet Service, the fixed-base operator for Rexsen Aircraft at John Wayne Airport, when the call came in. The Coast Guard had plucked David Wellington, unconscious and critical, from the helipad of an offshore oil platform just north of the Santa Barbara channel. He'd been pulled from the water by the crew of a supply boat dispatched by the platform's foreman in response to the distress call of the crippled Gulfstream. There were no other survivors.

Joe yanked the wheel into the parking lot of the Cedars-Sinai emergency department, threw the car in "park" and sprinted through the automatic sliding doors. His eyes scanned the crowded lobby. An elderly woman, parked against the wall, cradled her head and groaned as if begging for more attention. A frazzled mother sat beside her son, who held his forearm and cried while she eyeballed the nurse's aide manning the front desk.

*It's just a broken arm. Stop your whining.*

Fighting the sterile smell of cleaner, Joe trotted to the desk. The young freckle-faced girl appeared frustrated by Joe's arrival.

"Can I help you?"

"Yes, ma'am, you can. I need to see David Wellington. A chopper just dropped him here within the last hour."

The aide turned to her screen, pecked on the keyboard, and read the information displayed on the silver monitor.

"He's critical and the doctors are still working on him. No visitors." She refused to look back at Joe.

Joe remained calm. "I understand, ma'am. I would like to speak to his doctor as soon as he can give me some news."

The girl kept her eyes locked on the screen. "Are you family?"

Family, Joe mused. David Wellington had no real family. His father had been a hard-driving workaholic criminal defense attorney who'd dealt in the sanitized cesspool of the criminal behavior of spoiled stars and starlets of Hollywood and Beverly Hills until he died of a heart attack at the age of forty-two. His mother came from money and had attended Pepperdine, where she'd met David's father. But after twenty years of being ignored and cheated on, her money and religious convictions were not enough to stop the bullet she put through her head. Joe had known David longer than anyone and was the closest thing David Wellington had to a friend, let alone family.

"Yes, I am. I'm his brother." Joe decided a little white lie to grease the skids wouldn't hurt.

The girl huffed in disgust, shuffled through the pile of papers in front of her and produced a pen. "Name?" she said curtly.

"Joe Pirelli." Joe smiled.

The frustrated girl stopped writing and stared at Joe.

"I'm his half-brother," Joe proclaimed, still smiling.

"Whatever!" She returned her attention to the page and jotted his name. She pointed the pen toward the rows of chairs cluttered with would-be patients. "Wait over there, and the doctor will see you if and when he has time."

"Thank you, ma'am, and have a *nice* day." Joe couldn't resist the jab.

He found a seat in the back corner of the room and waited. Alone with his thoughts and nothing to do, he prayed as his Catholic mother had taught him. He prayed for his boss and his friend. He prayed for Adam Rexsen, who had died in the crash. Joe had great respect for the old man. He wished he could have said the same for his offspring. It was ironic that a man who'd dedicated his life to hunting and fixing genetic imperfections could have a pair of them for children. He despised both Priscilla and Prescott Rexsen, Priscilla for cheating on his boss and Prescott for his spineless whining.

He prayed for David to live, not just because he didn't want to have to deal with Priscilla and Prescott. He believed that the death of David's son had made him the cold driven man he'd become, but somewhere deep inside David Wellington was a good-hearted human being. The kind of person who knew the right thing to do, the kind of person Joe had pledged his loyalty to.

Joe finished his prayers with the sign of the cross.

"*Semper fi,*" he whispered as he kissed the cross he pulled from around his neck. The words were Latin for "ever faithful" and emblazoned on the Marine emblem. Joe was ever faithful to two things: the United States Marine Corps and David Wellington, and he never took either pledge lightly.

# CHAPTER 5

PRISCILLA WELLINGTON FELT the Southern California sun warm her glistening skin. The smell of coconut oil drifted on the fresh ocean breeze. The tall palms gently swayed, and she watched the emerald waves of the Pacific lap against the soft white sand of Laguna Beach with a steady pulse. Priscilla loved her life, at least most of it.

She'd dealt with the only difficulty in her life with her morning phone call to her husband in San Francisco. Now she could enjoy the life she deserved and the luscious young man lying next to her. She'd seen him three weeks ago in New York. She had watched him escort one of those rail-thin models who wore the plunging necklines and flowing silk of Oscar de la Renta. He was tall, with a dark complexion and steely blue eyes. She'd watched him strut with bravado, and his Grey Vetiver cologne beckoned her as he turned just a few feet from her table beside the runway. With a hundred-dollar bill discreetly passed to the nearest waiter, the introduction was arranged.

Now he was here. It was almost too easy. Concealed behind black-rimmed Ray-Ban's, she shifted her eyes in his direction. His body was strong and tanned. His muscles were chiseled but curved in all the right places. The oil glistened on his chest while he napped. At thirty-five, she was proud of the fact he needed the rest. She guessed he was fifteen years younger, though the subject of age never came up. Still, her sexual appetite was superior to his eagerness and youth.

He began to stir, and she closed her eyes. She knew he thought she was a beautiful woman. She'd caught him staring at her long tanned legs, compact waist, flat smooth stomach, and perfect round breasts that were as firm as any twenty-one-year-old's, thanks to the finest Beverly Hills cosmetic surgeons money could buy. Her gold bikini top stretched tightly across her, and the chill of the breeze hardened her nipples just enough to seductively reveal their outline. She knew he wouldn't be able to resist, and soon they'd be entwined in the soft comfort of the bed inside. She opened her eyes and watched the breeze toy with a line of pelicans floating in the afternoon sun. She decided she would send him back to New York this evening in style.

She quietly rose and left the deck of the beachfront home. After retrieving the pitcher from the refrigerator, she poured another Bacardi daiquiri. The staccato ring of her iPhone interrupted her first sip. She checked the small digital screen and recognized the number. She slipped the phone to her ear.

"I thought you forgot about me," she said, smiling with her rum-wet lips.

She knew he'd never forget her. None of them ever did. And her latest affair held a special ranking on the list. Royce Brayton was handsome, strong, and arrogant, but they all had that. Brayton, however, worked for her husband. He had been handpicked to replace him, her brother had told her, and he would make them all richer than they imagined. The added tension and excitement of sleeping with the man who'd get rid of her husband and push her father aside made him special.

"I'd never forget a beautiful, sensuous woman like you," Royce Brayton playfully replied.

Brayton had had a way with women ever since he was fourteen years old. He was handsome and confident, traits he inherited from his father, who'd been a successful banker until he was sent to prison for skimming millions. While Brayton's mother was trophy wife number two for his father, he'd used his smooth charm and good looks to bed numbers three and four in his teenage years without his father's knowledge. Priscilla was a much greater challenge but still susceptible to his masterfulness.

"I guess that means you've been thinking about me," Priscilla said as she sipped her rum-laced frozen concoction.

"I've been thinking about last Friday. Your deep brown eyes, your long sexy legs, your luscious round breasts, and that long night of lovemaking."

Priscilla squeaked out a sexy girlish giggle. "Where are you?" She had to check. It would be a messy scene if Brayton suddenly showed up at his own home and found Priscilla with her latest twentysomething boy toy.

"Still at the office. But I can't wait to see you tonight. You and I will pick up where we left off."

"I'm not sure, Royce. I talked to David earlier and he said he would be back tonight."

Royce chuckled playfully. "So? He'll never know."

The certainty in his voice caused Priscilla to pause for a moment. She'd been told why Brayton was here. She knew he'd take her husband's job and gain control of the company. She'd decided to steer clear of anything between David and Royce to preserve her innocence in the eyes of her father. After all, David was the son he'd always wanted, and there *was* the trust—the trust that would soon balloon to billions of dollars when the company went public. She and her brother were the sole heirs, and the controlling share of the trust would pass to them once their father died. She'd do nothing to prevent that from happening.

"You still there, Priscilla?" Royce asked after the long silence.

"Yes, I'm still here."

"Okay. I'll see you tonight around eight at my place."

Priscilla choked back a laugh. He didn't know she was already there.

"And wear that sexy little number again for me."

"I will, but only for a little while. I plan on taking it off, taking it all off for you."

She ended the call, tossed the iPhone onto the table, smiled and sipped the third drink in her rum parade. She slipped off her gold bikini top and returned to the chiseled young model who had just been caught admiring her legs again. It was a little after five—she was sure she had more than enough time to give him a proper sendoff. Maybe one he'd never forget.

# CHAPTER 6

ROYCE BRAYTON HAD looked forward to Friday night all week. The headlights of his bright red Ferrari 360 Spider illuminated the iron gates guarding the entrance to the exclusive neighborhood perched atop the seaside cliffs of Laguna Beach. The gates opened, and Brayton pressed the gas pedal down. Powered by an engine able to go from zero to sixty in four seconds, the car leaped forward and he sped down the short winding drive past the multimillion-dollar homes whose occupants included Hollywood stars, NBA bad boys, and the wealthiest businesspeople in Southern California.

To say he was eager was an understatement. Priscilla was waiting for him at his tri-level home overlooking the seascape of the Pacific. The thought of the silky soft lingerie clinging tightly to her firm tanned figure had his body throbbing with testosterone. He'd already demonstrated he could manipulate Prescott, and in five minutes he'd be in bed with the only other heir to the Rexsen Family Trust and the best lay he'd enjoyed in years. Life didn't get much better.

He turned into his driveway and pulled next to the red Mercedes SL500 convertible. The house appeared to be designed by an exhibitionist. Massive glass windows on every wall were framed in white stucco and provided magnificent views of the ocean or the rugged

Pacific coastline from every room. The house was topped by a sunburst terra cotta tile roof and surrounded by exotic palms, ferns, and hydrangea. Brayton swaggered to the glass doors at the entrance to the home and entered as a conquering hero.

The sprawling black granite floor led to walls of light gray. The furniture and cabinetry were all ebony, and the hand-rubbed finish made them sparkle in the sparse light. Its furnishings were smartly accented by chrome frames and glass tabletops. Obscenely priced artwork and fine ceramics from around the world were displayed on chrome-framed tables and tripods and filled the remaining empty spaces. Some would call the décor cold, but he called it masculine.

He turned left into the kitchen, which was covered in jet-black granite with rarely used sparkling chrome fixtures. The stairway leading to the second floor reached along the back wall and was silhouetted against the view of the Pacific through plate-glass windows that ran the entire length of the house. He stopped and gazed at the lights from tankers and cargo ships glittering across the water. Soft music drifted down from the second-floor master bedroom. Brayton threw his keys onto the table and headed upstairs. He slowed his gait when he topped the marble steps.

The smell of jasmine was faint at first but grew stronger as he turned down the hall to the master bedroom. The room was dark except for the soft yellow light flickering from the granite-framed fireplace. Priscilla lay in the soft firelight in a sea of fluffy silk linens.

Her sleek legs stretched from under the black silk sheet, exposing just a hint of her beautifully shaped hip. Brayton's knees weakened, and his desire grew out of control. He followed the silhouette of her body, tightly wrapped in the silk sheet. The end of the sheet revealed her large round breasts, scantily covered by a deep red negligee draped loosely between those two works of art. She smiled and her red lips glistened in the firelight. Her dark brown eyes invited him in.

"Hello, Royce. I've been waiting for you." She gently patted the bed.

"And I've been thinking about this all day," he said.

He tugged his dark blue tie from side to side and snapped it from around his neck. He twisted the top button and released his starched collar. Priscilla rose to meet him. Her eyes locked on his as she fondled each button on his cream-colored shirt with her sleek, red-nailed fingers and caressed his body between each tug on his shirt. His body tingled with anticipation while she massaged and stripped him at the same time. Brayton thrust her onto the soft sea of silk, and in a moment the two were lost in the fiery passion of adulterous sex.


As they completed their last act of passion, the black cordless phone next to the bed rang. Brayton reached across Priscilla, grabbed the phone and checked the digital display.

"Brayton."

"It's me." Brayton immediately recognized the voice of the head of Rexsen's security team. "We may have a problem. Not sure yet."

"What do you mean a problem?" Brayton said. Priscilla sat up in bed, and she examined Brayton's face for any indication of what was being said. Catching her gaze, he turned his look away from her and did his best not to give anything away.

"I just got notified by the Coast Guard that Wellington's plane went down just off Point Conception at the northern tip of the Santa Barbara Channel."

"What?" He twisted out of bed and started pacing with the phone.

"There's more, Royce. They said the Eleventh District dispatched an HH-65A rescue helicopter out of Los Angeles to search the site."

Brayton shifted the phone to his left hand and slid his shirt sleeve over his right and tried to conceal his joy. With Adam Rexsen and

David Wellington gone, the company was his. All of his problems were solved. He would take Rexsen public as the CEO and be on the covers of *Forbes*, *Fortune*, *Money*, and *Business Week*. He'd join the elite circles of power and experience the riches Wall Street could provide.

"And there's a survivor."

Brayton froze in mid-stride and clenched his teeth. He locked his blank stare on Priscilla.

"What! A survivor from twenty-six thousand feet! That's impossible. They're full of shit. It can't be."

Royce raced through the possibilities. Did Adam Rexsen survive or was it Wellington? Maybe he was lucky and it was one of the pilots. His dream of Wall Street riches disappeared in the fog of uncertainty.

"I've confirmed they've picked up someone through my sources monitoring communications in the area. The person is near death and broken up pretty bad. They don't think he'll make it. But they've flown the victim to Cedars-Sinai in Los Angeles. They won't release a name until the family has been notified."

As if on cue, Pricilla's iPhone rang from across the room. Naked, Priscilla darted from bed and fumbled through her purse. While staring at Brayton, she grabbed the phone and held it to her ear.

She listened for a moment, then spoke. "Okay, I'll get there as soon as I can." She stuffed the phone into her purse.

"Shit! It's David. He's been pulled from the waters off Santa Barbara by some offshore oil workers. He's almost dead. They want me at the hospital now. My father was killed in the crash."

Brayton thought for a second and put the phone back to his ear. "You get that? It's Wellington." He pressed the button disconnecting the call and threw it onto the bed. It was the worst option: Wellington was alive. He hated him. Not for any character flaw or anything he'd experienced under Wellington's leadership. After all, Wellington was a money-hungry, no-prisoners type just like he was. It was simply that David Wellington stood between him and everything he thought he deserved: Priscilla, the CEO job and the money. It was nothing personal, just business.

"He'd better die," Priscilla said. She slipped her dress over her head and it unfurled along the curves of her tanned body. Brayton chuckled at Priscilla's inability to hide her disappointment.

They'd never talked directly about her husband and didn't want to. The less they talked about him the better. Royce tried to read her face. Her dark eyes flashed and darted away when she caught Royce's stare. There was something in her look that kept Royce on edge. He didn't trust her. But that was not surprising to him. There was no woman he trusted; his long line of sex-driven stepmothers had seen to that. Priscilla was the means to an end. Still, he understood they shared a common enemy. There was one obstacle that kept both of them from getting what they wanted. And David Wellington was still breathing—barely.

# CHAPTER 7

IF PRISCILLA WELLINGTON had handpicked a hospital to
have to visit, Cedars-Sinai would have been her first choice. Priscilla
guided the convertible red Mercedes SL500 off of Santa Monica
Boulevard and onto Rodeo Drive. She couldn't help herself. Cedars-
Sinai was less than a mile away, and sure there were faster routes, but
none as elegant as this. This was the Golden Triangle of Beverly Hills.
Each boutique was adorned with sparkling walls of glass, polished marble, and glittering stainless steel. Prada, Cartier, Tiffany, Armani,
Versace—the names elicited an affection a woman should only have
for her children. Even at 11 p.m., Porsches and Mercedes still roamed
about. No, Priscilla decided, she wouldn't mind this hospital visit at all.
From her luxury suite in the Peninsula, Beverly Hills' most exclusive
hotel and spa, she would be steps from the Golden Triangle shops and
within a sympathetic three-quarters of a mile of her dying husband's
hospital bed.

    With Beverly Hills still in her mirror, Priscilla maneuvered along
Beverly Boulevard and turned right onto George Burns Road, then
down Gracie Allen Drive to the valet parking near the emergency
room. As she approached the entrance, the glass doors parted, and she
crossed the polished white floor to the admissions desk.

"I'm Mrs. David Wellington." She tried to pretend she enjoyed the title. "I received a call that my husband was brought here."

She was politely ushered into a waiting area and told a doctor would be with her momentarily.

She tried to forget she was Mrs. David Wellington; the thought of her marriage made her stomach sour. She hated all those years of acting as if she liked David just to please her father so he might let her run the company one day. With her father now gone and Prescott next in line, she'd undoubtedly wasted her time.

She sat alone on the uncomfortable steel-framed chair. The chill of the ER began to seep in. No one sat with her. She maintained her outward air of superiority, but uneasiness churned deep in her heart. The father who'd given her everything, except the one thing she'd wanted, was dead. She raised her head and was actually happy to see her brother Prescott enter the ER. He immediately spotted her and slinked down the sanitary corridor.

"Hi, Pris. Just got the news. Looks like the old man's gone." Prescott smiled and rubbed his hands together.

The words hit hard and deep. Her father was gone. She remembered how he'd always made time for her as a young girl. He'd been a great dad. She got whatever she wanted as a child. He spent lavishly and never said no. Despite the long hours required by his job, he'd always found the time to make her feel special. Lunch at school, those little Saturday morning errands with just the two of them, basketball in the driveway, making Sunday morning breakfast and sitting next to her at church, all said how much he loved her.

But she'd wanted more. As she got older, the jealousy grew. She convinced herself there was something he loved more than her. He'd talk about his purpose in life and how Rexsen Labs filled that purpose. She couldn't remember when it happened, but soon a hunger for power and money replaced her hunger for her father's love. Tears filled her eyes, but she refused to let them fall.

"From what I hear, your hubby may be next." Prescott smiled and attempted a hug that Priscilla successfully dodged.

"The nurse instructed me to wait here and said the doctor would be down to speak with me," Priscilla said. "Can you believe they want me to wait? I don't think they know who we are." Priscilla glared at the young girl behind the desk.

"So you don't know his condition?" Prescott said, his greasy-haired head cocked forward, attempting to play the very unfamiliar role of the man of the family.

"No—only that he's like a cockroach. Who survives a plane crash in the ocean?" Priscilla looked away in disgust in an effort to hide her sadness.

"Ah, be careful, sis. Someone might get the idea you don't want him to survive." Prescott grinned.

"I don't! He's been nothing but a pain the ass for the last ten years."

"Why don't you divorce him?"

"That's a stupid question. Sometimes I wonder about you."

Priscilla wanted to punch her brother. He knew that the only reason she had stayed with David was to please their father. And now with the trust passing to the two of them, any divorce would result in an equitable split of the marital assets. That meant David would get half of Priscilla's ownership in the trust. No divorce; she was rooting for the angel of death.

"Mrs. Wellington?" said a handsome young doctor in teal scrubs and booties.

"Hello, doctor," Priscilla said. "This is my brother, Prescott Rexsen."

The doctor shook his hand. "First, let me say I'm very sorry about the loss of your father."

"Thanks," Prescott said and smiled. Priscilla couldn't believe he wasn't covering up his joy.

The doctor raised his eyebrows and turned his attention to Priscilla. "Mrs. Wellington, it's a miracle your husband is alive. He's taken in a lot of water and has trauma to his head and chest. He's unconscious, and we're not sure he'll make it. There's not much we can do. It's all up to him. It will be a long night. I wish I had more to tell you."

Priscilla lowered her head as if she cared.

"We'll let you know when you can see him." The doctor paused. "Do you have any questions?"

Priscilla looked up through her thick eyelashes. "No, doctor, just do everything you can." Again, what she thought she should say.

"Okay. I need to get back in there. Can you update his brother?" The doctor nodded to the back of the room, and Priscilla spotted Joe. She looked at him sharply, and he crossed his arms and stared back.

"Certainly I can."

The doctor disappeared behind an automatic door. Prescott leaned down with his arms folded, still keeping his eyes on the door. "Good job, sis," he whispered. "Even I almost believed you cared."

"Shut up, Prescott, you asshole."

Prescott kept his arms folded, stepped back, and looked at Priscilla. "Well, you won't be calling me names tomorrow. I called our lawyer and told him to get the papers drawn up tonight to have the control of the trust transferred to us first thing in the morning. That asshole said there wasn't a death certificate yet. I told him to just do it any way he can because the old man is gone. As the new trustee, I'll be able to vote the shares of the trust any way we want at the board meeting this weekend. And by the way, how does it feel to be a billionaire?" Prescott grinned.

"You'd better not do anything stupid with our money. The only reason you're trustee is because you have a penis—a very small one, I might add."

"At least I have one." Prescott stomped down the hallway and disappeared.

Priscilla hated the fact that their father had chosen Prescott as trustee. She remembered when her love and admiration for her father had turned to hate and jealousy. Although she'd attended college and graduated in theater arts, she'd asked to help him run the business. His reply was "no," and it was followed within a week by Prescott's getting a vice president position despite the fact that Priscilla knew he couldn't spit and hit the earth. A part in a television series from a friend of the family followed as an obvious bribe to let the issue go. It was clear what her father really thought of her: a girl who couldn't run the business—ever.

Ignoring Joe, Priscilla removed a silver bullet lipstick and a compact mirror from her purse and applied another layer of the glistening red gloss. She stood slowly, wriggled in her dress, and sauntered to the admissions desk. She gave her number at the Peninsula to the young receptionist.

She knew if she hurried she could still catch some of Hollywood's self-anointed studs at the Belvedere, hopefully with a few drinks already in them. While her father never thought she was good enough, younger men made her feel she was very good at something. It wasn't running a major pharmaceutical company, but it was one thing she had that nearly every man she met wanted. It was the only power she'd had until now.

# CHAPTER 8

THE BLOOD-RED NUMBERS illuminated the darkness: 3:37 a.m. The room's corrugated steel walls were lined with computers, video displays, radios, and other state-of-the-art communications and surveillance equipment. The video displays silhouetted three men dressed identically in black. They monitored the displays and listened to the latest chatter regarding the events of the past twelve hours. A fourth man stood hulking over them and stared at a display over the shoulder of one of the men. The pulsating ghostly shadows exaggerated his square jaw, protruding cheekbones, and ruddy complexion. A scar formed a dark canyon on the left side of his thick neck, signaling his deadliness.

"Sorry, sir," the red-haired man in the chair said crisply while he awaited an ass-chewing from the man he regarded as his superior officer.

"Forget it. We got the old man, and Wellington is not out of the woods yet. What's the latest?" He slapped a meaty hand on the man's shoulder.

"One of the two marks is dead. Wellington somehow survived. I've never heard anything like this, sir. I've been on crash sites of F-15s that dropped from much lower altitudes, and we had to gather the pieces of the crew. You can see here on the screen, the last report from the transponder came from twenty-six thousand feet. The HH-65A out of Los Angeles reported to the Coast Guard command center that they picked up one survivor, male, between forty and fifty years old. He has a few broken ribs, chest and head trauma and was in critical condition when they dropped him off at Cedars-Sinai heliport facilities at 7:04 p.m."

"Any word from the hospital?"

"They received the patient, and he's still critical. He's in a coma, no surgery. I've got three of my men there. One has infiltrated hospital security and is undercover as an orderly. It's pretty hot inside. Media got wind of it as quick as we did. They know a corporate jet went down. Coast Guard will confirm it's one of Rexsen's pretty quickly."

"Well, keep an eye on Wellington for now. Your people need to get in position and be sure we can neutralize him if we need to."

"Understood, sir. Our plan is already underway. It may take a little time, but we'll get to him if we have to." The man shuffled a few papers on the table and pulled out a photograph of Tori Clarke. "What about her, sir?"

"Where is she now?"

"Still at home. We have her under surveillance. My guys got into her apartment and got the lights on, so to speak. So far she's called home and bragged about how well she did today."

His superior held the photograph in the light from the screen. "Seems like such a waste to be home alone, I'll bet she's great in bed."

Both men chuckled.

"Keep an eye on her. I don't want too many accidents at once, but if she starts to act suspicious or contacts the regulators, do what you have to. I want to get this one done cleanly. Our client is getting a big payday based on our work. This is the one we can retire on."

"You can count on it, sir."

He knew there were two ways to retire from this business: get the big kill or be killed. This would be the big kill. If they completed their missions, their client would have access to over $1 billion. And the remaining marks were in the crosshairs. They were nearly halfway there. He could taste the rum and feel the Caribbean sun warming his face. After a career in the darkness, it would be nice to finally see the sun.

# CHAPTER 9

AT FIRST, THE high-pitched tone was barely audible and repeated every few seconds. David Wellington's mind seemed to float, as if in a dream. He could sense his body, but it was heavy, and every limb, finger and toe was weighted down. The tone grew louder and became intermixed with a soft gentle voice that called his name. It was higher than most men's voices, but it definitely was a man.

The voice came closer, and David struggled to see. He'd had no sensation of sight. Still, he tried to see. A blurred white light filled his eyes, and an image began to form ever so slowly. Someone stood at his side. He struggled to clear his mind. The person moved closer, and as the image came into focus, David saw a younger man dressed in light blue scrubs, who repeated David's name. He was in his thirties and had thick brown, curly hair cut neatly above his ears and brushed cleanly back away from his round face.

David noticed a name tag but couldn't see any writing on it. Every image was filtered through an opaque haze affecting his vision. The young man smiled and a dimple appeared on the left side of his cheek.

"I've been pulling for you. Glad to see you're still here," he said.

"What is this place?" David said. "Heaven?"

The young man chucked. "Not quite."

"Am I alive?"

The young man just smiled.

"What is this place?" David's mind was a blank page.

"My superior won't let me say."

How strange, David thought. His mind was slow and clumsy and his speech was awkward and difficult. "How did I get here?"

"He decided to give you a second chance."

David's vision slowly faded again. He struggled to make sense of what the young man was saying. "What?" David said in frustration.

The figure faded into the milky white light, but his soft gentle voice continued.

"You need to know there is a reason. It's His reason. Listen to your heart; open it up to everything; listen. The reason is within each of us. It's as unique as every person on earth. Some never find it. You've been given a second chance."

The voice was barely audible and was being drowned out by the rhythmic beeps that grew louder and louder.

"Remember His reason is not always obvious. Seek it."

The image was gone, and the white light faded to black. But the beeping became loud and clear. David noticed the smell of cleaner, like the Spic and Span his mother always used. He felt a hand wrap around his wrist and lift it.

"Mr. Wellington. Can you hear me, Mr. Wellington? Try and open your eyes."

David could feel the weight of his eyelids, and he used all his energy to lift them. They would barely open. He could see clear tubes leading into his face and dangling from around his bed.

"Hi, Mr. Wellington. You've been injured, and you're in Cedars-Sinai Hospital in Los Angeles." This time it was clearly a woman's voice. He rolled his eyes in the direction of her voice and saw a woman dressed in blue scrubs gently smiling at him.

"How did I get here?"

"Your plane crashed in the Pacific, Mr. Wellington. The Coast Guard brought you here yesterday evening. You've been in a coma since then."

"Where's the young man?"

"Mr. Wellington, I'm the only one here. You must have been dreaming."

It seemed too real to be a dream, but he accepted her explanation. "Will I be okay?"

"I think so. Your doctors will talk to you in detail later. Right now you need to rest. We don't want anything to happen to our miracle man."

David was confused and closed his swollen eyes, trying to comprehend the nurse's comment. She apparently sensed his confusion.

"They're calling you the miracle man," she explained. "The news, the papers, they all say no one could have survived that crash. You're our miracle man."

He kept his eyes closed, and his mind began to float again. The young man's final words replayed over and over in his mind: *His reason is not always obvious. Seek it.*

# CHAPTER 10

TORI DROVE NORTH along Highway 1, as she did every Saturday morning. While there were much faster expressways, the coastal route helped clear her mind of the clutter of the week so she could focus solely on her little brother, Aaron. He was nine the last time she saw him in the hospital. Even as he labored to breathe, he cracked his mischievous grin and looked as if he were about to do something he shouldn't. She replayed their final conversation as she drove: how they both hated the sickness inside him for what it did to him and to their family; how God would take care of him in heaven and what fun he would have there. But she always came back to the promise she made him that day. That promise was the reason she headed north to the cemetery outside of Camarillo every weekend.

The sun was well above the Santa Monica Mountains as she turned right and drove through the stone pillars of Our Lady of the Angels Cemetery. She wound along the smooth blacktop road lined with majestic queen palms. After passing the shimmering granite fountain marking the entrance to the small chapel nestled against the green hillside, she turned left and drifted to a stop. After slipping her Prius into "park," she leaned forward and gazed out the passenger's window at the small granite tombstone. Over the years, the sadness of the site had given way to the joy of talking with her brother again. She smiled, grabbed the fresh daisies on the seat and headed out to see her brother. Tori pulled her gray cardigan tighter as the chilly breeze tugged at her lapel.

"Hi, Aaron. Looks like another great day," she said as she knelt down and pulled the wilted daisies from the planter. She instinctively brought the fresh bouquet to her nose and smelled the subtle sweetness of the flowers, just as she and Aaron did when they'd come upon them at their ranch outside of Fillmore, a few miles north of the grave site. Tori slipped the fresh bouquet into the planter, stepped back and sat down, legs crossed, on the smooth green grass.

"So this week was a weird one, AC."

She'd given Aaron that nickname when he was five and he'd discovered that all of his kindergarten classmates had them but they couldn't think of one for Aaron.

"We were so close to getting CGT to the other kids, but then I found a problem. I had to present my findings to that jerk I told you about last week and he said he'd have to have someone else verify my work!"

Just then, she heard another car approaching. She glanced over her shoulder and the black Chevy Suburban drifted past her car. Through the heavily tinted windows, she saw the driver lean forward and spot her, but he kept going and disappeared over the next hill. Tori turned back to her brother.

"But don't worry, AC. The work I've done to find the problem also gave me the solution." She leaned closer to the tombstone and smiled. "I won't let you down."

Tori tilted her head to the heavens and felt the warm sun on her back. She scanned the few clouds roaming the sky. Aaron was there somewhere watching. She wanted to tell him that something didn't feel right: things just didn't add up. But she remembered him as the nine-year-old he was and decided not to worry him. She'd made a promise and she was keeping it. That was good enough.

Startled by the growl of an engine to her right, Tori looked across to the adjacent hillside and spotted the plume of black smoke hovering over the backhoe. The yellow arm began to claw at the ground like a deadly predator digging for its prey. But the hole would be empty until filled with perhaps another victim of a genetic imperfection—worse yet, another child. She looked back at the words engraved into the tan granite inlay on the gravestone.

*Loving son, joyful brother, God's little angel*

"No matter what, AC ... I'll have the answer soon."

She stood and glanced back at the backhoe piling the brown dirt on the grass.

"No more children will die from this—no more!"

# CHAPTER 11

THE SATURDAY AFTERNOON sun hung directly overhead and brought welcome warmth to the groups of golfers making their way around Pebble Beach Golf Links. A light salty mist drifted in on the ocean breeze, scented with the smell of freshly cut grass. Sea lions lounged on the offshore rocks while otters playfully tangled with the kelp beds. Brown pelicans patrolled the shoreline in tight formation. One-hundred-year-old cypress trees silently kept guard over the fairways and landing areas. White golf balls emblazoned with the Rexsen Labs name in bright blue letters filled the air and littered the beaches. An unexpected memorial service for Adam Rexsen had been hastily arranged and held earlier in the morning. The sudden death of Rexsen's founder while many of the board members were in the air themselves hit too close to home.

But under the banner of "Adam Rexsen would have wanted us to carry on the business of realizing his life's dream," eloquently spoken by his only son, board members somberly displayed their best slices and hooks and occasional water balls, as originally scheduled.

Royce Brayton restrained a chuckle as William Walters, one of the most powerful men in investment banking, fed another ball to the sea lions playing in Stillwater Cove. After the customary cursing, Walters placed another ball on the tee, opted for an iron, and chopped one toward the left side of the sixth hole.

"Nice one, William," Prescott Rexsen said in a silky tone.

"Claire, you're up," Brayton said, showing the way to the tee with his outstretched gloved hand.

Claire Armstrong stepped to the tee. She was a lanky battle-weathered woman notorious for her sharp tongue. She headed Armstrong Investments, one of the largest mutual funds in the country. Together, Walters and Armstrong were the most powerful force on the newly formed Rexsen board. It was not by chance they were in a foursome with Prescott Rexsen and Royce Brayton.

After Claire outdrove Prescott and Walters, Brayton covered another chuckle and the four headed for the carts.

"You see, William, the problem is the lack of edge and focus," Brayton said, dropping his driver into the blue bag strapped to the rear of the cart. "It's been that way for a while. But as you both know, going public will require that Rexsen clean house and reorganize. The entire process from research to marketing has to be streamlined. The time to market has to be cut significantly."

After placing their clubs in their bags, both Armstrong and Walters paused and listened intently. Brayton had been leading the conversation toward this point since the first tee. He'd explained the competitive market for gene therapy treatments, outlined the competition, described the investors' needs and suggested how they would not be happy with Rexsen Labs' performance going forward. He'd given the appropriate credit to old man Rexsen and Wellington but also subtly questioned Wellington's ability to return to health and lead a publicly held company. It was now time for the punch line.

"Claire, you know it's nearly impossible for insiders from a private, closely held company to do what's necessary to restructure a company they built. I can name company after company that has failed to perform because of that lack of objectivity and willingness to change or get rid of their life's work. And besides, David Wellington is near death in the hospital."

"I understand what you're saying, Royce, and the changes you've outlined make sense, but we need to be realistic here. In order to make the changes, the trust would need to support your position."

Prescott Rexsen had the opening he needed. "I can guarantee you my family will support the action that will deliver the greatest value to our investors. Once public, my sister and I will support Royce on this one. That's enough ownership to get the majority behind Royce's plan. And we all know his track record. He's made shareholders *and* board members at his last three companies *very* rich."

"Shall we play on?" Brayton led the group into the carts, and they glided to the next hole.

The play continued while Brayton skillfully outlined his plans to reorganize Rexsen and then merge with a major pharmaceutical company. With their marketing muscle and pull with the FDA, other drugs in the pipeline would only increase in value, and the investors would view the merger with great favor. The change-of-control provisions for the board and its executives would be triggered and result in millions of dollars in cash payments to the elite group. In addition, significant bonuses would be paid upon successful completion of the merger.

"I understand the value proposition here," Walters said as the group prepared to tee off on the seventeenth hole, "but your plan would require that the deal be completed just after we went public. Not to mention the hundreds of Rexsen employees who would be laid off in a merger. You'd have to add to your group of bodyguards to protect us from the employees. We already told them no layoffs." Walters pulled his driver from the bag and stepped to the tee.

"I have to tell you, Royce, I'm with William on this one," Claire said and reached for her driver. "It's a risk to permanently replace

Wellington just after we go public. I know the investors pretty well, and they're a jittery, suspicious bunch."

Brayton protested coolly. "David Wellington is in no position to lead this company, and as you've heard, I have full support of the trust. That's a 61 percent block of stock once we go public, so I have the support. This is about shareholder value and how to maximize the value of this company for its owners." Brayton paused as Walters hit a low line drive about 150 yards down the left side. Satisfied that he missed the beach on the par three, he retrieved his tee with a smile. Armstrong outdrove Rexsen and Walters again, then rejoined the group at the carts.

Brayton pressed on. "The reason I wanted to talk to you two about this plan is to see where you were on the matter. I've discussed it with Effingham, Kerrigan, O'Reilly, and Moreno and they all said run it by you two. If you see merit in the plan, they'll support me." Brayton knew how to play to egos. After all, his was the biggest he knew.

Armstrong and Walters shared a glance. Armstrong nodded, and Walters answered for them both. "We'll support your plan, but it has to be with the full support of the board and the trust."

The foursomes cycled through the course, then settled on the veranda of The Terrace Lounge for a late afternoon lunch of ahi tuna, fresh Caesar salad, and, of course, a wide selection of California chardonnays, merlots, pinot noirs and cabernets. As the sun dropped behind the clouds prowling the Pacific, they left the lounge and retired to their rooms scattered around the resort, all under watchful eyes of Brayton's security team.

Brayton watched as Prescott gave a warm bon voyage to each of them, shaking their hands, accepting sorrowful condolences and words of support. As they watched the last pair of inebriated board members disappear into the shroud of dusk, Prescott turned to Brayton and extended a hand. Brayton knew he was one step closer to buying back his life. The board had bought it. The vote would take place tomorrow afternoon. And the greasy weasel of a man whose limp hand he was now crushing would put the full support of the Rexsen Family Trust behind him in his bid to replace David Wellington as CEO. Prescott showed his crooked yellow teeth as he returned Brayton's sinister grin.

"See you at the board meeting, Royce," Prescott said, hoping to be recognized as Brayton's newest buddy.

"Yep, see you there," Brayton said and tried to not to laugh at the ludicrous thought of Prescott even thinking he was on Brayton's level. Prescott spun and disappeared into the lobby of The Lodge. Brayton wiped his right hand on his trousers, disgusted with the exchange. He's a means to an end, he reminded himself, and the end was worth billions.

# CHAPTER 12

IT WAS SATURDAY evening and Priscilla stepped out onto the sprawling deck of the Mediterranean-style Malibu home of the latest Hollywood bad boy, Danny Flynn. She was joined by Brittany Rogers, a thirtysomething platinum blonde and her longtime friend and occasional actress. The party inside was going full tilt. Champagne flowed from a center fountain just inside the open sliding doors. Ozzy Osbourne's *Crazy Train* blasted from the integrated home entertainment system. The private party in the upper bedroom had become too much. The cocaine use was excessive, and Priscilla knew the sex would be rough. It was time for a breath of fresh air.

The sea air felt cool and refreshing, and the view from the beachfront estate was relaxing. Priscilla and Brit, as her friends called her, had spent the day at the Grotto, the finest Spa in Beverly Hills. The seven-hour Tahitian Treatment Special had done the trick. The warm oil sugar glow massage, the Tahitian milk bath and collagen treatment followed by a pedicure, a full haircut and style accompanied by island music and Champagne had the pair looking sexy and feeling like a million dollars.

Both women wore tight, short white silk Versace cocktail dresses that clung to their youthful figures, which had been sculpted by the most expensive plastic surgeons in Southern California. Their tanned skin was smooth and soft, and the fragrance of lavender completed the aura and attracted the handsome young actors, lawyers, and moguls in attendance.

"That Danny is a real hottie, Brit."

"So's his friend Robbie. I'd like to continue our little foursome after the effects of the coke wear off a little." Brit stuck out her chest and shook her upper body as if twirling a pair of pasties. Both girls giggled and smiled.

"So what's up with that hubby of yours? Looks like you're not as single as you thought you were, girl."

"God, I know. That bastard is like a cockroach. That jet fell from twenty-six thousand feet and disintegrated on impact, and he's still alive!"

"The miracle man—that's what they're calling him."

"Oh, bullshit! He's the pain-in-the-ass man to me." Priscilla leaned against one of the large concrete pillars that surrounded the pool. "If he pulls out of this, it will cost me billions."

Brit leaned against the other side of the column, stirred her Kahlua and cream with her finger, and licked it through her bright red lips. "How's that? Didn't you talk to Michael Glick?"

Brit had recommended Glick's services as the finest family law attorney in Beverly Hills. He'd handled all the high-profile splits, including Brit's three.

"He makes it so it's just like breaking up in high school. No pain and you're on the prowl the day you file."

"I talked to him this morning, Brit, but he said under California law, we'd divide up the marital assets in half. He said since my father was killed in the crash and half the trust immediately passed to me, it would be included in that total. I'm not about to give him three billion or more just so I can continue what I do every day anyway."

Priscilla downed her Champagne in one big gulp. "Thank God we don't have any children."

"So whatcha' gonna do, hon?" Brit took a sip and batted her eyes at Priscilla over the rim of her crystal flute.

"That asshole Brayton said not to worry." Priscilla crossed her arms and peered into the darkness.

"I thought you liked him."

"I said I like the sex." Priscilla's eyes locked on Brit. "He's just another arrogant asshole. But he's going to make us rich, so I'll keep him around until he finishes the job."

"Whatever," Brit said, rocking her head from side to side. "I don't worry about money. Daddy took care of that for me."

Brittany Rogers was the daughter of one of the most powerful producers in Hollywood. Burt Rogers gave his only daughter anything she wanted. He could afford to.

"My father took care of nothing."

The ring from the iPhone in Priscilla's small white clutch purse interrupted the two. She pulled the phone from the purse, checked the caller ID and shook her head before answering.

"This is Priscilla." Brit gave her an inquisitive look. Priscilla covered the phone with one hand and whispered, "The hospital." She listened for a moment. "Okay, I'll be there in a little while." She jammed the iPhone into her purse. "Shit. I told you he's a damn cockroach."

"What's up?"

"They say he's out of his coma and I can come see him."

"Now?" Brittany said, nodding toward the soft bluish light seeping from the upstairs bedroom window.

"I've got to. It won't look good if I don't act like I'm happy he's alive."

"Just all the more for me, Pris." Brit smiled and returned to the party.

Priscilla knew she'd miss out on a wild night, but Brit would represent Priscilla well. She was great in the sack, and in their drug-induced horniness, she would easily handle both Danny and Robbie. Priscilla figured Danny would suspect that if Brit was that good, Priscilla, with her firm sculpted body and more experience, would be better. She convinced herself he'd be back.

Priscilla slipped around the side of the estate, found her Mercedes and headed for Cedars-Sinai. She hoped it would be a short visit—followed by a tearful graveside service.

# CHAPTER 13

IT WAS LATE Saturday night when David heard the light tapping on the door. Still suffering from the effects of hitting the Pacific at several hundred miles an hour, he'd been drifting in and out of consciousness. The muffled sounds of voices, the mechanical clicks and beeps, and his terrifying thoughts of the empty life he'd wasted all combined into one horrendous nightmare. Stuck somewhere between hell and eternal darkness, nothing seemed real except the recent visit from the orderly. He struggled to open one swollen eye and saw a figure silhouetted by the soft light from the hallway.

"David?" He could barely hear the whisper of his name over the hissing of the oxygen rushing into his nose and the steady beep of the monitors. He held his eye open while the figure moved steadily closer and into focus.

"David, it's Priscilla."

Priscilla. *There* was a name he wouldn't forget. It had a strange empty, cold ring to it now. The thought of her presence made him shut his open eye. Maybe it was part of the nightmare or his sentence to eternal damnation. Either way, the strain wasn't worth it. If it really was her, she'd only shown up to look good and circle like a vulture waiting to pick his corpse, and probably his bank account, clean. He decided she might be real, and if so, he'd better respond before she flipped a switch or tripped on a cord and ended his life for sure.

"What are you doing here?" he said in a dry scratchy whisper.

"I'm your wife, David. Don't you remember?" Priscilla said, cutting her eyes toward the nurse standing within earshot.

"Let's cut the act," David said, still not opening his eyes. Despite the fact that every word was accompanied by a piercing pain in his chest, he took in another breath and efficiently finished his revelation. "We've been acting the part for years."

Priscilla kept her eyes on the nurse, who kept her back to the pair and pretended not to hear a word. "I'm not sure what you mean, dear."

David opened his left eye again and looked at Priscilla. Even through his foggy vision, she looked beautifully sexy. Years ago, she'd dressed that way for him. Now he knew she'd been somewhere trying to attract her next bedmate. He hadn't minded much until now. He remembered how he always used to think about how she looked on his arm. Now he couldn't think of a reason they were together. There was none.

"I mean you and I have no love and no respect for each other. This has just been an arrangement of convenience for both us. There's no meaning in our lives together."

David coughed once and winced in pain. The nurse turned from the bank of monitors and glanced at David. She turned back to the monitors as his breathing settled back into a steady rhythm.

The look on Priscilla's face was worth the pain. Her nose was wrinkled, and he swore she was holding her breath as her face began to turn red. She hated to look bad in front of anybody, including an attending nurse. He'd never seen her speechless. After a minute, she exhaled and gathered her composure.

"David, you don't know what you're saying. It must be the medication."

"It's not the medication," he snapped back. The beeping of the heart monitor sped up quickly. "It's you."

Priscilla recoiled and stepped back from the bed.

"There's no need for you to come back. We're through!" he yelled in his hoarse dry voice. The heart monitor was now beeping at twice the frequency from before. David began to cough uncontrollably. The nurse stepped to his side and looked up at Priscilla.

"You'll have to leave now, Mrs. Wellington."

Priscilla gave her an indignant look and stormed from the room. The nurse raised the head of the bed and injected a clear liquid into one of the IVs.

David's respiration and pulse dropped, and he began to slip back into a drug-induced sleep. A smile spread across his face. For the first time, he'd spoken the truth to Priscilla. Part of the sadness and regret lifted. He wasn't sure if it was the medicine. Suddenly, a song from his favorite childhood movie echoed in his head. *Ding dong! The witch is dead! Which ol' witch? The wicked witch* …

# CHAPTER 14

LATE THE NEXT morning, Prescott Rexsen paced past the marble fireplace, crystal chandeliers, and tall bookcases of the Card Room,
the elegant conference facility overlooking the eighteenth hole and the
waters bordering the exclusive Pebble Beach Resort. He stopped at the
sliding glass door of the terrace and watched the ominous beginnings
of a Pacific storm slam frothy breakers against the jagged rocks as they
fought a losing battle against the angry sea. Prescott smiled when he
thought of David Wellington, who'd lose his own hopeless battle to
retain control of Rexsen Labs in just a few minutes. He enjoyed his
newfound feeling of superiority. He watched the golfers who had paid
$600 for a hurried round before the storm broke scurry for cover and
curse. Rain, driven by strong gusts of wind, clicked against the glass
and began to blur his view.

In a few minutes, he would make the most important speech of
his life. He moved his lips, practicing the words that would accompany
his slides, words that would lead him to riches and power far greater
than the old man ever had. He marched to the head of the mahogany
table and dropped into the chair.

That old bastard was gone, and today it was his show. Prescott
now represented the trust, and he had control of Rexsen Labs. With
the IPO scheduled for a week from Tuesday, he had only nine more

days until his net worth ballooned to $6 billion. He'd propose to put Brayton in control, since Wellington was incapacitated by the unfortunate accident. Most of the work had already been done with the board, but he needed the formal approval from the members, including Claire Armstrong and William Walters.

Representing a large mutual fund and a prominent investment bank, they were the most influential members, brought in by Prescott's father to bring credibility to the board as Rexsen Labs prepared to go public. With a little pressure from Prescott and Brayton, the other board members had easily fallen in line and agreed to support the change. Although technically they didn't need Walters's and Armstrong's approval, Prescott knew he needed it to preserve his fortune. If they didn't vote to replace Wellington, Armstrong and Walters had the option to resign just before the IPO. Prescott knew that would put the huge run-up in stock price, currently predicted by Wall Street insiders, at risk. With the Rexsen Family Trust holding over one hundred million shares, that equated to a $9 billion bet Prescott was not willing to take.

One by one the dark-suited board members filed into the room. All had been contacted and knew precisely the issue to be decided: Wellington out and Brayton in as CEO—permanently. The meeting began and Prescott nervously droned through his prepared remarks. He described how they were in the quiet period, the time where the SEC would allow no information to be released other than the prospectus for the IPO. The prospectus could be amended in time to still go public a week from Tuesday. The lead underwriter had quietly contacted the largest institutional investors, and the change to Brayton as CEO, with his reputation to run stock prices up in the short term, actually seemed to increase interest in the already-oversubscribed stock.

Prescott stood as he prepared to make his final statement.

"Therefore, I propose we elect Royce Brayton CEO in accordance with the terms provided to you in your packet. David Wellington remains incapacitated and would be unable to maintain the pace necessary to continue to lead Rexsen Labs through this critical time in our company's history. He will, of course, receive a very generous severance and be retained on a consulting basis for three years at his current salary. Any discussion?"

Most at the table remained silent and shuffled papers. But William Walters fired the first salvo. "What the hell are you up to, Prescott? I've known your father for years. He was a good and trusted friend. I know he wouldn't support this change at any point, let alone nine days before we go public."

Prescott sat back down in his chair. "I simply have our new shareholders' interests in mind." Prescott knew Walters and his father were close. He was sure his father had talked about him behind his back. He hoped Walters would make a good public showing for the rest of the board and beat his chest like the biggest gorilla in the jungle but, as he'd promised, ultimately support the change.

Claire Armstrong slammed her fist on the table. "Has anyone talked to David? Have you talked to David?" she said, pointing her finger at Prescott. He was surprised by her challenge, considering her promise of support on the golf course.

Prescott raised his crooked index finger and returned fire. "He's out of the picture," Prescott whined. "He's in the hospital, and who knows when he'll get out. Even then, my sister has said his brains are scrambled. Do we want him guiding this business with mush for brains? Brayton has the track record. He's an integral part of the management team. He's had a prominent role in all our management presentations to the investors, and the underwriters say naming him CEO will actually improve the performance of the IPO."

Prescott had been well-briefed by Brayton on how to cut off Armstrong and Walters. He crossed his arms and delivered the punch line.

"Each of you will gain significant wealth with this plan. And I assume I don't need to remind you who will control 61 percent of the company when it goes public."

Armstrong and Walters were finished. The Rexsen Family Trust would control 61 percent, Wellington 10 percent and Brayton 2.5 percent after the IPO. The remaining 66.7 million shares were being offered at $30 to an elite group of investors. And with the IPO demand much higher than the shares available, the stock would pop to $120 in the first day or so of trading. Brayton was holding an unofficial offer of $200 from a major pharmaceutical company. Prescott knew Armstrong and Walters had no support to press the issue, and if their positions were made public, even if only in the elite circles they traveled, their reputations as tough advocates for the shareholders would be destroyed. Too much money was on the table for all concerned, especially the institutional investors. They owed the old man's honor one try, but that was all.

"Now I need a motion to elect Royce Brayton CEO."

There were no smiles, and no one hurried to make the motion. A fainthearted motion from board member John Durham was seconded by longtime board member Robert Effingham. The vote was unanimous. David Wellington would no longer run the company he built. It was in the hands of a vindictive son, a scorned daughter, and a wannabe Wall Street cover boy. They'd cash out with $12 billion, and CGT, with its undetectable flaws, would flood the market. Hopes of cancer patients and their families would soar—at least for a while. Then the unsuspecting patients would receive their death sentences one at a time, victims of CGT's genetic imperfections.

# CHAPTER 15

DAVID FLUNG THE covers off and perched on the side of the bed. It was Monday morning; he'd been in the hospital for three days. The door to his private room was propped open and the whispered chatter at the nurse's station drifted in. The room was washed in dim florescent light. The dry air filled his nostrils, and for the first time, he smelled the effects of three days without a shower. He winced as he raised each arm, testing their effectiveness for the first time since the crash. He looked down and plucked at the rumpled, dingy white hospital gown hanging loosely from his shoulders. Priscilla's visit had him worried—she'd never been that concerned for anyone except herself. With her father gone, she and her idiot brother had inherited billions—and as long as he was *alive*, he'd be entitled to half. He needed to get out of here.

"Mr. Wellington, you're up," the nurse said, entering with a small plastic cup and a glass of water. "Time for your meds."

David studied the nurse as he reached for the cup on the tray in her hand. Her wrists were thick and her forearms were strong and well-defined. There was no wedding band and no tan line on her ring finger. He guessed she was in her late forties, and she carried herself with an air of confidence—she'd been at this awhile. David smiled and threw the pills down his throat and chugged the water.

"Mmm, my favorites!"

"You're certainly feeling your oats," she said, taking the cup from his hand and circling the bed.

David held his grin. "Any chance I can I get out of here?" he said, scratching the stubble on the side of his chin.

"Whoa, tiger. You've had a pretty rough time, and we're still checking you out. The doc has a few more tests to run, and you need to get back on solid food and get more mobility back."

David twisted at the waist to stretch and quickly covered the pain in his side with his hand. "I just assumed with all your great care I'd be out of here pretty soon."

She stopped at his bedside and gently took his wrist and slipped a pulse oximeter onto his finger and smiled.

David sheepishly looked up. "How much longer?"

"I don't know. It depends on you and your test results." The nurse was firm.

"Can I at least get some fresh air?"

"Do you think you're ready to try walking?"

David nodded and the thick-bodied nurse extended a strong arm.

David shifted his weight to his arms and pushed himself to his feet. He held his breath as the pain shot through his legs, but the payoff was worth it. He wanted to get out. There was a reason he miraculously survived, the orderly had said. Now, despite the threat from Brayton, Prescott, and Priscilla, David was desperate to find it.

The nurse guided him to the door, and he propped himself with the IV stand. Moving under his own power, he let go of the nurse's arm.

"I'll be right here if you need me," she said, stepping aside.

The steps were hard at first. The bruises and cuts burned with each step. He shuffled along the linoleum floor and listened to the noises emanating from each room he passed, but he resisted looking in at the occupants. He passed the nurses' station and managed a smile at the young woman seated at the desk. A TV blasted from the room to the right. A reporter was giving a recap of David's miraculous survival of the horrible crash. "The miracle man," he called him. David had to glance in.

"Hey, mister! It's you!" The voice was high-pitched but pleasant. He recognized the unpretentious tone of a child, a young girl. He paused and leaned into the room.

"It *is* you. You're the miracle man!" A mountain of pillows propped up the girl, maybe nine or ten, as she sat upright in bed. An IV at her bedside was attached to her arm through a clear tube. A metering device clicked and beeped at her bedside. She wore a red Anaheim Angels cap, obviously hiding a hairless head. She grinned in excitement, her large blue eyes locked on David.

"I'm sorry, she just saw a picture of you on TV," a woman's voice said from behind the curtain of the semiprivate room.

"No problem. I guess I'll have to get used to that," David said, shuffling into the room. "I'm David Wellington."

"Mr. Wellington, I'm Faith Carlton." The woman was in her thirties, fit and lean like a runner. There were dark, tired circles under her bloodshot eyes. Her short dark hair was tousled. It was the same ragged look his wife had as they watched Connor die. She stepped from behind the curtain and extended her hand to help David.

"And who is this pretty young lady?" David asked with a smile.

"I'm Amy."

David stood by her bed. Something drew him to her.

"The news said you should have died," Amy said.

"Amy!" her mother said.

"It's okay. She's right. I should have." He took a seat at the foot of her bed.

"So, how come you didn't die?" Amy asked.

"Now, that's a good question. I've been asking myself the same thing."

"You know what I think?" Amy grinned with a knowing look.

"No. What do you think, Miss Amy?"

"I think the TV was right. It was a miracle. And since it was a miracle, God saved you."

"Well, I guess that makes sense," David said, glancing at Faith.

"And if God did it, there must be a really good reason. Do you know what it is?"

David shifted uneasily in his seat. The discomfort was not from his injuries. It came from inside him. Amy had hit the nail on the head. *There must be a really good reason.* But what was it? If Amy was right and it was God, could he have made a mistake? After all, David knew he hadn't lived his life to this point in accordance with God's teachings.

"I guess I don't know yet," David said.

"That's okay; I know you'll find out." Amy's confidence made him feel a little better.

"So what brings you here, Miss Amy?" David asked.

"Well, I have a cancer. This stuff here fights it off. I come here every now and then to fight the cancer. It tires me out, but I know it's good for me."

David, impressed with her frankness, offered encouragement. "Well, you keep fighting."

David started to get up and Faith stepped in to help. He shuffled out the door.

"I'll see you later, Miss Amy."

"Bye, miracle man." Amy giggled.

Faith followed David out the door. Both stopped just out of Amy's earshot.

"Mr. Wellington, I've read about the gene therapy treatment your company developed and is testing. Is it really that promising?"

"Absolutely. We hope to have FDA approval next week and make it available within a month or two."

Tears welled in Faith's tired eyes and she reached for David's hand. "Mr. Wellington, Amy may not have that much time. I know I have no right to ask you this, considering your condition, but I'd do anything to allow her to get the treatment now. They've told us this is her last treatment. The cancer seems to have stopped responding to the chemo. If there's anything you can do ..." Her tired eyes begged him.

Without thinking, David stepped closer and wrapped his arms around her. Normally, he'd have blown her off and given her some phone number of a contact buried deep in the company and that would have been the end of it. But he'd met Amy, and that made a difference.

The nurse stepped into the doorway. "There you are. The doctor wants to see you. It's time for another test. Excuse us—I need to get him back to his room."

"Of course," Faith said, wiping her cheek.

"I'll ... I'll look into it," David said as he was led away to his room. He wanted to cry, too. It was a feeling he'd nearly forgotten. He remembered how he'd begged for his young son's life and how no one could help. Some of the doctors, nurses, administrators and researchers had seemed concerned and had looked at him with helpless pity, but others were either too busy or just didn't want to get involved and had brushed him off. Life flickered in his young son's eyes, and then, late one evening, the little boy's big blue eyes rolled to the top of his head and closed. His breathing grew shallow and tears filled David's tired eyes. He held his little boy's hand and watched him surrender his last breath. His heart hardened that day, and he promised he'd never rely on or care for another person again. It was a promise he'd kept for over fifteen years—until today.

# CHAPTER 16

TORI CLARKE WEAVED through the Monday morning traffic along the wide tree-lined boulevard. The clear blue sky held a brilliant sun, which peeked over the mountains to the east. A light offshore breeze filled the air with the fresh smell of cypress and salt water. The wind from the open driver's window toyed with her dark brown hair. Any other day, she'd be singing to the radio and reveling in the beautiful weather that Newport Beach seemed to deliver more days than not, but not today.

The breeze cooled her reddened eyes and helped her fight the fatigue of a sleepless night. The call from Rexsen's human resources department had come the previous evening. The project manager for CGT, Jeff Reese, had been killed in a tragic accident. There would be some immediate changes, and Tori was to report directly to Brayton's office first thing this morning. She considered the possibility that this may be her last day on the job. Brayton had told her to turn her work over to an outside contractor. She'd seen him grimace for a moment when he first heard the news that CGT had a problem, but then he smiled and dished out a few compliments. After what she'd heard about his slick reputation, she wouldn't put it past that asshole. To make things worse, when she'd asked the caller what the subject of the meeting was, she was told to just be on time.

Now she looped around Newport Center Drive, turned right onto Santa Barbara Drive, pulled to the security gate at the entrance of the Rexsen Labs complex, and displayed her security badge to the elderly guard in the booth. The guard leaned out and gave her a somber smile.

"Terrible news about Mr. Reese. He was a nice man."

Tori dropped the badge into her purse and did her best to return a smile, but a lump in her throat choked off her attempt to reply. She swallowed hard. "He certainly was." She focused on the lifting gate and got back under control. "Thank you."

Numbly, she drove along the four-story white marble administration building and then hunted up and down the rows of parked cars between the lab complex and the admin building until an open space appeared. She pulled her Prius into the spot and stepped out and glanced at the lab. She was close to the cure—and close to fulfilling her promise to Aaron. She took a deep breath and prepared to face whatever Brayton had to say. Either way, she convinced herself, she wouldn't let it stop her. Turning her back on the lab where she'd worked for three years, she marched into the main office building that housed Rexsen's executives, lawyers, and accountants. With her chin up and ready for battle, she cleared security and headed to the elevators without making eye contact with anyone.

Once on the executive floor, she walked the long hardwood corridor and listened to the clicking of her own heels. She entered Brayton's office suite and abruptly stopped when she noticed the parade of managers and company lawyers lined up outside his office in the waiting area.

"Hello, Ms. Clarke," Brayton's secretary said, stepping from behind her desk. "I'll let him know you're here. He's expecting you."

Tori stood firm, like a statue, as she watched Dianne bypass the long line of managers waiting for Brayton's attention. After a quick knock on the door, Dianne opened it just wide enough to announce,

"She's here." Dianne stepped aside, held the door open, and gave Tori a polite smile. "Come in, Miss Clarke."

Tori focused on the door and tried not to catch the annoyed looks from the managers lining the walls of the suite's lobby. She took a deep breath and stepped past Dianne and into Brayton's office. She heard the door close behind her. She prepared for the worst.

Brayton looked up from his neatly organized desk and smiled. His obvious attempt to use his legendary charm disgusted Tori. She never knew why people said he was charming.

"Ah, Miss Clarke, please have a seat."

"No, thank you, Mr. Brayton. I'll stand."

Tori moved quickly to the desk, stood in silence and mustered as much emotional armor as she could. Her blue eyes were wide open and locked on Brayton's as she braced for another dose of bullshit from this arrogant bastard.

He smiled again, ignoring her refusal to sit. "First of all, please accept my apology for my shortness with you last Friday. There was pressure to get ready for the board meeting, and I wasn't ready for the news you delivered."

"That's okay, Mr. Brayton. I understand."

Tori listened to the words tumble out of her mouth. That was not the response she'd promised her friends she'd give him, if given the opportunity. He'd been the topic of discussion for Friday's happy hour session at McGinty's. Everyone agreed with Tori's assessment that he was just a hired henchman who would get his someday. The next time she had a chance, she'd tell that bastard off in a second, she'd bragged. This was that chance.

"Well, now that that's out of the way, I wanted to give you some good news. With the events of this past weekend, we have to make some changes in the research division. Effective today, you're the new group leader for Proteus 40."

Tori tried not to react. Proteus 40 was the next high-profile advance in the oncology line of gene therapy treatments. It was entering phase one testing and would be fast-tracked to get FDA approval within the next eighteen months. She'd made several requests to Reese to transfer into the section. She had an even greater passion for the effort than she had for CGT since it was targeted at several other forms of leukemia, the disease that ended her little brother's life at the age of nine. Obviously, Brayton had been well-briefed.

"I ... I don't know what to say."

Brayton laughed. "I'll take that as a 'yes.' I've taken the liberty of setting up your new office in Laboratory C. You're to report there for your first briefing in fifteen minutes." Brayton stood and extended his hand across the desk.

With her head still spinning, Tori shook his hand. "Thank you," she heard herself say.

"Congratulations, Tori. I know you'll be a terrific asset to the team."

He dropped back into his seat and picked up a memo and began to read, making it clear the meeting was over. She headed to the door, but as she grabbed the brass knob, she turned back to Brayton. He was still ignoring her presence.

"Mr. Brayton?"

Brayton raised his head, looking a little aggravated. "What?"

"What's going to happen with my findings on CGT?"

"Don't worry about that. We already have a team charged with confirming your results. Your job is Proteus 40. Focus on that."

"Thank you," she repeated and left.

In a daze, she weaved her way through the people who were nervously shuffling through documents in the outer office of the suite. She didn't remember the elevator ride, the trek across the parking lot to the lab, or the strange walk to her new office. She tried to figure out what just happened. Brayton just gave her a great promotion. He never mentioned anything about Reese's death, though—no sadness, no re-morse, no sympathy. On Friday, he seemed ready to fire her and then he had praised her, and now she was leading the next blockbuster can-cer treatment team.

She entered her office and dropped her bag. All of her personal items had been moved over the weekend, including her desk. She headed to the conference room for her first briefing. No time for sort-ing things out right now. Her distrust for Brayton and the motives be-hind her promotion was secondary. She had more important things to do.

Things like finding the cure for her little brother's killer.

# CHAPTER 17

IT WAS MONDAY morning and Prescott Rexsen was finally at the top the Rexsen empire. He sat on the edge of his brown leather executive chair, faced the huge oak desk and, for the tenth time, adjusted the phone, leather blotter, and thirty-inch flat screen, which boldly displayed the Rexsen Lab's screen saver. He gazed at the view once reserved for his father. The sailboats bobbed in the blue Pacific just beyond Newport Beach Harbor.

Rocking him from his daydream, Priscilla stormed into the office and slammed her purse on his desk. Prescott spun from the window to face her.

"Christ, Pris! What the hell is your problem?"

She hadn't planned on starting this conversation red-faced and flustered, but the sight of her idiot brother, seated in her father's chair and playing king for a day, boiled her blood. "My problem is David Wellington."

"What else is new? He's been chapping your surgically enhanced behind for years." Prescott snorted as he chuckled at Priscilla's expense.

"Keep laughing, you slimeball. We'll see how you like dealing with him as a member of our trust!" Priscilla wouldn't take any guff from her older brother. Their father had favored him just because he was the only male successor. The human genome had randomly given *him* the Y chromosome instead of her. She was smarter and more cunning and he knew it. Now her problem would become his problem, Y chromosome or not.

The smirk left Prescott's face. "What?"

"You heard me. David asked me for a divorce, from his hospital bed. He'll get half of everything I have, including my share of the trust."

Prescott put his elbows on his desk and cradled his greasy head. Calmer now, Priscilla dropped into the side chair.

"So, my dear brother, what do you have to say about that?" The smirk had passed to Priscilla's face.

Prescott paused and rubbed his slicked scalp with both hands. In disgust, Priscilla watched the white flakes that fell onto the blotter.

"He's not out of the woods yet. Still in intensive care, isn't he?"

"He was Saturday night, but I wouldn't bet against him making it. He's just survived a jet crash from twenty-six thousand feet."

She kept the pressure on Prescott. She'd always been able to get him to do what she wanted. Her plan was simple: since divorce would give David half her fortune and the possibility to build his shares to a controlling interest in Rexsen, she needed to get him out of the way for good, and Prescott represented means to that end. Priscilla knew all the right buttons to push. While he exuded an air of superiority, she knew the soft underbelly of his armor. He couldn't stand the reality of his own limitations, especially those reflected in his father's reluctance to hand him the reins of the company.

"I'm quite certain you'll be answering his questions for the rest of your life. I'm sure our father would have loved that. He seemed to favor David."

Prescott turned a bright red. Priscilla had pressed another button.

"Wellington's an ass! I'm the son. Not him. The trust belongs to us and I will run it the way I see fit." Prescott's tone turned sarcastic. "Now that our loving father is gone, I'll make us richer than ever."

Priscilla continued to play her role well. Acting school was paying off. "I just don't know how you'll do that with David having a quarter of the trust under his control."

"Don't worry about that, little sister," he said, trying to sound arrogant.

"So you think you're tough enough do what it takes to get David out of the way? To beat him?"

The hook was baited and she waited for him to bite.

Prescott shot up from his chair. "You're damn right I am," he yelled. "With my connections he'll be done before he knows what hit him!"

Satisfied that his warped ego was sufficiently inflamed, Priscilla grinned and waved him off. "Whatever you say. I'm off to the divorce lawyer's office anyway. I'll believe you've handled things when I see it."

Priscilla grabbed her purse and pranced out of the office. She smiled when she cleared the doorway. She had no intention of seeing a divorce lawyer—she wouldn't need one. After all, she'd always been the smartest one in the family.

# CHAPTER 18

DAVID WELLINGTON DUG into Monday's afternoon meal. The boiled carrots, mashed potatoes, and brown mystery meat covered in gravy were the first solid food he'd had in four days. He was so hungry, finally, that it might as well have been a filet mignon served at 21 Oceanfront in Newport Beach.

For the third time that day, he called his private line at the office. Carolyn always picked up on the second ring, but not today. And why hadn't she come to visit him? Or anyone from Rexsen, for that matter? Searching for news about his company, he picked up the remote and surfed the business-news channels.

Nothing.

He wasn't sure if his stomach was unsettled by the meal or by Carolyn's mysterious absence from her post.

The bang on the door startled David, and Prescott Rexsen slithered in with Patrick O'Reilly, his corporate secretary, in tow. O'Reilly avoided eye contact and Prescott stopped at the foot of the bed and stared at David. Prescott smiled, showing his yellow teeth. David knew from the look on Prescott's face the news was bad, and he braced himself.

Ignoring the pain, David crossed his arms. "Well, what's up, guys?"

"Mr. Wellington, as the head of the board's executive committee, I regret to inform you that you've been voted out of the CEO's job for Rexsen Labs. Our legal staff will negotiate your severance with the law firm of your choosing."

"What?" David screamed, feeling searing heat rush to his face. "What the hell did you just say?"

Prescott kept grinning.

"Look, Rexy boy," David scoffed, using a nickname he knew Prescott despised. "I was playing this game when you were still having your mommy wipe your ass. I'm still running things here."

Prescott turned red. "You're fired, you bastard! You and that sorry old man I had for a father can't freakin' tell me what to do anymore!"

*The asshole is enjoying this. He wanted to deliver the news.* David grabbed the plastic tray and fired it at Prescott. He followed the tray out of the bed and throttled Prescott by the throat.

"I'll kill you, you little greasy bastard."

Wellington, well over six feet tall, hammered the stringy man into the linoleum floor. The nurse stormed in just as O'Reilly began to pull David off Prescott, who screamed like a little girl. The two finally got David up and onto the bed while Prescott sat on the floor and straightened his ruffled clothes. He looked ready to cry.

"What's going on in here?" the nurse demanded.

A security guard entered the room and helped Prescott to his feet. David glared at Prescott and huffed and puffed to catch his breath while the nurse straightened the covers.

"Nothing," he said, his eyes locked on Prescott. "This asshole was just leaving."

"You're lucky I don't sue you!" Prescott whined.

The nurse nodded to the security guard. "Please escort these gentlemen out of here, Frank."

"You haven't heard the last from me," David shouted as Prescott
and O'Reilly left the room. Prescott leaned back in and gave David the
finger and shot a mock smile at him. The guard yanked Prescott out of
the doorway.

"Now, there'll be no more of that here, Mr. Wellington," the nurse
said.

David glared at the door and shook his head. Prescott was a
pompous ass. He wasn't smart enough to get the board to abandon
David in favor of Brayton. He must have had help. Now, five days
before the planned approval of CGT and a week before Rexsen Labs
would go public, Prescott Rexsen, the smelly, slinky mouse of a man
whose own father had wanted him on the sidelines, had David's life's
work in his hands.

But it wasn't the power or the money that burned the fuse to the
anger about to explode inside him. Ever since the plane crash, his reason for living had changed. Now his need to get out of the hospital
bed and regain control of Rexsen Labs came from another place. An
image of a bald ten-year-old in an Angels cap, with her body being
ravaged by cancer, gave him his answer. He had a promise to keep.

# CHAPTER 19

MCGINTY'S WAS THE place to go for professionals in Newport Beach. Its low profile and dark glass exterior, nestled among the banana palms, birds of paradise, and Torrey pines, gave an air of understated elegance. Its location just on the outer rim of Newport Center Drive placed it directly in the path of the high-tech professionals and sophisticated financial types who worked in the corporate offices and campuses in the immediate area. Inside, a bevy of framed photographs of public figures hung on the richly stained walls of the lobby. Deep crimson leather booths trimmed with brass buttons circled the long brass-railed bar. On any given night, men and women, still wearing their power suits, mingled, dined and drank.

On Monday nights, Tori Clarke and her friend Kelly always took the stools at the end of the bar. Tori had sworn off men since she was seventeen. A summer fling with a ranch hand at her father's ranch ended in rape. She'd never told a soul. Tori couldn't trust any man now, and it created a tortured loneliness she filled with work. Six months ago, Kelly's husband of three years walked out to trade up to an even younger model. Kelly had worked with Tori for the last three years at Rexsen as a research assistant. While she was a few years older than Tori, her bright eyes, short dark hair and smooth skin made her appear younger. The secluded corner allowed the privacy necessary to discuss anything and keep the suited wolves trolling the bar at bay.

"What's happening in the CGT section?" Tori said. "I'm sure gonna miss you guys."

"It won't be the same without you," Kelly said. "With Reese gone, they shook up the whole team today. Said we needed to focus on the next treatment in the pipeline. CGT was sales', marketing's, and manufacturing's focus now. A few of the team were assigned to do long-term testing, but the rest of us were moved to CGT II."

Tori sipped her pinot grigio, leaned in close and squeezed Kelly's shoulder. "You're kidding me, right?" Tori couldn't say much more. She couldn't talk about her findings regarding CGT, so she bit her lower lip and took a long gulp of her pinot. Everything was covered by the confidentiality agreement she'd signed on employment. If she did talk about the findings, she'd be fired and blackballed in the industry. "What happened to my work? Where did it go?"

Kelly slammed her drink on the dark wood bar and leaned closer to Tori. Her eyes grew wide in disbelief. "You didn't hear?" she whispered. "It was all gathered up. We thought you took it with you."

Kelly nervously flicked her glass with her finger. She seemed worried she'd said something she shouldn't have.

"Brayton didn't tell me anything. Just promoted me and told me to get to work immediately on Proteus 40. I haven't had time to even think about anything else with this new position as director for Proteus. He told me there was a team already assigned to confirm my work."

"If it is, it must be subcontracted to another lab," Kelly said as she took another sip of her drink and eyeballed Tori over the rim of the glass.

"Watch my seat for a minute." Tori jumped from the stool and marched to the lobby as she dug into her purse. She produced an iPhone and dialed Brayton's number. It was 7 p.m. and she knew he'd still be in the office.

"Brayton," he answered.

Tori turned her back to the bar and huddled against the wall so no one could hear her words. "Mr. Brayton, this is Tori Clarke. I'm sorry to bother you this late."

"No bother, Miss Clarke. What can I do for you?"

"I just hadn't heard anything about my work on CGT and was curious how the team was doing."

"Miss Clarke, that's no longer your area, and you know we don't share information unless there is a need to know," Brayton said.

"I know, Mr. Brayton. Can you tell me anything?" Begging might work, she thought.

"I can tell you this. Your work is being reviewed. The outside lab found one flaw in your method already. Anything else?"

Tori swallowed hard. She couldn't ask the next question. She knew her work was solid. She'd followed widely accepted protocols, from the preparation of the DNA samples and isolating the mRNA right down to the base pairing with the cDNA on the microarrays. There was nothing wrong with her work. Her assistant verified it, and Reese had signed off on it. She didn't trust Brayton. If he was dismissing her data, he was planning on going forward with CGT. But now was not the time to confront him. She needed time to think.

"No, Mr. Brayton. Sorry if my work caused any undue concern." Tori was trying to remain calm and sound apologetic. She knew Brayton was lying. The phone shook in her trembling hand.

"Not to worry, Miss Clarke. You were just doing your job. Good night."

Brayton hung up and Tori slid the iPhone into her purse. She understood the havoc CGT would cause within the human genome if it was not fixed. It would raise the hopes of patients and family members just long enough to make the deadly diagnosis that would follow the treatment by a few months that much more devastating to patients, mothers, fathers, brothers, and sisters—and she knew that devastation all too well. She marched back to the bar and stopped behind her chair.

"I gotta go, Kelly."

"What? We just got here."

An explanation would require sharing all the facts, and there was no need to pull her friend into this and risk both their jobs. "I gotta go now. Sorry, I'll call you." Tori threw a twenty on the bar and left.

A man at the far corner of the bar with a three-day growth, very short brown hair, and a black T-shirt and leather jacket chugged his scotch and followed.

# CHAPTER 20

THE GLOW FROM the flat-screen monitors was the only light in the warehouse. The alert chirped at 6:32 p.m., indicating the recording device had been voice-activated. The jagged pattern on one of the five screens visually displayed every inflection in the voices. The name in the frame on the lower left hand side was Clarke. A man dressed in black sat at attention in front of the monitor and slipped on the headphones and listened.

The listening post was buried within the shabby warehouses of Long Beach Harbor. Butch Donovan and his team had manned it twenty-four hours a day. They'd used it for every assignment. Surrounded by the huge cranes and weathered shipping containers stacked three high, its location was unknown to all except Donovan and three of his men.

Derek Lane, Donovan's deadliest mercenary, who led the surveillance on Clarke, listened closely to the conversation between Tori and Kelly at McGinty's, and then he clicked the "play" button on the second screen and listened to the phone call from Clarke to Brayton. He immediately pulled out his smartphone and called his superior.

"Go ahead," Donovan said.

"Got something you need to hear, boss. Are you close to a secure computer? It's about eighteen minutes of audio."

"Yeah, send it over."

Lane clicked the "send" button.

"What's up?" Donovan said.

"Clarke met with a coworker from the old CGT team. Asked about follow-up on her work. Clarke called Brayton, and I think he gave her the slip. She sounded like she believed she made a mistake in her data, ashamed and all that."

"Awe, shit! She called Brayton? Uh, I'm opening the file now. Let me listen to it."

"Affirmative. I'll stand by for your call back." Lane ended the call and sat silently in the darkness.


Butch Donovan, a massive muscular man who, according to the records of the U.S. government, died twelve years ago in Bogotá and no longer existed, was doing what he did best. His client had set him up quite nicely in a contemporary three-bedroom home overlooking the Pacific in Laguna Beach. His home office was equipped with state-of-the-art surveillance equipment. His three computers were connected through a secure line. His client had spared no expense in ensuring he had the tools to track their targets and take whatever action was required to ensure their control of Rexsen Labs. He clicked the icon on his screen, and he turned his ear to the speaker and listened to Tori's voice above the din of the bar crowd.

He jumped when his phone rang. He dashed across the room to the smartphone on the kitchen table and waited one more ring while he tried to catch his breath.

"Donovan."

"Damn it, you said Clarke would not be a problem!" the synthesized voice said.

"My guys are on top of it. I'm just reviewing the audio now."

"There's no damn reason to review the audio. I'm telling you, she's starting to nose around. Now, what are you doing about it!"

"Look. She thinks she screwed up. I've got a man tailing her 24/7. If she makes a wrong move, we'll take care of it."

"Like you took care of Wellington?"

"Don't worry about Wellington. He's history. Tonight he attacked that weasel Prescott. Got a security guard in our pocket. He saw the whole thing. Wellington has been fired, and we have an insurance policy."

"I don't give a shit what you have. Just do your damn job."

Donovan jerked the phone from his ear as his client slammed it into the cradle. He shook his head. "Asshole." He'd worked for assholes for the past ten years and made a ton of money, but he didn't have to like the bastards. He pressed a button and held the phone to his ear. "It's me. Look, we need to stay close to her. If she makes another move and starts snooping around, let me know."

Donovan set the phone down, clicked the mouse and continued to listen. The conversation with his client was still on his mind. He fantasized about being Wellington in the hospital room and pounding Prescott's head into the floor. No one would have been able to pull *him* off. Then it hit him. The solution to the problem was so obvious. It was clean, it was clever and it would be fun. He hit "redial" and watched the lights of the freighters slowly tracking across the dark Pacific.

"We need Waters—now."

He threw the phone onto the table and grinned. He loved the hunt. He identified with the soul of the great whites surely lurking in the depths of the black waters sprawling before him to the horizon. He was just as undetectable and even deadlier. He sure liked his job.

# CHAPTER 21

DAVID WELLINGTON WATCHED as Monday's evening business news reported the change. It was then that the reality hit hard. Rexsen's CEO, the news anchor explained, had been replaced by Royce Brayton. Mr. Wellington was unable to continue as CEO due to injuries sustained in the unfortunate crash of Rexsen's corporate aircraft that took the life of its founder, Adam Rexsen. Royce Brayton had a great track record for increasing shareholder value, he said. Then, in a well-planned sound bite, Brayton appeared on screen and said he planned to take the company public immediately, out of respect for Adam Rexsen's commitment to fighting cancer with CGT. The room seemed to close in on David. He pressed the remote harder and harder, switching from newscast to newscast, until he finally threw the remote, and it shattered against the wall. He repeatedly crushed the nurse call button in his hand.

"What can I do for you, Mr. Wellington?" she asked.

"You can get me the hell out of here!" David locked his arms across his chest and scowled.

"Now, there's no reason to take that tone with me, Mr. Wellington."

David looked away from her and took a deep breath. "I'm sorry, but have you been watching the news?"

The nurse chuckled. "No, I've been taking care of my other patients."

David had to laugh at himself. Millions of people probably saw the broadcast and said, "So what?"

"Well, it was pretty bad stuff," he said, losing some of his self-pity.

"I know it seems that way. Sorry about your job, but you'll get another. And I understand you guys at the top get a pile of money when you leave anyway."

*So much for sympathy. What did she know? She didn't build the company from a ten-person firm to one of the largest in the country.* "When can I get released?"

The nurse came over to his bedside and checked the readings on the monitor beside his bed.

"You can ask the doc on rounds tomorrow morning. I think he'll want to run more tests."

"No more tests."

"That's between you and the doc. He'll be here around eight."

She straightened his pillows and gently pulled the sheet up to his neck.

For a moment he was reminded of his childhood and how his mother gently tucked him in each night. That is, until his father's carousing finally caught up with her and she put a bullet in her head. He'd never felt more alone than on that night. The same emptiness now gnawed inside him.

The nurse left the room. David turned to the phone on the nightstand and dialed Joe Pirelli's number. He was the only friend he had.

"Joe here."

Joe had been David's driver for fifteen years. When they first met, David sensed Joe was not a great fan, but over the years the two grew closer. One evening, after a few drinks, Joe told David how he hated

Priscilla and Prescott and how poorly they treated everyone, especially the hired help. Joe wondered out loud why David tolerated Priscilla's cheating. He even absolved David for his trysts with several Newport Beach beauties onboard David's yacht. David wasn't sure if Joe genuinely liked him or just felt sorry for him, but Joe was trustworthy, and he needed someone he could trust.

"Hi, Joe."

"Hey, boss. How the hell are you? I thought you might be taking a dirt nap!"

David smiled. Joe's sense of humor was tactless but still funny. "Nope, I'm still looking at the grass from the right side."

David heard Joe chuckle.

"So what's up boss? I saw the news. Looks like the inmates are running the asylum."

"You're right there. Speaking of asylums, I want you to be here at eight tomorrow morning to get me out of this one."

"Cedars?"

"Yup."

"They letting you out already? Damn, you *are* a miracle man."

"Just be here at eight sharp. Pack some clothes for me. We'll be going to the beach house."

"I love that place."

"Me, too."

The beach house had been David's third extravagant purchase after his annual earnings reached the more-money-than-you-can-spend level. It was his private hideaway. He spent as much time there as anywhere, to escape both the job and Priscilla. Joe and he spent many nights on the deck swapping stories. David would explain the mysteries of the human genome and the backstabbing of corporate politics, while Joe told of clandestine missions in faraway places that officially never happened. Each took an oath that what they said on the deck never went any further. It helped build a strong bond of loyalty and trust.

"Be sure to keep this quiet," David said. "I want you to bring my briefcase from the office at the house. Buy a phone for me, too, but not in my name."

"Got it, boss. Be there at eight. And, boss, sorry about Mr. Rexsen. He was a nice guy."

"Thanks, Joe. I miss him more than you can imagine."

David put the receiver down and turned off the TV. He recalled his last conversation with Adam Rexsen just before the crash. They had reached cruising altitude, and, as he always did, the old man monitored the pilot's communications with ground control. David assumed it reminded Adam of his days as a highly decorated Vietnam War pilot. Apparently satisfied that the cockpit crew had the flight under control, the thin white-haired man removed his headphones.

"David, how do you think the meeting went?" he had asked, leaning across the aisle.

David made a quick check of the aft cabin to make sure Jeff Reese was still out of earshot.

"I think it went well, Adam. Our presentation went very well. Reese was convincing and left no doubt that the Center for Drug Evaluation and Research, the directors at the FDA, and all the critical subcommittees will be in support of our CGT treatment. We already had the nod for Treatment Investigational New Drugs, which allowed the critically ill to start treatment right away, and I expect formal FDA approval next week."

Adam gave a gentle smile. "That's really important to me, David. Those people suffering from that terrible disease need hope, and that's why I started this company in the first place." His eyes softened as he went on: "I know you guys were taught differently about business. I was taught you're in business for a purpose, to do something noble for society, to improve our way of life. I understand Harvard Business

School taught you you're in this to make money, create value for the shareholders as measured in the stock market. But I think that's how Enron got in trouble and ruined hundreds of thousands of lives. They believed that hokey pokey about 'virtual assets' and 'creative accounting'—all kind of legal, mind you—but they lost sight of why they existed in the first place."

David chuckled. "You're right there, Adam. But that's what it takes these days. Fact is, your board and your kids would send me packing if I didn't deliver earnings any way I can."

Adam's eyes turned sad. "My kids—now, there's a pair. Did you see that son of mine slithering around this week? He's up to something."

David was surprised by the comment. "He was a little strange."

"You're too kind to this old man. I know a lot more than you think. But it's nice to know someone respects my feelings."

"What do you mean?"

Adam leaned farther into the aisle. "I know all Prescott wants is the money," he whispered. "I know your 1980s MBA says you want it, too, but at least you know how to make it. He just knows how to spend it."

David acknowledged the comment with a nod.

"And that wife of yours, if you can call her that, is just as selfish."

Wellington felt uncomfortable. The old man knew a lot more than he let on. He didn't reply.

"Yes, I have connections, too. I know she fools around, and I know you've put up with her to keep me happy. But you don't have to please me. Priscilla is my daughter and I will always love her, but she's greedier than Prescott. She's also much smarter and much more cunning."

David stared into the brandy in the Waterford crystal glass.

"I don't know what to say, Adam."

"Just keep doing what you're doing. Whatever happens to me, don't let them get control of this company. They have no sense of purpose. Their mother died of cancer. Still, they don't care about all those men, women, and children who are dying needlessly from that insidious disease. They don't care about our employees, many whom have worked their entire career for us. They'll sell out to some big pharmaceutical company for the money, lay off our people, and we'll lose our sense of purpose for sure."

David reached across the aisle and gently squeezed his forearm. "I promise I won't let you down. They won't get the company."

The old man looked frail and tired. He leaned deep into the back of his chair and closed his eyes. He was done talking. Those were the last words he'd ever speak.

At the time, David didn't know why Adam Rexsen's words hit him so hard. Before the crash, success was all about the earnings and the money, but now something deep inside him said the old man was right. He wasn't sure if it was the crash, the loss of his job, or the little girl down the hall who bravely faced death, but he was sure of one thing: he wouldn't let Adam Rexsen's dream die, at least not without a fight.

# CHAPTER 22

TUESDAY MORNING TOOK forever to arrive. David checked his watch and sighed; it was almost eight. Since he'd placed the call to Joe, David had checked the time nearly every hour. He knew Prescott and Brayton would move quickly to solidify their positions and probably planned to sell out to the highest bidder. He wouldn't lie there and let them get away with stealing *his* company.

He paced his room in his well-ventilated hospital gown. Although he still winced when he took a deep breath, he was ready to go. He'd cleaned his breakfast dishes to the bone and stacked them neatly on the tray. The bed was made, with each corner tightly tucked into the frame. Each time the sound of footsteps in the corridor approached, David prepared to make his case to the doctor. He'd make sure it would be a short conversation.

A crisp knock on the door announced the doctor's arrival. A neatly groomed fortysomething man with graying black hair entered the room. He wore a white lab coat and stethoscope. As with the last two visits, he appeared confident and David immediately knew he would not be easily intimidated. The nurse trailed him.

"I'm ready to go, Doc. Just sign me out," David said.

The doctor looked at his chart. "Good morning, Mr. Wellington," he said. "We have another MRI to run before we let you go. You've had a rough time. We need to be sure you're in shape to go home."

The doctor's tone was unemotional. David thought he should have been a corporate lawyer with those negotiating skills. Still, David pressed his case.

"I'm ready to go now. I don't need an MRI to tell me that I feel fine, and I want out now. As I see it, we can stand here and argue about this or you can just sign me out now and save yourself some valuable time." David smiled.

The doctor shook his head. "As your attending physician, I cannot release you in good conscience. However, if you insist on taking this foolish risk, I'm obligated to let you know you can sign a release and go."

"Where do I sign, Doc?"

The doctor frowned and turned to the nurse. "Get Mr. Wellington the forms, and I'll give you the patient instructions." He turned back to David. "Since you insist on leaving now, I want you to follow my instructions and schedule a follow-up within a few days for the last test."

"No problem, Doc."

The doctor marched out and nearly ran into Joe in the doorway.

"Sorry, Doc," Joe said, stepping aside.

The doctor just gave Joe a nasty glance and left.

"What's his problem, boss?"

"Me," David said, laughing.

Joe laid a change of clothes on the bed. "I'll be just outside when you're ready."

He closed the door, and David stripped off the gown and slipped into the tan slacks and yellow polo shirt with a pair of Sperry Topsiders. He heard a knock on the door.

"Damn it, Joe, just a minute!"

The door opened just a crack and a squeaky voice said, "Who's Joe?"

David slipped on his last shoe and stepped to the door.

"Amy?"

Amy stood in the door clutching an Elmo doll and wearing her red Angels cap. "Mr. Wellington, sir, I just wanted to see if you wanted to come down and visit today." Her big blue eyes begged him to stay.

"I'm sorry. I'm leaving today."

Amy dropped her head. David wasn't sure what to do. Amy looked weaker in the morning light. Her face looked drawn and pale. Her eyebrows were gone, victims of the chemo. Despite his years in the business, he hadn't been this close to a child with terminal cancer since Connor died. He remembered the old man's lecture on purpose in life. The image of his young son entered his mind.

"Uh, do you have a phone number where I can call you?"

Amy raised her head and smiled. "Yes, my mom has it. I'll go get it."

Amy ran down the hallway while Joe and David waited patiently. She returned with her mother in tow. Faith Carlton's golden brown skin and lean athletic figure reminded David of the girls at the marina. But Faith had a mature look about her; something the yacht hounds didn't have.

"Mrs. Carlton. How are you?" David smiled and extended his hand.

"Just fine," she said as she returned the smile and shook his hand. David felt her strong grip.

"I hear you're leaving already," she said looking down at Amy.

"Yes. I have to go. But I wanted to stay in touch with Amy."

"You don't have to do that. I know you're going through a tough time. I can't ask any favors." David knew she was referring to getting Amy into one of the clinical trials.

"It's no problem. I do want to stay in touch with you."

"Okay. I gave Amy our number. We'll be home tomorrow. She wants to tell you something."

Amy reached out and touched David's hand. It was a gentle, calming touch. She handed him the phone number and then motioned for him to lean down.

"I know you're someone special," she whispered, "and God thinks you're special, too."

David drew back slowly. For a moment he was speechless. *What the hell do I say to that?* He knelt down and looked at her at eye level.

"You're someone special, too. I'll call you at your house."

"Promise?" Amy said and extended her hand.

"Promise." David shook her hand and smiled.

Amy smiled and nodded to Faith as if to say, "I knew he'd promise."

Over his lifetime David had made many promises; some he kept, many he didn't keep, and some he made just to get rid of people. But he knew from the moment he spoke the words that this was a promise he'd keep—no matter what. To keep it, he needed to somehow regain control of Rexsen Labs. He didn't know how, but he knew time was now his enemy. Based on her looks, Amy didn't have long to live. And he understood the longer Prescott, Priscilla, and Brayton were in control, the more difficult it would be to get his company back. They'd voted him out behind his back, and he was certain they'd laugh off a request to help Amy. He needed to get on with getting his company back.

"We've gotta go, Amy. I'll talk to you soon. Let's go, Joe."

Joe helped David into the wheelchair, and the nurse pushed David to the elevator. He looked back at Amy. She stood in the hallway, clutched her red Elmo doll, waved and smiled. David waved back, and Joe rolled him into the elevator. He knew if he failed, this would be the last time he'd ever see Amy alive. He'd made a promise, and at that moment, he decided failure would not be an option.

# CHAPTER 23

IT WAS TUESDAY evening and Royce Brayton admired the orange glow surrounding the silhouette of Catalina Island. The breeze off the water was refreshing and steady. He felt the chartered yacht rock gently in the small swells. The skipper turned the three-deck pleasure cruiser parallel to Balboa Island and headed south. Brayton faced the shoreline, leaned on the brass rail, and took in the offshore view of Newport Beach. Sunset lost its battle with dusk, and thousands of lights brought the coastline back to life. This was the good life, he mused, and it only would get better from here.

Priscilla Wellington stepped from the cabin with two glasses of Dom Perignon cradled in her slender fingers.

"Well, Royce, here's to us," she said. She draped her arm over his shoulder and looked at the sparkling shoreline.

Royce glanced at her. She was irresistible. Her light silk dress waved softly in the breeze. The sweet smell of Pleasures drifted around him and drew his body closer. The silk loosely wrapped the full tan breasts she pressed against his side. He'd never been able to resist an opportunity for pleasure. Even as a young man, he was unable to resist the advances of two of his three stepmothers. All beautiful trophies for his father and the reason his father eventually threw him out.

"You look beautiful tonight. I hope the crew doesn't mind us disappearing after dinner."

Royce took Priscilla in his arms and they shared a wet, passionate kiss. Priscilla seemed to share his appetite for sex.

"Royce, now that you have control of the business, I sure hope you can keep it," she said.

Royce stepped back from the rail and held Priscilla by her shoulders, peering into her dark brown eyes.

"What do mean, you hope I can keep it?"

"Oh, I was just thinking about what would happen if David found a way to get his position back," Priscilla said, turning her gaze to the coastline.

"And how would he ever do that, my dear?" Brayton kept his eyes fixed on her.

"It's just that now he's asked me for a divorce and he's survived the crash, I'll have to split everything with him, including my shares in the new company. That gives him quite a bit of clout, doesn't it?" She still gazed at the lights glimmering in the distance.

Brayton joined Priscilla at the rail, sipped his Dom Perignon and looked silently across the swells. He drew in a deep breath of the fresh salt air. She peeked at Brayton to catch a glimpse of his expression, then quickly gazed back at the coastline.

"You know, I hadn't considered that a threat until now." *How did I miss that? No loose ends.* He knew Priscilla might be right. Wellington could gain enough leverage with his shares to persuade an institutional shareholder to join him. He wasn't sure if Priscilla was asking him to do something or just sharing a concern. They never talked about his plans, and now would not be the time to start. After all, she was just a good lay, not his partner.

He convinced himself he'd deal with Wellington later. Tonight was about his coronation as the winner. He had the company, and he had Priscilla. He was the victor. And to the victor go the spoils.

"Let's not let that spoil our evening," he said, raising the Champagne flute.

Priscilla raised her flute and, with a ring, clicked it gently against his. She smiled. It looked like it was a smile of satisfaction. But Royce didn't care. He had one thing on his mind.

He led Priscilla into the master stateroom. The room was paneled in teak wood. Two small lamps at the head of the wide bed warmly lit the room. The leopard-skin spread was tucked tightly into the bed frame. Brayton dimmed the lights and slipped closer to Priscilla. Gently, he unwrapped the silk that covered her smooth tan breasts. He felt her firmness, the smooth silky skin. He slid away her lingerie and exposed her sexy tan line.

This was his trophy. He'd defeated David Wellington, taken his company, and now he'd take his wife. He was certain he could handle Prescott, and the other half of the Rexsen Family Trust was now underneath him, groaning in passionate pleasure. He was firmly in control. CGT's imperfection would remain a secret, and in one week he'd be richer than he'd ever imagined. He drifted into a trance and enjoyed one of the forbidden fruits of his labor. To him sex was power, and tonight, he had all the power.

# CHAPTER 24

DAVID WELLINGTON ENTERED the darkened first floor of his Laguna Beach house and flipped the light switch. The soft light warmed the familiar surroundings, and for the first time in days, he felt safe and secure. The contemporary décor ran through the entire beachfront home. White rounded chairs were accented with soft pink pillows and draped with sand-white afghans. Every corner where walls or ceiling met was carefully rounded into a smooth gentle curve. The soft lines of the room drew the eye to the serene beach and sparkling blue surf outside. As he watched the ocean foam onto the long stretch of beach through the massive windows, he relaxed his labored breathing.

Everything about the place was soft and comfortable to David—$8 million worth of comfortable.

"Just leave the bags in the room, boss?" Joe asked.

"Yeah, I'll unpack later," David said as he stretched.

He kept looking outside as the Pacific churned wave after wave onto the beach.

"You gonna be okay, boss?"

David turned and saw the look of concern on Joe's face. It was the first kind face he'd seen since the accident. Joe always took care of

David, and David, in return, took good care of Joe. "You know I'm going to need some help figuring some things out," David said.

"You know me, boss. I'm ready when you are. I don't like what those bastards did to you, especially after your accident and all. That prick Prescott didn't give a damn about Mr. Rexsen dying, and he was his dad; the best damn man I've ever known."

David turned back to the ocean. Adam Rexsen was the best man he'd ever known, too. David couldn't shake the last conversation they had or the image of the old man's last moments. "Do you know what Adam's last words were?"

Joe walked up and stood next to David as they both stared at the surging tide. "No, boss."

"He said Prescott and Priscilla had no sense of purpose."

"Purpose?"

David looked out to sea. "He said the reason he was in this business was to give people hope. To help all the men, women and children who suffered or died from cancer. That was what drove him."

"Yeah, that sounds like Mr. Rexsen. He always felt that way. I heard him tell the employees the same thing when he'd visit with them."

"Well, he really believed it. You should have seen how peaceful he was just before the crash. He said one other thing, too."

"What was that, boss?"

"He asked me not to let his children get control of the company. It's like he had a premonition. I promised him, Joe." David stopped.

"Promised him what?"

"That I would not let them get control of the company."

David continued to stare out the window. He realized he'd let his mentor and friend down. He was out as CEO, and Adam Rexsen's greedy children had control of the trust and therefore the company. Maybe he could have headed this off if he'd listened to Adam years earlier. He'd been too caught up in himself and the money. Adam was right, David decided. Under the banner of creating value, he'd lost sight of the purpose of Rexsen Labs. His failure had cost Adam Rexsen his life.

He felt Joe's hand on his shoulder.

"It's okay, boss," Joe said.

David nodded and pulled himself together.

"Well, then," Joe said, "we'd better get to work, boss."

For the next several hours, they sat at the dining room table and shuffled through the mountain of papers. Using his contacts with the clerk in the corporate secretary's office, Joe had obtained news clips, David's employment agreement, and a bootlegged copy of the minutes of the last board meeting. They had read and reread each document, searching for any way to undo David's firing. They had also made dozens of phone calls.

"Okay, then," David said as he placed one hand on his forehead and reviewed his notepad, "the calls I made to the executive committee got us nowhere. The ones I could reach just clammed up. Said they couldn't speak directly to me on the advice of counsel. They all directed me to work through my attorney."

"What'd he say?" Joe said.

"He just kept apologizing about me losing my job and promising he'd negotiate a great severance."

"Sounds like an attorney," Joe said.

"What did you come up with?"

"My guys in the garage gave me what they could. They drove the board members to the Monterey airport after the meeting and overheard them talking about what went on."

"What'd they say?"

"First of all, they all hate Prescott. But apparently he used some strong-arm tactics to get the vote. He told them since he now owned the controlling shares in the company, they'd all be replaced within a month if they didn't vote you out. He told them you were incompetent to continue, from the crash and all. Then he had the underwriter and a few other investment bankers tell the board that the IPO would do better with Brayton at the helm. They all went along to save their own greedy butts."

"That's okay, Joe. I expected as much." David patted Joe on the arm.

"So what are we going to do, boss?"

David took a deep breath and scanned the table. "We don't have many options, do we?"

"We ain't got shi—"

David's personal iPhone buzzed.

After checking caller ID David answered it on the second ring. "Hello."

The caller paused. "Mr. Wellington? David Wellington?" a woman's voice said.

"Yes. Who is this?"

"Mr. Wellington, I'm so sorry to bother you after … you know, after your crash. Your old secretary gave me the number after I begged her for it. I didn't know where to turn."

David heard the stress in her voice. He looked at Joe and raised his eyebrows. "You worked for me?"

"Oh, I'm sorry. I'm Tori Clarke, a senior researcher for Rexsen. I think …" She hesitated, but David remained silent. "I think I may have discovered a problem with CGT … and maybe a cover-up."

David made a writing motion in the air, and Joe jumped up and delivered a pen and David's notepad.

"Okay. What's the problem?"

Tori hesitated again. "Not over the phone, Mr. Wellington. There's something weird going on. I need to meet you in person. Someplace where there are not many people."

David thought for a second. "Slip 29. At the Eagle's Nest Marina."

"Okay, but just you. What time?"

"Ten o'clock."

The phone clicked dead.

David slowly returned the iPhone to the table and stared at Joe. He knew that a problem with CGT, if exposed, would mean there would be no FDA approval. And without the earnings potential of CGT, the IPO would not go forward. Billions of dollars were at stake. If there were a conspiracy, David was certain Prescott and Brayton were the ones who were in control and would profit the most from it. Maybe Adam Rexsen's fears were a premonition. Maybe the plane crash was not an accident but a means to get control of Rexsen. David stiffened at the thought of his friend being murdered by his own son.

"Boss?" Joe said, breaking his train of thought.

David threw the notepad on the table. "We may have a plan."

# CHAPTER 25

THE FOG-CHILLED AIR seeped in from the moonless night and drifted along the bare tile floor. Shrouded in darkness, Butch Donovan hunched over the table and meticulously reviewed the checklist illuminated by a single halogen light. A razor-sharp dagger did an impression of a paperweight, and glistening parts of a disassembled Mark 23, including a sleek silencer and laser aiming device, were laid out like chess pieces on a soft square cloth. He felt in control. This was his office and he did his best work under the cover of darkness. He'd prayed for pitch-black nights like this on every mission he'd completed.

In less than an hour, he'd devised a flawless trap. The team had the necessary evidence, and he was certain he had the right pawns in play. His body tingled with a surge of endorphins when he moved to the last actions on the checklist and imagined using his knife with the precision of a surgeon. Leaning back and closing his eyes, he locked his hands behind his thick neck and savored the feeling.

The ring of the black cellular phone, neatly positioned to the right of the makeshift mini command center, interrupted his deadly daydream. It was a little after 8 p.m., and the display indicated the call was from Long Beach.

"Donovan."

"We got a problem," Lane said.

"Go on."

He loved problems. Problems meant action. He felt confident he'd anticipated this one.

"Just sending you an audio file from Wellington's beach house and another containing a phone call he received a few minutes ago. Sure glad we got our equipment in place. You'd better listen right away and call back."

"Will do," he said calmly.

Donovan stood, grabbed the knife and headed to the laptop tucked into the far corner of the room. Passing by the kitchen island, he picked an apple from a bowl and had gutted it into bite-size quarters before he reached the computer. He logged in and clicked on the first of the two audio files. The voices were identified in the window as those of Wellington and his driver. Their conversation was circular, Donovan thought, and going nowhere. No big deal. But the last few words caused him to reposition the cursor to play the last few seconds again.

"We may have a plan."

The words made him bristle in anticipation of hearing the next file. He closed the file and opened the remaining audio file containing the call. He carefully listened to Tori Clarke's voice and noted the tone and the inflections. He replayed it and confirmed his conclusion: she had information devastating to his client and his planned retirement.

"Shit!"

He knew they needed to move quickly. Much sooner than he thought, but still his planning had been clairvoyant. His adrenaline surged, and he grabbed the phone and crushed the numbers into the keypad.

"Let's get going on the contingency plan for Clarke and Wellington now," he ordered. "We only have until ten to set up our insurance plan. I'll brief you on the remaining details once you connect with Waters. It's sooner than we thought, so get the second team going, too. It's 8:17 now and they need to have the evidence and the weasel in place and be out of there by nine thirty, so this is a scramble."

"Affirmative," Lane said.

Donovan hung up the phone, retrieved the knife from the computer desk, and, with several huge strides, moved through the darkness back to the kitchen table. He picked up the polymer frame of the MK 23 and, in less than thirty seconds, methodically assembled the pieces and grinned. He unsheathed the knife and admired the blade glimmering in the shadowy light. He thought about the plan and imagined its smooth execution. It would be an enjoyable night.

# CHAPTER 26

IT WAS NEARLY 9 p.m. The Champagne was still cold, and Brayton gulped the half-full glass while he watched Priscilla wriggle into the silk teddy and disappear into the head. He felt the gentle rock of the yacht and sank back into the pillows, locked his fingers behind his neck and sighed. The smell of her perfume lingered in the soft silky sheets. He closed his eyes and smiled. He knew he was good in bed. He loved their compliments every time they left his bed. He replayed his last three conquests in his mind and concluded he was getting better with age.

The ring of his iPhone jolted him from his ego-building narcissistic self-review. He reached to the teakwood nightstand, glanced at the closed bathroom door, and answered.

"What's up?" he whispered.

"You have a problem."

He hated the implication that he was in this alone almost as much as he hated having to use this contact. The man he despised most in his life sat in his comfortable cell at Lompoc while Brayton struggled to pay back his debt to the deadly bankers his father had recommended.

He pushed himself up from the bed and swung his feet to the floor. His glance checked the closed door again.

"What is it this time?" he growled.

"That Clarke bitch you called me about earlier is on the move, and I think she's headed toward the marina as we speak. Looks like she's meeting with Wellington on his yacht."

Brayton shot up to his feet and stood naked, trying to keep his voice low while still making his point. "What the hell do you mean?"

Priscilla's words from earlier in the evening echoed in his mind. *Now that you have control of the business, I sure hope you can keep it.*

"We have to move quickly here, Royce."

Brayton felt the pressure build inside.

"What do you want me to do?" the voice asked.

Brayton checked the door again and turned away from the closed bathroom door, paced to the opposite side of the stateroom and raised his voice slightly. "You guys are supposed to help *me*. I'm paying you a ton of money so do your job."

"So, you want me to make them go away?" It sounded as if the voice were begging.

"Not now, you son of a bitch. We can't have any more accidents. It'll be too suspicious. We're going public in seven days. We don't need any cops sniffing around, and we don't need to draw any more attention to the deal."

"You may not have a choice!" the gruff voice said. "I'm certain Clarke is planning on telling Wellington about the problem with CGT. He'll take that and use it to stop the IPO and then work with the directors to try to regain control. Then you'll be out and get a visit from that nice Italian family."

Brayton knew he was right. Without the company going public and with a question on CGT, he'd lose his leverage with the directors.

It was either the IPO or Clarke and Wellington: one had to go. He paused, staring at the closed bathroom door. Prescott was difficult to deal with at best, but he could handle him. And he'd just proved he could deal with Priscilla in bed. With Prescott on his side and Wellington and Clarke out of the picture, he was certain the genetic imperfection on CGT would go undiscovered and the IPO would proceed as planned. And he'd live to see his next birthday.

"Keep your eye on both of them and do what you have to do," he said. Brayton tossed the phone onto the table and jumped back into bed.

He couldn't see Priscilla, smiling, her ear pressed against the thin teakwood door.

# CHAPTER 27

DAVID WELLINGTON ARRIVED at 9:45 p.m. at the parking lot of the Eagle's Nest Marina, an exclusive thirty-slip private marina at the entrance to Newport Harbor. The marine layer had drifted in, and the streetlamps that lined the path to the slips were shrouded in fog. He stepped from his BMW 740 and felt the chilly mist against his cheek. He peered through the mist and scanned the parking area. He saw the dark silhouettes of a few cars scattered in the parking lot, but no sign of life. He checked his watch. He pulled the collar of his dark leather jacket up and walked toward the water. He decided he would wait on board.

David was proud that Eagle's Nest was the preferred home to the multi-multimillion-dollar luxury yachts of Newport Beach. It was the playground for the super-rich, especially those who needed a home away from home to conduct affairs not appropriate onshore. Newport Beach had its start as a naval ship yard during World War II. Many servicemen returned to the area to live. But in the 1950s the tentacles of the Southern California freeway system reached to the coastal area of Orange County and the invasion was on. In recent years, David was happy to lead the charge, buying yachts and trading up year by year. Over the years he'd watched Newport Beach change from a small

seasonal beach town to a trophy room for the wealthy. And this was
his trophy room.

He hurried down the row of boats tucked tightly in their slips. A
few had their cabin lights on, but most were dark. Security lights dan-
gled over the gate to each dock. David approached the gate to slip
thirty at end of the pier. He'd paid a premium to get the last slip. The
isolation was well worth it. Just beyond his slip, the dark water
stretched to the Pacific. The fog glowed red from the lights on the
channel markers.

He removed the magnetic card from his pocket and inserted it
into the card reader. The magnetic lock buzzed, then released, and he
propped open the gate. He hoped Tori Clarke would be just a few
minutes behind him. The fog had thickened and now gently drifted
over the decks of the sleek Manhattan Sunseeker yacht. It was his pride
and joy, and it had cost him millions to buy the envy of Newport
Beach's fleet. The only noise was that of the harbor's ripples swishing
against the hull. He entered the yacht at the stern.

He unlocked the aluminum sliding door, slid it aside and flipped
the light switch, just inside the door. The recessed halogen lights came
to life, and he froze at a gruesome sight. A beaten and bloodied
Prescott Rexsen was bound, gagged and seated on the plush beige
leather sofa in the stateroom. Blood dripped from under the tape over
his mouth. Prescott's glazed gaze locked on David. Through the blood
and a pulpy swollen face, David sensed Prescott's terror as his eyes
begged for help. For the first time in his life, David felt compassion
for the broken man. He stepped closer, and Prescott cut his eyes to the
right, just over David's shoulder. David turned, then instinctively
jerked his head backward in self-preservation. He was face-to-face with
the black barrel of a Glock. He stumbled backward toward Prescott
until his heels hit the sofa as a black masked gunman emerged from
behind the drapes that flanked the sliding door. David stood frozen
next to Prescott, still seated on the sofa with his hands tied behind him.

"Mr. Wellington, I presume?" the masked man said.

David raised his hands and hoped to live another day. "Who the hell are you?"

"I'm no one. I'm a ghost. I'm not even here."

"Look, whatever you want you can have. Just let us go."

The man slowly shook his head. "You don't have a clue, do you? Some miracle man."

His chuckle, muffled by the black balaclava mask, sent chills rattling through David's body. *This guy won't think twice about killing us both.*

He heard several footsteps on the deck behind the gunman. The gunman didn't look around. He seemed to be expecting company. A man dressed in a tweed sport coat stepped through the door and pointed a .38 caliber pistol into the darkness outside. He was white, just over six feet, and well-groomed with tight-cropped brown hair and bloodshot green eyes. David spotted the shield on his belt and smiled.

*You've had it now, buddy. The cops are here.*

But the man stepped around the gunman and yanked someone in from the darkness. A woman raised her head, and her tear-wet face and apologetic look emerged from behind her thick brown hair. She stared in horror at the sight of Prescott's face.

She looked at David. "I'm sorry, Mr. Wellington," she cried.

David recognized her voice; it was Tori Clarke. He turned back to the detective in the tweed coat.

"Who the hell are you?" David asked again.

The detective shoved Tori toward David and a quivering Prescott.

"I see you have things under control," the detective said, pushing Tori a third time. She stumbled and David caught her in his arms. The gunman remained silent.

"What the hell is this about?" David said.

The detective turned. David saw the flash of a knife blade. The detective slashed his arm just above the elbow. David grabbed the wound, and blood dripped through his fingers to the floor.

"*Mr. Wellington,*" Tori cried out.

"Shut up," the gunman yelled and pointed the automatic at Tori. Bravely, Tori swallowed hard and stared back.

"You see, Mr. Wellington," the detective said, smiling, "tonight, in a rage about being fired, you forced your way into Mr. Prescott's home." The detective moved next to Prescott and patted him on the head. "And you can see how you beat him, bound him and brought him here." He pulled Prescott's head back by the hair. Prescott's eyes stretched wide and appeared to plead silently for his life.

"And when my forensic technicians go to his home and get your blood off his carpet, we'll have the evidence we need to arrest and convict you."

The detective raised the knife in his left hand and yanked Prescott's head backward by his hair with his right, exposing his neck.

"Then ..."

The detective paused and with a quick movement drove the knife into Prescott's neck, just above the breastbone. Blood spattered and Prescott's eyes froze. His body contorted and wriggled while the detective kept his grip on his hair. Prescott's body suddenly stiffened and became still, and he slumped on the sofa as the detective released him and began to speak.

"You see, you killed Prescott with this knife that happens to have your fingerprints on it, thanks to the fine work of this gentleman in the hospital, while you were unconscious." The detective nodded to the gunman behind him.

"Please let us go," Tori said, sobbing.

The gunman stepped closer and pressed the black barrel of his gun to her head. Shocked and hopeless, David shook his head, silently protesting the horrifying scene unfolding before him.

The detective continued as he threw the knife into the blood pooling on the sofa. "And you, Miss Clarke, just had a very large sum of money deposited into your account by Mr. Wellington here."

The detective carefully stepped backward until he was shoulder to shoulder with the gunman, and together they backed to the sliding doors. David suspected he and Tori would not leave the yacht alive. He channeled the anger roiling inside him into every muscle. He knew he couldn't just stand there and let this asshole kill them.

The two men stopped in the doorway, and the detective finished his matter-of-fact description of the end of David's life.

"And I responded to an anonymous caller who said they saw you board your boat with a man bound and gagged, and"—the detective smiled and pointed the .38 at David and cocked it—"I called for backup, but unfortunately, I had to shoot both of you when you attempted to attack me."

David shifted his weight to his toes and prepared to lunge like a vicious cornered animal. He expected to be shot, probably fatally, but hoped his rage would continue his assault and give Tori at least a minuscule chance to run. Time seemed to shift to slow motion. He clearly saw the detective's finger pull back on the trigger, and his eyes closed in anticipation of the blast. David threw himself forward and listened to his own animal-like roar as he attacked. Before he reached the door, a bright red fire extinguisher suddenly appeared out of the misty darkness behind the detective and bounced off his skull. David adjusted his trajectory, aiming for the masked man, whose attention had cut to the commotion. The gunman spun toward the noise, and a huge hairy fist slammed into his jaw. At the same time, David hit him head-on, and he dropped to the ground.

Facedown on top of the motionless attacker, stunned and gasping to catch his breath, David heard a familiar voice above him.

"*Semper fi*, asshole."

Joe Pirelli bolted into the room and quickly eyeballed Prescott, dead and bloodied on the sofa. He returned his attention to David and waited for direction. Tori stood in the middle of the blood-soaked carpet, shocked and speechless. David regained his senses and struggled to his feet. He knew this was not a place to stay and sort things out. The cops were in on it, and he'd been framed for a murder. Better to run and live another day.

"Let's get out of here now, Joe," David said.

"But, boss, what about Prescott and these jokers?"

"Prescott's gone and we've been framed. We gotta go now!" He turned to Tori. "You've gotta come with us now, Miss Clarke."

She seemed to be anchored in a pool of blood still dripping from Prescott's gory corpse, unable to move.

"We don't have time for this. The backup will be here any minute. The cops are in on this. You can't trust them. You've been set up. So have I. I don't know what you have to tell me, but it's obviously worth killing you. If you want to live, you have to come with us."

David ran to her, grabbed her arm and dragged her to the door. She stumbled in a daze as they followed Joe out of the cabin and onto the deck.

"Sure glad you don't take orders well, Joe," David said, thanking Joe for not staying at the beach house. Joe just smiled.

As they made their way to the parking lot, David quickly assessed the situation. Prescott Rexsen, head of the Rexsen Family Trust for only three days, had been murdered on David's yacht. A Newport Beach detective had attempted to frame him for the murder and then tried to kill Tori and him. He figured if they were trying to kill her, too, what she had to say was a threat to someone, a threat worth killing for. Most disturbing was his final conclusion: the plane crash was no accident, and someone involved with Rexsen Labs wanted Adam Rexsen and him out of the way permanently—and they were halfway there.

# CHAPTER 28

AROUND MIDNIGHT, THE black Lincoln Town Car sped down Interstate 5 into the fog seeping onto the southern California coast as it always did. The eerie glow of the halogen streetlights, spaced evenly along the expressway, caused the passengers' compartment to pulsate between darkness and an opaque dusky gloom. David noticed that Joe had his attention split between the road ahead and the rearview mirror, probably scanning constantly for patrol cars. David sat next to Tori in the backseat. As her face appeared and disappeared in the intermittent shadows, he saw that her eyes were glazed and her stare was fixed ahead, oblivious to her current surroundings. He felt her shivering, and her eyes were puffy and wet with tears.

"I can't believe this is happening. Who are these people?"

His guilt for getting her involved forced an explanation. "Ms. Clarke, I'm sorry you're involved in this. But the fact remains there is someone out there wanting you and me dead, and they are powerful enough to have a police detective on their payroll."

She broke her trance-like state and looked at David.

"They stabbed that poor man, right in front of us. He's one of the Rexsens. They own our company. Who would do that?"

"Unfortunately, I think I know. I'm guessing that bastard Brayton is behind all of this somehow. First, the plane crash kills Adam Rexsen, then I'm fired, and Prescott is murdered. He wants it all, the whole company!"

What started as a seed of anger grew quickly into rage, fed by the thought that his mentor and surrogate father figure had been murdered. Now that he'd said it out loud, it seemed so obvious. Brayton had slinked around Rexsen for the past six months. At times, David had sensed Brayton was avoiding him. He'd seen Brayton and Prescott together on more than one occasion, talking softly and darting their eyes about the room, ensuring they weren't overheard. He'd suspected Brayton was a braggart and a slick corporate huckster who'd sell his own mother, any one of them, to make money, but he never pegged Brayton as a murderer.

"Where are you taking me?" Tori said.

Joe answered without taking his eyes from the road. "We need to get you two where they can't find you. Not the cops and not those assholes that have had us under surveillance. I pulled this off the car tonight." Joe held up a micro-transmitter. "They'll be checking every hotel from Ventura to San Diego. They'll be watching the border into Mexico. I'm sure your descriptions are being broadcast as we speak."

Joe's frankness seemed to further upset Tori. David surmised from Joe's matter-of-fact tone that his training from his service in the USMC Marine Expeditionary Unit, followed by some mysterious assignments with the CIA, had kicked in. It had been the shortest but most compelling part of Joe's résumé when David hired him as a driver and part-time bodyguard.

"So what are we going to do?" Tori said. "Where can we go?"

"Don't worry, miss. I've got the perfect place."

Joe took the Dana Point exit and wound his way down the dark tree-lined boulevard past the sprawling landscape of resort hotels and conference centers and into the large marina and restaurant complex.

Joe entered the gate to the marina parking lot, turned into an open space and threw the car into "park."

"We've got to hurry," Joe said as he opened Tori's door.

David followed Tori from the backseat and they hurried through the thickening fog and past the few dew-covered cars remaining in the lot. Other than a few late-night revelers leaving the waterfront watering holes, the marina was quiet. David heard the hum of generators from boats in their slips. Joe led them down the pier and turned down one of the wooden docks. The smell of diesel hung heavy in the mist that was still blanketing the coast. They passed a small fishing boat in one of the slips, and David tried to clear his nostrils of the pungent odor of rotten fish parts.

"Okay, here it is." Joe said, extending his hand to guide Tori down the slip to their left.

The catamaran stretched the entire length of the slip. Its white hull glistened in the dull light that reflected off the black water lapping at the waterline. The rear deck was partially covered by a blue tarp. Joe pressed the button, and the tarp uncovered the entrance to the catamaran's expansive cabin. Joe extended his hand to Tori and helped her onboard. David followed.

David shot Joe a questioning look.

"My buddy lets me take it out any time I want. He's out of the states on business. Fellow Marine, you know. Owes me big time."

Joe flicked on a light and scoured the cabin with his eyes. He seemed quite familiar with it. He inspected the catamaran's main deck, then disappeared below deck and returned in seconds.

"It's all yours, boss. I think you ought to head to Catalina at first light. The chart is on the desk next to the helm. Take one of the moorings marked on the map on the north side of the island. Call the Isthmus harbormaster's office, and use the name listed on the card stuck on the helm. No one will find you up there. And use the phone onboard if you have to, but keep it short. Beer and provisions are in the galley. Hope you like Corona." Joe smiled and stepped to the dock.

"What are you going to do, Joe?" David said.

"They didn't see me," Joe said, extending his palms. "Had these gloves on, too." Joe scanned the cabin one more time and stepped to the door. "I'll just do my thing and deny, deny, deny. You two be safe. Let me know if you need anything, boss. But call on the secure line you installed last year at the house." Joe hopped off the rear deck and disappeared into the fog, well before his footsteps faded. David pushed the button, and the electric motor unwound the tarp over the deck. He focused his attention squarely on the young woman still shivering in front of him. He was certain she held the key to their survival, and he needed answers. Time was not on their side. Joe's plan was solid but still risky. The authorities had most likely started a manhunt. They'd check airports, train stations, bus stations, and soon, marinas. They'd have roadblocks, and eventually they'd be caught or killed.

Tori Clarke might be his only hope. Maybe she had the information he needed to expose Adam's Rexsen's murderer and the conspiracy behind it and get his neck out of the noose that seemed to be already choking him.

He pointed to the lacquered pine table at the side of the main cabin, dimly lit by an overhead light, and eyed the trembling researcher.

"Now, Miss Clarke, about the information you had for me ..."

# CHAPTER 29

BUTCH DONAVAN WIGGLED a felt-tipped pen between his thick fingers and waited in the darkness of the Long Beach warehouse. His ruddy face was lit only by the soft light from the five monitors. Obsessed with the thrill of the hunt and the anticipation of the kill, he'd decided to leave the house in Laguna. At times like these, he longed for the old do-it-yourself days. Since he'd become the commander of his own private little group of mercenaries, this was the closest he got to the action.

Lane, his second-ranking merc, had gone on this one himself. And Lane never missed. He was Donovan's best. But there had been no call. Donovan stared at the red numbers on the wall: it was 12:34 a.m. Wednesday. The trap had been set at 10 p.m., and two and a half hours had passed without a word. He didn't dare try to contact Lane. He knew from his own experience that any distraction could be disastrous. After all, Lane was the best, and the money he'd spent to put a Newport Beach detective on the payroll should have assured a winning result.

The smartphone is his jacket pocket vibrated, and he checked the number on the display. The client—again. Donovan hated meddlers.

"Just pay me and let me do my damn job!" he wished out loud before answering. He put the phone to his ear. "Donovan."

"Any word yet?" the synthesized voice warbled.

"No," Donovan said bluntly, "nothing since the last time you called."

"What the hell's going on there, Donovan? What type of operation are you running? I pay you well to do your job."

"Look. Lane is the best. He'll get the job done. He's probably just cleaning up before he calls."

"Call me!" The phone clicked dead.

"Asshole!" Donovan said.

The man next to him, monitoring the consoles, chuckled. "You know, Butch, it's not like Lane to be out this long. And we lost our ears on Wellington's limo just before ten. Still have them on his Beemer. No movement."

"Probably just a technical problem on the limo," Donovan said.

The two sat silently in the darkness, scanning the bank of monitors. Donovan understood why the client was upset. There was a ton of money riding on this operation. He wasn't sure exactly how much, but after you get to nine zeros, he thought, it really doesn't matter. His cut would be chump change to the client, but it meant a life of leisure. He looked forward to seeing the sun again on a regular basis and not worrying about asshole clients and overzealous law enforcement officers. The phone on the console rang and Donovan snatched it.

"Where the hell have you been!"

"We've got a problem," Lane said. His voice seemed weak, and he fumbled to find his words.

Donovan knew bad news was about to be delivered. "What?"

"We ... we lost them. Prescott's dead, but someone jumped us before we got Wellington and Clarke."

"Both of you! They got both of you!" Donovan shot out of his chair. "Where are they?"

"We hoped you had something on that. Someone clobbered us from behind. We've been out of it since ten."

"You mean they're together and on the run, and we don't know where they are?"

There was no answer. Lane probably knew Donovan's penalty for failure.

"Shit! Tell that bastard cop Waters he ain't getting a cent until they're gone!" Donovan pointed his finger as if Lane stood in front of him. Donovan knew he'd gotten Detective Waters of the Newport Beach Police Department at a discount, courtesy of his coke-snorting bitch of a wife. Why Waters felt obligated to feed her habit was a mystery to him, but he expected to get his money's worth anyway.

"He's on it already. Said he'd personally track them down and kill them. He's pissed. Said he'd use the department's resources."

"You stay with him and do whatever you need to, but find them!"

Donovan returned to his chair and leaned forward. "How did Prescott get it?"

Lane gave a halfhearted chuckle, still groggy from Joe's right. "He cried like a baby all the way to Wellington's yacht. Waters got him good in the throat."

"Good. Wish I was there. Now find those bastards! We'll fire up things here. Get the whole team involved."

"Everyone?" Lane said.

"Everyone!" Donovan shot back and slammed the phone down.

Donovan stood and rubbed his chin. He looked at the man at the console, who looked up and shook his head. Donovan, too, shook his head in disgust. He had to call the client. There was no way around it. He pulled his smartphone from his pocket and put it to his ear.

"We've got a problem."

# CHAPTER 30

THE DANA POINT Marina was home to several thousand boats tightly packed into their slips. They formed an endless forest of masts, reaching into the cover of darkness and fog. The fog was even thicker in David's mind as he wondered what this young woman had to tell him and where and when the next assault on his life would take place. He understood that finding the catamaran would be like finding a needle in a haystack, but the thought didn't comfort David. He'd just witnessed a murder that would surely be pinned on him. And the woman who sat across from him was his accomplice.

They'd find his fingerprints on the knife, carefully obtained from his limp hand while he lay unconscious at Cedars-Sinai. He wouldn't have felt the prick of the needle draining the blood from his arm—the blood that was now spread around Prescott's waterfront town home. The rogue detective, if he recovered from Joe's blow, would provide the proof of a financial tie between Tori and David. They'd find thousands of dollars electronically transferred into her account from one of the many accounts David had access to. They'd be wanted murderers on the morning news and the front page of the *L.A. Times*.

David closed the sliding glass door to the main cabin and moved to the lacquered pine table tucked neatly in the corner. The white molded fiberglass glistened in the light that seeped in through the windows. The entire cabin was white except for the jet-black controls at the helm and the pine countertops, tables, and trim. Tori dropped into the built-in seat across from David and rested her forearms on the table. Her shoulder-length dark brown hair framed her face. Her eyes were puffy but still open wide. Streams of mascara meandered down her cheeks. Still, he found her attractive. David shook off the chill from the sea air, still lingering in the cabin, and handed Tori his black leather jacket.

"How are you doing, Miss Clarke?"

She leaned forward and widened her eyes even more. "How do you think I'm doing?" she snapped. "I just witnessed a gruesome murder and was told I'm being framed for it, along with you. And two thugs, one a detective, were going to kill me."

She pulled back from the table, crossed her arms and glared at him. David didn't blame her for her anger. It actually helped ease his guilt.

"I'm sorry, Miss Clarke. I'm sorry you're in the middle of this. But apparently the information you were planning to give me must have something to do with all of this." He leaned back against the cushion and waited for a reply.

Tori shifted her gaze out the window of the catamaran. "The information I had for you regarded a problem I think exists with CGT, hardly worth murdering three people for." She shook her head.

David drove his fist into table, and Tori jumped in her seat. "CGT, the IPO, Brayton—that bastard. I knew it!"

Tori's disclosure of a problem with CGT confirmed David's suspicions. Brayton had Adam Rexsen killed.

"What?" Tori said, wrinkling her nose in frustration as she eyed David.

"If there's a problem with CGT, the FDA will not license it," David said. "Depending on the problem, we'll have to go back into the pipeline, maybe even phase one clinical trials. The IPO will be delayed because the anticipated run-up in the stock price is tied to the FDA approval of CGT and the profits that would follow. Brayton won't be able to go public and claim his cash bonuses. His restricted shares and options will be worthless, at least for now, and with his history, he'll never stick around to fix things. He breaks up companies and sells the pieces, then cashes out. He's got two-thirds of the Rexsen family out of the way. The only one left is my lovely wife, and he's been sleeping with her for six months."

Tori sat up straight and rested her head against the white wall of the cabin. "Oh, my God," she said.

David saw it was nearly too much to handle. The employees knew little of his personal life or the web of deceit and hate within the Rexsen family. It was in everyone's interest to keep all that in the dark.

"It would help if I knew the problem with CGT," he said.

Tori leaned forward again and folded her hands on the table. She looked stronger now. David sensed a strength and determination he'd missed earlier. She glanced at David, then stared into her hands as if they held her notes.

"We had been using the established methods for using micro-arrays to determine the genetic expression profiles to predict the pre-cursors to cancers at the molecular level. My work took that process one step further. We improved the method to allow us to identify cancer subtypes at the molecular level, improving the expressed tag sequence."

David furrowed his brow and tried hard to remember his training in genetics. Tori saw his struggle and clarified.

"You know, we could spot changes in chromosomes that caused cancer, well before the symptoms would develop."

David nodded. "Yes, I see."

Tori continued to stare into her hands. "I wanted to test the process, so I used the post-treatment DNA samples from the phase three clinical trials on CGT, since it was readily available. The results showed the previously damaged chromosomes were repaired, but 70 percent of the patients in the trial had new chromosomal damage caused by the treatment consistent with the precursors to pancreatic cancer."

David was speechless—stunned. His hope for CGT had been high. It would have been the crowning achievement of his life's work, both financially and emotionally. But more important, he'd convinced himself CGT would save Amy.

"So CGT is a failure?" he asked in disbelief.

Tori looked David in the eyes. "No. No. Not a failure. We couldn't see the genetic imperfections CGT was creating until I developed this new sequencing process. The results showed we simply had to modify the process that repaired the damaged proteins in the targeted DNA and use our unique combination of fullerene-based nanotechnology and virus delivery system to deliver the gene. It would take some time, but I think we could make CGT work."

David couldn't take his eyes off Tori. It was more than just knowing how to fix the flaw in CGT. They shared something else—a connection stronger than anything he'd felt before. David reached across the table and cradled Tori's hands. She moved her gaze to the hands covering hers. She gently smiled and glanced at David. He regained his composure when he reminded himself that because of Tori's work, Amy could be saved, and there just might be a way to get his company back to do it. He gently slipped his hands from hers.

"Who did you tell? Who knows about this?"

Tori eased back. "I made a presentation to Mr. Brayton last Friday with Mr. Penn. I could see Brayton wasn't happy, but he tried to hide his disappointment. He told me how wonderful my work was and then he asked me to leave the meeting before I finished the presentation. I think he jumped to the same conclusion you just did. I didn't get to tell him we could fix CGT. He transferred me to the Proteus 40 pipeline team. On Monday, I called him to talk more about it, but he cut me off. So I guess just Mr. Brayton, and now you, know. Oh, and Mr. Penn."

David rubbed his chin and sat silently, listening to the rhythmic creaking of the hull as it rocked gently in the water.

Brayton had control of the company. They were wanted for murder and probably would never be taken alive. Brayton would see to that. Clearly, he planned to bury Tori's work and go public, cash out, and claim ignorance later. David knew Tori was the key to their survival. He had to keep her alive and safe. He also had a strange and wonderful desire to keep her close to him. And there was Amy, too. He was no good to her if he was wanted for murder. One thing became clear: if he didn't stop Brayton, CGT would go to market and then, once the FDA recognized the problem, they'd yank it from the market. It would be their worst nightmare: the first gene therapy treatment for cancer approved by the FDA would be killing its patients. It would be years before they gave the nod to any other treatment.

It was clear that Brayton and his henchmen had orchestrated the airplane crash that killed his only friend and mentor, Adam Rexsen. The anger building inside him grew when he looked at the brave woman across from him. He knew he needed to get to Brayton to protect her and avenge Adam's death, but they needed to buy some time. Most of all, he knew they needed a plan—a very good one.

# CHAPTER 31

DETECTIVE SKIP WATERS checked his watch: it was 3 a.m. He scanned the marina parking lot. Illuminated by the red and blue gumball machines flashing on their roofs, a dozen patrol cars were scattered on the damp black asphalt with complete disregard for the carefully painted lines. Sitting next to Lane in Lane's black Suburban, shrouded in the fog outside the marina, he was sure they were invisible to the investigative team.

He rubbed his throbbing head, and he fumed at the thought of being taken out by a fire extinguisher. While his head ached, his ego hurt worse. He'd been certain this would be easy money. He'd knock off a couple of the rich bozos from Newport Beach, answer a few questions, file his carefully prepared report, and get paid. But instead some amateur had taken out a nineteen-year veteran detective and a supposedly highly trained assassin.

Waters couldn't wait to get his hands on him.

This was the first homicide of the year and the victim was from one of the wealthiest families in Newport Beach. With the victim's father killed in a plane crash just days before, the entire Newport Beach Police Department was on hand. The Newport Beach detectives immediately called in the Orange County Sheriff's Crime Lab. The crime lab staff of four technicians, a supervisor, and two cadets scurried around the yacht, gathering evidence, getting prints, and snapping dozens of digital photos. He spotted two technicians, guided by detectives, as they examined the two suspects' vehicles at either end of the marina's parking lot.

One by one, the plates on the few cars in the parking lot had been run through the Department of Motor Vehicles. The computer had been efficient in identifying the two cars registered to David Wellington and Tori Clarke. They were searching for two murder suspects, Waters had told them, and they'd assaulted a detective in the process: him.

Lane shook his head. "Christ, Waters, you guys don't get much action here, do you?"

Waters knew the answer. Homicides were nearly nonexistent in Newport Beach. It was a town run by haves served by have-nots. The haves drove around in their Mercedes and BMWs in their velour track suits, sporting bodies designed by the best and busiest plastic surgeons in the country. The have-nots served the haves and slugged through life trying to make ends meet, enjoying tying one on, and if the ends didn't meet, they enjoyed stealing from the haves. As a result, most of the action consisted of public drunkenness, DUIs, domestic simple assaults, and drug violations. Waters considered himself a have-not, but this deal would make him a have.

"Yes, we're rather civilized here," he said, looking at Lane. He used a handkerchief to blot the blood still oozing from the back of his head.

Lane ignored the jab. "Okay, what do your guys have so far on the two marks?"

Waters pointed through the steamed-up windshield. "Wellington's BMW over there hasn't been moved in at least three hours. Same story for Clarke's Honda. We pulled the history on the meter at the gate, and it shows three vehicles entered after ten but a dozen have left. One left right at ten fifteen. Probably them and whoever assaulted you and me."

Waters had listened to Lane responding to the calls coming in from the command center.

"Your guys have anything?"

"Yeah. The bug we put in Wellington's limo stopped working just before ten. No activity in Wellington's and Clarke's cars here. So I bet they're in the limo heading somewhere."

"Shit, let's go," Waters said. "My guys can run it down in minutes!" He'd love nothing better than to come face-to-face with the bastard who bounced the fire extinguisher off his head.

"All right, call it in. Just be sure you keep control of the situation if your buddies here make the stop. You're not getting paid if you screw this up."

Waters stepped from the Suburban and slammed the door. He thought of the mess he was in, all thanks to that coke-snorting bitch at home. She was a great lay, but her habit strained their finances. Do this one thing and he'd be free, he'd told himself. He could stop skimming from his drug busts and the property room, maybe even dump his wife and get the hell out of his rental shack in Costa Mesa. But things weren't going to plan. Wellington and Clarke were on the run and no-where to be found. It didn't seem as simple as when he'd agreed to participate. Of course, the fact that Lane's boss had him on tape, steal-ing from the evidence room, made the decision to accept the proposi-tion easy. Take one hundred thousand in cash or go to jail—a real no-brainer.

He dropped into his unmarked Impala, picked up the radio mike, and made the call to dispatch. The APB was issued for the Lincoln Town Car. Waters replaced the mike, shoved the car into "drive," and headed back to the crime scene. After all, he *was* working.

# CHAPTER 32

DAWN BROKE OVER the San Gabriel Mountains, and David carefully maneuvered the sleek twin-hulled catamaran through the calm waters of Dana Point Harbor. He stood at the helm, dressed in a white nylon windbreaker, white shorts, and a blue polo shirt he'd found in the stateroom of the catamaran. He knew he looked just like the other sailors who scurried about the decks of the expensive sailboats and yachts, getting ready for their weekly therapy. He tipped his head back as an offshore breeze cooled his face. The fresh salty air and the first hues of sunlight refreshed his weary mind and battered body.

He actually smiled, a bit grimly: he had lived to see another day.

He noticed everything as though for the first time: the brown pelicans perched on the piers, standing guard over the waterway, the bright white seagulls circling above the procession of sailboats as they made their way to the open waters, the smiles on the boaters' faces as they waved to him as if he were part of some special fraternity. Beyond the breakwater of the harbor, he could see the long silhouette of Catalina Island, barely visible in the early-morning mist. He'd overlooked all this beauty before the plane crash. Now he was seeing a world he'd ignored during his first forty-five years on earth.

He pulled the Ray-Ban sunglasses from the console and slipped them over his eyes. The sun had cleared the mountains behind him and warmed his back. Tori stepped from the stateroom. David adjusted the glasses and hoped they concealed his stare. At David's suggestion, she'd changed from her conservative pantsuit to the white shorts and midriff top they'd found in one of the dressers. A white body wrap made a vain attempt to conceal her shapely body. She was freshly showered and smelled of lavender. Her silky dark brown hair was pulled into a tight ponytail and highlighted her high cheekbones and lightly tanned skin. Her legs were long, and her toenails revealed her fondness for French pedicures. But David focused on something else. He was happy to see that the fear and shock from the events of last night had faded. Tori seemed confident and committed. This was not the same woman from last night.

"Good morning, Mr. Wellington." She smiled at David for the first time.

Her renewed energy was contagious.

"It's David, and good morning." David returned the smile. "Wow, you look great. Feeling a bit better?"

"Yes, thanks. How long to Catalina?"

"Just a couple of hours."

David tried to keep looking ahead, but his eyes were stealing another look at Tori. He wanted to protect her, and that strange connection he noticed last night created a gravity he couldn't escape. She stepped closer to David, leaned against the helm's console and crossed her arms. Her brown eyes flashed and examined David's face.

David regained his senses and continued his description of the route. "We'll head around the north side of the island and duck into Hamilton Cove. It's outside the busy traffic of Avalon, but it'll be a short shot to catch the Flyer to the mainland."

Tori shifted her weight and cocked her head. "The Flyer?"

"The Catalina Flyer."

"I know what the Flyer is. I'm wondering why we're going back to the mainland."

David heard the tension in Tori's voice. He shared her concern about going back so soon into harm's way, but time was running out. The catamaran began to roll gently over the waves as it moved into the open water.

"Let's get the sails up, and then we can talk. Here, take the helm, but keep us on this heading." David pointed to the display on the console and bounded onto the deck. He skillfully unfurled the sails and returned to the cabin.

"You look like you've done this a time or two," Tori said, impressed with David's seamanship.

"Yup. After you live in Newport Beach long enough, sailing gets in your blood."

He smiled and confidently stepped back to the helm. As he had hoped, the diversion of raising the sails broke the tension between them. Tori returned to her position leaning on the console but continued to watch him. David settled into the captain's chair.

"I think I understand what happened last night, Tori."

Tori cocked her head and listened.

"Your work on CGT scared Brayton. I don't know how he did it, but I don't think the plane crash was just a coincidence."

Tori refolded her arms. Her eyes grew wide. "You mean your plane crash was planned?"

"It kind of makes sense now. Brayton knew about your work. You told him on Friday, just before the board meeting. If he could get rid of Adam Rexsen and me at the same time, he'd be able to get control of Rexsen Labs and hide your work. The company would go public, and he would reap hundreds of millions of dollars. If he doesn't know CGT can be fixed over time, he thinks the IPO would be canceled and there would be no payoff for him."

David glanced up to examine the sails. They billowed in the strengthening breeze.

"So last night was about getting rid of me?" Tori said and bit her lower lip.

"I'm afraid it was about getting both of us."

David shifted his gaze from the bow to Tori. She turned her head and stared at the open water. A tear ran from the corner of her eye, and she quickly wiped it away.

"This can't be happening to me. I haven't done anything wrong."

"I know—it's terrifying. But I think I may have figured out a way to save the research, based on what you told me last night."

Tori shook her head furiously. "You may be used to having people wanting to kill you, but I'm not—damn, damn, damn. You're not even scared. The police want you and me for murder and one of your high and mighty executives wants you out of the way, and you just sit there and tell me you have a plan to save the research!"

Tori stepped even closer. David drew back into the captain's chair. "And us as well," he said.

"I'm just a researcher," she said softly. "I'm a biochemist who thought she could find a cure for the cancer that killed her nine-year-old brother."

David leaned forward and placed his hand on hers. "You'll still have that chance, I promise. In a couple of hours we'll be safe in Hamilton Cove. I used to hide there when I wanted to get away from Rexsen Labs. We'll find a way out, I promise. You had a brother who died?"

"My little brother. He was nine when he died of acute myeloid leukemia. It came out of nowhere. He and I were always together. He'd loved to make me laugh. Even at the end, he loved to make everyone laugh. It crushed my mother. Now every time I see her I can see the sadness in her eyes. I know that when she sees me, she thinks of him."

The catamaran was at full sail now, and the boat sliced through the blue swells. They were halfway to Catalina Island, which grew larger as they approached. David listened to the rigging that kept beat with the rhythm of the sails. He glanced up at the mainsail and then glanced at Tori.

"So that's why you became a biochemist?" he said.

Tori stared toward Catalina. "My thesis was on the use of micro-assays for genetic mapping. I would have gone to medical school, but I thought the answers to the cancer problem would come from bio-technology. I was very excited when I was named to the CGT team, but I was crushed when the new microassay method I discovered showed the treatment repaired the targeted gene but unintentionally modified another." Tori paused.

"I'll bet you were," David said. "I was, too."

"And then I was shocked when the expression profile of the post-treatment DNA, the profile that shows which genes are switched on, matched the one in the national database for pancreatic cancer."

"But you said you know how to fix it?" David said.

"I think so. We identified the proteins in the genes damaged by the treatment, and we were able to modify the treatment to avoid the problem. All of the mice we tested showed complete remission and no side effects. Their genetic expression profiles checked out." She stopped talking and seemed to be gazing out to sea.

David looked at Tori. Her dark brown curls waved in the breeze. She was beautiful, brilliant, and committed. Her little brother shared the same terrible fate as his son. They'd fallen victim to a common enemy. He now understood why Adam Rexsen was right. There *was* a purpose to this business. It was clear as the brilliant blue sky before him. He remembered Amy's hopeful blue eyes and how they had si-lently begged him for help. He was committed and determined to help—not just her but thousands of sufferers. His jaw tightened, and he squeezed Tori's hand.

"We'll find a way to get your work to the people who need it, so help me God."

He never wanted anything as much as he wanted to help Tori get the treatment to the thousands of kids who suffered every day and whose families carried the invisible scars for life.

A pair of sleek bottle-nosed dolphins appeared and frolicked in the bow waves. David remembered the words that haunted him each night.

*You need to know there is a reason. It's His reason. Listen to your heart; open it up to everything; listen. The reason is within each of us. It's unique to every person on earth. Some never find it. You've been given a second chance. Remember His reason is not always obvious. Seek it.*

# CHAPTER 33

BRAYTON SLAMMED THE Wednesday morning *L.A. Times* on the table and startled the servant standing a few feet away on the top deck of the luxury yacht. Wellington and Clarke were on the run, and Prescott's murder had been pinned on the pair. To top it all off, Brayton read about it on the front page of the morning news, just like everyone else in Southern California.

He hated surprises, especially considering what he had paid to be kept informed. With Prescott dead, Priscilla had control of the trust, and he knew the calls from concerned board members would start soon. The bigwigs from Jones-Frederick wouldn't be far behind. As the underwriter for the IPO, their investors would be clamoring for information regarding the strange series of occurrences that put control of the Rexsen Trust in the hands of a woman with no business experience.

The wind gusted and knocked over the crystal flute filled with orange juice. Brayton noted the clouds building to the west. The twin diesels surged between the growing swells. No question this would be a bad day.

"Good morning, Royce," Priscilla said, announcing her entrance onto the sky deck. The attendant stepped to the chair facing Brayton and gently guided Priscilla into her seat.

For the first time that he could remember, Brayton's stomach churned as a little doubt about his ability to control her entered his mind. Dressed in a smart dark blue pantsuit, she appeared calm and confident. For the first time since he'd known her, she appeared to be going for the strong, not the sexy, look. He didn't like it. She looked too composed for just having learned of the death of her only sibling less than a week after the death of her father.

"Good morning, Priscilla," Brayton said.

Priscilla's eyes dropped to the paper on the table. "I see Prescott's murder made the front page."

The lack of remorse in her voice raised Brayton's suspicions. "Yes, it did, and your husband and his girlfriend are wanted for the killing." Brayton pushed the paper across the table.

Priscilla ignored it. "I sure hope they get him and don't give him a chance to explain his way out of it," she said.

Brayton wondered where the conversation was headed. "I'm not sure what you mean."

Priscilla leaned on her forearms and Brayton could see the coldness in her brown eyes. "If he lives and divorces me, he'll have half the trust, and you'll have to deal with him, too."

Brayton felt as if he'd stepped into a trap. The gusts had become stronger and swirled around the table. The sun disappeared behind the approaching squall line. He squirmed in his chair under the weight of Priscilla's silent stare. He wasn't sure anymore if he was the hunter or the hunted.

"He won't make it." Brayton tried to sound confident.

"What makes you so sure?" Priscilla said.

He tossed his linen napkin onto the table and knocked his chair away from him. "Trust me. I gotta catch the jet to New York." Certain he could bull his way out of the discomfort of Priscilla's pressure, he turned his back to her.

Priscilla slapped her hand on the table as the gust blew the hair away from her face. "I'm not done with you yet!"

Brayton spun and squinted to protect his eyes from the rain beginning to sting his face. How dare she threaten him like this? "You forget who you're talking to!" He closed the distance between them with one giant step.

Priscilla shot up from her chair to meet him. "No, Royce. *You* forgot who you're talking to. I'm the head of the Rexsen Family Trust, and I'm going to New York with you."

He leaned on his knuckles and met Priscilla face-to-face in the center of the table. "*What?*" he roared.

"You heard me," she said. "The underwriters will have questions, and they will ask to delay the IPO because of all this negative press. I'll go and show them I'm in firm control, and by Tuesday we'll all be a hell of a lot richer."

Brayton tried to rein in his temper. A damn woman telling him what to do, especially one he slept with. Who the hell did she think she was? He hadn't had that happen since his second stepmother, and she was a better lay.

"Shit!" Brayton said and clenched his fists. "Okay, but let's get one thing straight: you need me to make this thing happen. I'll call the shots until we all can cash out."

"Of course, Royce." Priscilla smiled. "I wouldn't want it any other way."

# CHAPTER 34

DONOVAN'S INSTRUCTIONS WERE clear: fulfill the contract or become a mark. Lane wiped the sweat beading on his forehead. He knew Donovan would follow through with the threat, and based on his firsthand knowledge of Donovan's work, Lane knew being the mark was no fun. The rain pecked at the windshield of the black Suburban. Waters sat in the passenger's seat, sleeping. Some detective.

He checked his watch. It was noon, and the beach traffic, slogging down Balboa Island Boulevard, had been thinned by the rain. They'd been positioned just off the boulevard at Eighteenth Street for two hours, outside the sixties-vintage bungalow owned by Wellington's driver. Lane could see the beach at the end of Eighteenth and the surf just beyond the sand. Find the driver, find the limo, and find Wellington—a simple but effective plan.

The screen door on the aqua one-story opened. Lane sat up, elbowed Waters in the side and tossed a black balaclava mask in his face.

"There's the mark," Lane said. "Let's go."

He started the Suburban and pulled quickly behind the 1969 SS 396 Chevelle in the driveway. Both men bolted from the truck and sprinted to Joe Pirelli. Dressed in sandals, black gym shorts and a gray tank top, he dropped his bags and prepared to defend himself.

He acquiesced when Lane showed him the compact but deadly MP5K under his jacket. Lane slipped a hood over Joe's head and pushed him into the backseat of the Suburban next to Waters who'd entered the SUV from the other side. The handcuffs were on in a second, and Waters pressed his service revolver against Joe's ribs. The Suburban raced down Eighteenth and turned left on Balboa to Newport Boulevard, then headed out of Newport Beach to their destination.

Joe had expected this. Maybe not this soon, but he knew it was coming. His training had already kicked in. Remain calm, assess the threat and make a plan for escape. Then wait for a break; timing was everything. Although the hood kept him in darkness, it heightened his other senses. He counted turns and noted the direction. He traced each one on the mental map emblazoned in is head from the years of driving for David Wellington.

He felt the left turn on Balboa and the merge onto Newport Drive. He felt the car rise over the bridge to the mainland, followed by a sudden stop. Must be the light at Coast Highway, he figured. They proceeded straight onto Highway 55 and took a left onto the 405, north. Joe sang his favorite Jimmy Buffet beach song, "Margaritaville," to keep time. Three times meant he was twelve to fourteen minutes up the interstate when they exited. The twisted route and the foul smell of sulfur from the refineries told him he was in Long Beach. The pungent odor of harbor trash cooking in the sun and the rumble of the huge cranes told him he was at the docks.

He knew what came next.

The Suburban came to a stop, and Joe heard the door open. A gun barrel stabbed into his ribs.

"Get going," Waters said.

Waters's voice confirmed what Joe already suspected. These were the two jokers he'd taken care of on Wellington's yacht. His confidence grew along with his resolve. As a veteran of the Marines Special Ops, with a stint with the CIA, he had been in hellholes around the world. Most people underestimated him because of his five-foot-six height, and most viewed him as an Italian limo driver. But he knew his training and strength gave him a distinct advantage.

He was shoved through a doorway—a warehouse, he guessed, based on the metal-on-metal echo of the closing door. He was slammed into a chair. Still in handcuffs, he winced when he felt the cutting pain as plastic ties were tightened around his ankles, anchoring him to the chair. The rustling noises around him ceased.

He closed his eyes in anticipation of the hood being ripped off his head. He didn't anticipate the brass-knuckled fist slamming into his left cheek. The blow stunned him, but he still felt the pain rip through his jaw and the blood run down his neck.

"That one was just to get your attention," the masked man said, bending down to be face-to-face with him. "Now, where is your boss?"

"Don't know," Joe said. Short frustrating answers, he thought.

He saw the flash of the brass knuckles announcing the arrival of the second blow to his left cheek and went with it this time. The pain was the same, but Joe assessed the damage as survivable.

"I'll ask you one more time. Where is Wellington?"

"I told you, I don't know." Joe braced for another blow, but it didn't come.

Instead, the man in the balaclava nodded to the pugilist with the knuckles, and he handed him a large dark object. Joe squinted through the blood running through his eyes; it looked like a gun—with a cord. The power drill roared to life, and the spinning bit closed in on his left eye. Joe knew he needed to get to work. With his hands cuffed behind him, he slipped his index finger and thumb into the waistband of his shorts. His tank top hung long, about halfway down his thighs, and provided the appropriate cover.

Joe could see the half-inch bit in the drill spinning as it stopped just under his eyebrow.

"You know, these things go quickly through bone, but they get tangled up in muscle and tendons," the man said.

Joe concentrated on his hands and pulled on one of the two safety pins he always kept in his running shorts. He used them to pin race numbers onto his shirt at the recreational races he loved. Once at the proper angle, he twisted his hand toward the keyhole on the cuffs.

"You'll talk. Most do. Usually once we start with the thigh," the masked man said, "but a few are a little tougher and don't break until we try the eyesocket."

"I'm a high achiever," Joe taunted, trying to buy some time.

"Well, it's time for your final exam." The man guided the drill into position just above Joe's right thigh. He heard a chuckle behind him. He felt the drill tugging at the material on his shorts. The click, followed by the release of the pressure on his wrists, said his hands were free, and he put his twenty-inch biceps to use.

In one motion he grabbed the drill, thrust it into the masked man's eye and stood with his feet still anchored to the chair. The man reeled in agony and collapsed to the floor screaming. Joe twisted on both feet and caught the man behind him by the throat. The chokehold dropped him to his knees in less than four seconds. With the drill still spinning in his left hand, he drilled through the plastic ties on his legs and sprinted to the door.

In an instant he was streaking down the 405 in the Suburban, wiping his face and checking his wounds.

"Not bad," he said as he pressed the cuts on his cheek while looking in the mirror.

He knew they were professionals; he'd run into enough of them in his time with the CIA. Someone had to be paying them, and they didn't come cheap. Whoever they were, he was convinced they'd caused the plane crash; they'd killed Prescott Rexsen, tried to kill his boss and nearly killed him. He promised himself he'd see they didn't succeed.

"*Semper fi,*" he said looking at his image in the rearview mirror again and smiling.

He loved that motto. It always gave him great strength and determination. Joe knew he was always ever faithful to the Corps—and now to David Wellington's survival.

# CHAPTER 35

TORI CLARKE CLUNG tightly to the brass rail she considered a lifeline. It was the only thing between her and the angry black waters attacking the hull. The storm seemed to have been waiting for them behind the horizon, then pounced, making the huge catamaran insignificant in the endless waves. Dark clouds rumbled and the sea chopped at the deck. With one eye focused on David and the other on the water, she fought her fear of the ocean. Who knew what roamed beneath the waves, watching and waiting for the unsuspecting prey to hit the water? Cold rain stung her face and announced the leading edge of the storm. She shivered and watched David skillfully guide the catamaran into Hamilton Cove.

As the storm worsened, the chill sank deeper into Tori's body, and her heart sank deeper into an abyss. She battled the debilitating power of her lack of trust in men, and she knew that now, without trust in David Wellington, she'd be doomed; cast out to sea to fend for herself, with no direction or skills for handling the troubled waters.

Bundled in yellow rain gear, the pair worked in unison to stow the sails and snag the mooring that bobbed in the dark waters. David guided Tori with his directions. Tori sensed gentleness in his orders that firmly guided her actions. It was a caring she'd never seen when watching him in his role as CEO. She'd seen him in employee town hall meetings where he would bark out financial results and cut off those brave enough to ask challenging questions, somewhere just above the ankles. But this was a different man. She wondered if the change was due to the current circumstances and his need for her expertise and eventual testimony, if they lived, or just a result of his near-death experience in the waters a hundred miles north of Catalina. She knew her life was in his hands now, and she decided his reason for changing didn't matter.

Rain dripped from the hood of her yellow slicker as she entered the cabin ahead of David. She felt his hand against her back, gently guiding her across the slippery deck. They pushed back their hoods in unison and shared a smile.

"You did great out there," David said as he pushed the water droplets off his cheeks. "Thanks for the help." His dark eyes and warm smile comforted Tori. He pulled the slicker off by the sleeves, and for the first time, Tori noticed the slight rippling of the muscles in his arms. Tori kept her slicker on and looked at the sheets of rain washing over the boat outside.

"Are we going to be okay here?"

David hung the coat on a hook beside the cabin door and surveyed the stormy waters for a moment. "Nothing to worry about now," he said, smiling. He stepped behind Tori and lifted the slicker from her shoulders. "This cove is secure, both from the storm and those clowns trying to kill us. This storm will blow itself out in a few hours. And thanks to Joe's connections, we are registered with the harbormaster under the owner's name. It's a private mooring, so no one will know we're here. Even the cops can't find us."

David shook the rain from Tori's slicker and tossed it over his on the brass hook hanging on the wall. He opened a cabinet and pulled

out two white towels. After tossing one to Tori, he rubbed the water
from his salt-and-pepper hair, looking more like a little boy fresh out
of the pool than a CEO. She admired his athletic build and blue-green
eyes, and for the first time she was attracted to him. In minutes he had
two steaming cups of coffee ready and set them on the table in front
of Tori.

"Thanks, Mr. Wellington," she said.

David chuckled. "I think you can call me David now."

Tori didn't answer. She couldn't. She wanted to, but her fear was
holding her back. It was always there, telling her to trust no one. She
was smarter than any man she knew. She'd proved that every time one
tried to get close to her. It protected her. But it wasn't protecting her
now and it wouldn't get her out of this mess. Only trust; trust in David.
He was not the young stable hand her father had hired for the summer.
He was not the one she chose for a romantic summer fling. He was
not the one who took something that was supposed to be the ultimate
act of intimacy and turned it into the criminal violation of a woman's
body, mind and soul. Worried that her mind would win the argument
again, she decided to plunge into the unknown.

"Okay, David. I want to thank you for helping me back there."
she smiled and patted the seat beside her. David sat and gripped his
coffee with both hands, never taking his eyes from Tori's. Tori felt her
need for self-preservation begging her to retreat; the free fall in the pit
of her stomach tried to convince her that if she uttered another word,
it would mean certain death. Despite her mind's warning to run for
cover, she pushed through her fear and forced a shaky smile.

"I was kind of scared back at Dana Point and wanted to apologize
for what I said to you."

David smiled and shifted his gaze to his coffee cup. "Actually, I
wanted to apologize for getting you in the middle of this." David hesitated, still looking into his cup. "I want you to know you don't have

to do this. I can get you to the mainland and get you out of town until this thing with Rexsen Labs is settled, one way or another."

Tori felt her courage slipping a little but caught herself. "Actually, as I remember, I called you, not the other way around." They shared a chuckle. "Besides, I have other reasons for doing what I'm doing."

David shifted his gaze back to Tori. She felt his eyes searching for an answer one.

"This is my life's work. CGT was my life's work. I believe it can save lives. Not just of the people who suffer from cancer but all of those who suffer with them."

Tori's mind drifted to a distant dark place. This was getting dangerously close to a fragile corner of her heart.

"People like your little brother?" David said.

Tori shook her head, still afraid of what she'd do if she allowed David to see the pain in her eyes. "And every mother, father, sister and brother who die a little bit with them."

David reached for her hand. "I need to warn you, it will only get more dangerous from here on out. But I'll protect you the best I can."

"Our odds of surviving this are better than what my little brother faced."

Tori felt strength in her own words. Her fear was nothing compared with what Aaron must have felt. She remembered him lying in the hospital bed, his small body ravaged by leukemia and the chemo. His eyes were nearly colorless and had sunk deep into his skull. His skin hung on his bony cheeks. He was in terrible pain, and he knew his young life was slipping away. His eyes begged his big sister to rescue him as she'd always done; he didn't understand that no one could help. She'd watched his eyes close and in an instant become nothing more than a body; his life had ended, and no one could have helped—no one until now. She thought about her commitment back then to search for the answers no one had, so that no other big sister had to endure the agony and helplessness she'd endured back then.

Her resolve returned. She locked eyes with David's.

"Just tell me what you want me to do."

# CHAPTER 36

THE SHINING WHITE hull of the Zodiac planed through the waves and hugged the Catalina coastline. The rain had passed, but the red hue that outlined the thunderheads to the west warned that storms were still roaming the open water. With a black ball cap pulled down over his eyes, David held a firm grip on the throttle of the fifteen-horsepower outboard and traced the coastline in the fading gloom of sunset. He guided the boat south through Descanso Cove. Tori gripped the gray plastic handrail of the shiny white craft with one hand and held her wide-brimmed straw hat on her head with the other.

Entering the Avalon Harbor, David sped the Zodiac past the Casino, a huge ballroom built in 1929 that stood like a sentinel guarding the harbor. Huge white columns held the ballroom twelve stories above the water. It dwarfed the Zodiac. David glanced up at the tall dark windows as they passed. *Could anyone be watching?*

He negotiated the sleek craft through a maze of expensive yachts and sailboats moored in a haphazard pattern in the harbor. He skirted the harbormaster's office at the end of Green Pier and ducked into the dinghy dock, just a few hundred yards from the Catalina Boat Terminal. David and Tori sat still for a moment and surveyed the shore along Crescent Avenue. Most of the tourists who had been sent scurrying for cover in the storm were now emerging from the string of gift shops, restaurants, and bars lining Crescent. They streamed like ants to the Terminal to catch the four-thirty departure to the mainland. Some looked soaked as they returned the glorified golf carts that littered Catalina's roads and provided a healthy income for the rental companies.

"Let's go," David said.

Tori grabbed the straw beach bag resting on the fiberglass deck of the Zodiac. David stood on the dock and extended his hand to steady Tori as she stepped from the bobbing boat. Their hats were pulled low, and their eyes were covered with dark sunglasses. White shorts, nylon windbreakers, and a straw beach bag helped them blend in perfectly with the Wednesday afternoon crowd. They ducked into a dive shop and purchased two sets of diving gloves. David led them through the wandering horde of tourists and day-trippers, and they boarded the Catalina Flyer for the hour-and-a-half trip to Newport Beach.

As the four Cummins Marine engines roared to life, David and Tori moved to the upper deck of speeding aluminum-hulled catamaran. Billed as one of the largest and fastest on the West Coast, it would have them in Newport by 6 p.m.

"So far so good," David said as he leaned on the rail and pointed across the channel to the mainland. "I think we'll be good until we hit Balboa Pavilion. Then we need to be very careful not to be recognized."

"They'll have our pictures everywhere, won't they?" Tori said.

David chuckled and plucked at his Hawaiian print shirt. "Not like this. The only photos they have of me will be in a suit. Even my driver's license photo is in a suit."

"That makes me feel better. My DMV photo is the ugliest photo I've ever seen."

"Ugly is hard to believe, but if that's the case they'll never recognize you."

Tori blushed.

David pulled his cap farther over his eyes as a uniformed security guard passed. "We'll need to get a cab at the Pavilion and then have it drop us at Fashion Island. Rexsen headquarters is just a short walk from the plaza. We'll need to pick up a few things at the fountain where Joe stashed them—then it's a go." David turned to Tori. "It will be the point of no return. Once we enter the Rexsen Lab complex, there's no turning back. You sure you're up for this?"

"Those morons tried to kill us," Tori said. "They're counting on exploiting people's hopes of a cure with CGT. If they succeed, my work was for nothing. Based on what you said last night, they'll cash out and leave the dying patients and their families holding the bag. The lawyers will file suit against Rexsen when they find the defect in the drug, but Brayton will be long gone. They'll destroy any chance for the cure. We'll be dead or in jail for life, and they'll never try to fix CGT."

David was surprised by the change in Tori's mood. She was far from the helpless young researcher he'd thought he'd drawn into this mess. Tori stared at the thunderheads that flashed with lightning in the distance.

"My brother puked his guts out, couldn't eat or sleep for months. After what he went through, this is nothing. I'm in—for good!"

David smiled as he remembered Adam Rexsen again and his lecture on purpose. He recalled the calm look on Adam's face while he plunged to his certain death. It brought to mind the mysterious orderly's words.

*You need to know there is a reason. It's His reason. Listen to your heart; open it up to everything; listen. The reason is within each of us. It's as unique as every person on earth. Some never find it. You've been given a second chance.*

"There is a reason," David mumbled to himself.

Tori smiled and put her hand on his. "Yes, there is."

# CHAPTER 37

THE BELL LONG Ranger helicopter banked left over midtown
Manhattan. The skyscrapers arrogantly jutted into the evening sky and
boldly challenged the night with their luminescence. The gaudy spire
of the Chrysler Building led the charge, quickly followed by the Empire
State Building and a supporting cast of thousands. Royce Brayton surveyed the scene and realized the insignificance of Rexsen's IPO to this
center of power and money. He knew that ten times more money was
made at lunch in Manhattan today than Rexsen Labs would deliver in
the next ten years. Still, it was his money—money he deserved—and
with the proceeds from the IPO and the immediate sale of the company, he'd be able to share in the city's arrogance.

The touchdown at the East Thirty-fourth Street Heliport was
smooth, and Brayton and Priscilla were ushered into the waiting black
limo. The driver deftly maneuvered the car through the maze of traffic
and within minutes stopped at the entrance to Pouvoir, a midtown restaurant reserved for the rich and powerful.

The driver opened the back door of the limo, and Priscilla, elegantly outfitted in a black sequined evening gown, extended her hand.
The driver stood at attention, looked straight ahead, offered his white-
gloved hand, and helped her exit the car. Brayton, bow-tied in a plain
black tuxedo, rudely popped out and marched through the entrance

ahead of Priscilla. In the past few days, his lust for her had disappeared and been replaced by visions of his bossy, greedy stepmothers.

"Royce Brayton here for dinner with Mr. Thomas," he announced to the host.

"Certainly. Mr. Thomas is waiting for you."

Weaving elegantly through the tables, the host guided them to the back of the room. Dark-suited older men seated with much younger women represented New York's business society. They dined on over-priced entrees off linen tablecloths and sipped from crystal goblets filled with Bordeaux and Champagnes so expensive the prices were never mentioned and never asked. Brayton's gaze drifted around the room. He recognized the faces of several of Wall Street's current cover boys. He was convinced he deserved a seat at those tables, and knew his chance was only days away. He sensed the stares following him. He knew that the intelligence network that connected the investment bankers to the moneymakers on Wall Street was intricate and accurate. The word was surely out about his ascension to CEO and the money about to explode into the shares of Rexsen Labs upon its public offering. Those willing to pay the price of admission were already counting their profits. He knew that only the already-rich could pay that price. The lowly individual investors would never get a chance. Controlled by the investment bankers working as underwriters, they only allowed those who would return the favor into the elite club that would own shares at the outset and ride them to the top.

And the hottest investment banker in New York City stood to greet Brayton and Priscilla. Jeff Thomas was the senior vice president at Jones-Frederick. His strong jaw, deep-set blue eyes, and dark brown hair with gray highlights immediately drew Priscilla's smile.

"Good to see you, Royce," he said.

"Good evening, Jeff," Brayton said.

"And this must be the most important woman of the night." Thomas turned to her.

"Pleased to meet you, Mr. Thomas," Priscilla said, batting her eyelids.

"The pleasure is all mine," Thomas said, not taking his eyes off of Priscilla as she took the seat next to him.

Brayton was unnerved. Priscilla seemed more important to Thomas than he was. Again, he considered the possibility of Priscilla as a threat instead of a bedmate. He knew the drill well: Power followed money. Period. And Priscilla had the money now. With control of the trust, her personal wealth would swell to $12 billion if the IPO took off as Thomas's firm had projected. Were the gazes and stares following him across the room, or was it her? Brayton felt his power draining. He'd identified with the concept of a shark in business, a cunning and relentless predator, but he was now in a room full of great whites, and power followed money.

The trio sipped scotch until the entrees, three filet mignons, arrived. Most of the conversation, led by Thomas, was about the tragic incidents that had taken the life of Priscilla's father and brother in less than a week.

"I've read your husband is wanted for your brother's murder," Thomas said. "Have they caught him yet?"

"No, Jeff. But it's just a matter of time. They found his prints on the knife and his blood was at the scene. He's working with a disgruntled employee he was probably sleeping with. They'll catch him, and they'll convict him."

"Sorry to hear that, Mrs. Wellington."

"Please call me Priscilla. As you can imagine, I don't want that last name now." Priscilla and Thomas shared a smile.

Enough of this shit, Brayton thought. That was his piece of ass and Thomas had better keep his hands off.

"Let's get down to the IPO," Brayton said.

Thomas's eyes lingered on Priscilla a little too long and then focused on Brayton as he spoke. "Well, we've polled our investors, and they want assurances that the trust is solidly behind this deal. They're confident Jones-Frederick can do our part, but they need to be certain the company is under competent and stable leadership. They have confidence in you, Royce"—Thomas turned back to Priscilla—"but to be frank, they're concerned about having a chairman of the board who has no business experience. They want assurances there is firm control of the trust."

Priscilla's eyes flashed, and her flirting smile intensified. "You mean a woman with no business experience?" she said, cocking her head.

She'd simply stated what Brayton had always thought. He was the brains, and she just pulled the lever to vote the trust's shares the way he told her. Apparently Thomas had drawn the same conclusion.

"As Royce can tell you, I'm fully capable of running things here and you can tell your investors not to worry. If a woman with no business experience doubles their share price in less than six months in this market, I think they'll be thrilled you gave them the opportunity," She leaned in and touched his forearm. "And you get all those fees—and if you're as smart as I think you are, you'll invest yourself."

Brayton wanted to laugh. Priscilla had done her homework. *No billion-dollar roll in the hay for you, my friend.* He felt the power return and electrify his body.

"If you'll excuse me, I need to freshen up while you and Royce discuss the details," Priscilla said.

She rose from her chair, and the two men joined her in courtesy. She strolled among the tables drawing several stares. Both men watched her prance out of the dining room while her eyes flirted with every stare in the room.

"Okay, Royce, here's the deal," Thomas said. "I don't trust some hot-blooded woman. You tell me you have this thing under your control or we'll pull the plug. This business is built on success.

One screw-up and we'll be selling savings bonds and cold-calling schleps making minimum wage."

Suddenly things weren't so funny. The IPO was three business days away. No IPO, no payoff. No payoff and the Marcosa boys would be fitting Brayton for concrete overshoes, and he'd get a permanent underwater tour of the Pacific. His bow tie tightened around his neck. In desperation, he'd sold his soul to the only source of funds he could find through a connection arranged by the father he despised. He'd borrowed millions from the family who silently controlled most of the West Coast docks, and his life was the only collateral he had left.

Brayton leaned across the table. His stare narrowed, and he pointed his index finger past the stem of his empty wine goblet.

"I've got it under control. You just calm the investors. That's what you're getting your forty million for."

It was a bluff, but Thomas didn't have to know that. Or did he know? Brayton tried to keep his face neutral.

Thomas leaned back and scoffed. "One more thing, Royce. I want in on this little side deal you're cooking up or we delay IPO."

Brayton felt the screws twist and the vise tighten, but still his face remained deadpan. Caught off guard, he remained silent. Thomas's minions had found a leak. No one was supposed to know about flipping the company to the highest bidder after the IPO.

"Well?" Thomas leaned back in his chair and waited.

Brayton's starched collar now felt like a noose. The clock was ticking, and there were still too many loose ends. Priscilla had to be kept happy—not an easy task, and David Wellington and Tori Clarke were still out there. Wellington could regain control of the company if he somehow dodged the murder charges and divorced Priscilla. Now this asshole wanted in and was holding Brayton's life in his hands.

Brayton had no choice.

"You're in."

Priscilla returned with her lips glistening with fresh lipstick and remained standing. Both men stood.

"Our car is waiting," she said, extending her hand. "It was a pleasure to meet you, Jeff."

Thomas gently shook her hand.

Brayton folded his napkin on the table and shook Thomas's hand. "I'll call you, Jeff."

He guided Priscilla to the aisle and they walked out of the restaurant. He was sure the same stares followed him out. Hopefully, they didn't see the blood gushing from the bite he'd just received from another great white. Otherwise, there'd be a feeding frenzy, and he'd be the prey.

# CHAPTER 38

DAVID WELLINGTON KNELT on one knee and checked his digital watch; it was 2 a.m. Thursday. The streets were deserted, and nothing moved in the still night air except the changing colors emanating from the traffic lights attempting to direct nonexistent traffic. In the shadows, Tori crouched beside him, and he listened to her shallow breathing as he scanned the perimeter of their target.

Nestled among the canopied evergreens and stately palms at the corner of Newport Center Drive and Santa Barbara Avenue, the Rexsen Lab campus glowed under the soft yellow light of the city streetlamps. The landscape concealed the eight-foot wall topped with three strands of barbed wire. The natural barrier of trees parted at the corner of Rexsen's ultramodern administration building that faced west and looked over Newport Harbor. The first floor was taller than the rest. Alternating layers of Italian marble and dark glass marked each of the remaining three floors, which grew successively larger and appeared to lean over the sidewalk and peer down on all who passed by. David thought the structure looked like a stadium from the outside, and with the fourth floor leaning out the farthest, it gave the impression that someone at the top was watching.

It used to be him. Now it was someone else.

David had approved the design and, at the time, thought the sub-liminal message was appropriate. *The power is at the top. You're wel-come at the front doors during business hours, but otherwise stay out—we're watching.* He knew information was money in this busi-ness and security and intimidation protected information.

Within the walls of the compound and behind the administration building stood their target: the lab. Two stories tall with only two ways in and four ways out, counting emergency exits, it was the heart of the company. Here the brightest minds that money could buy postulated, studied, and experimented with the human genome. In recent years the scientific community had mapped the thirty thousand or so genes that make up the blueprint of mankind. The infinite permutations made each person unique. At the same time, misprints and truncations in the four proteins making up the strands of human DNA determined each individual's fate. The secrets of disease, birth defects, aging, and other genetic imperfections were being revealed at an accelerating rate. Billions of dollars were chasing the answers to questions previously considered the realm of the Almighty.

CGT was intended to lead the fight against cancer at the molecular level. The clinical successes were unmatched and the treatment had raced through the FDA approval process. Now he was determined to stop it. The flaw Tori had identified would repair the targeted imper-fection but create another. Cancer patients like Amy would trade one cancer for another even deadlier.

He carried the black knapsack carefully packed by Joe and led Tori along the south wall of the complex. They disappeared into the thick landscape along the compound's back wall. Once concealed, Tori helped David wriggle out of the pack and remove a rope ladder and a thick black wool blanket. David tossed the blanket over the barbed wire and quickly followed it with the nylon rope ladder. Tori ascended the wall first and dropped undetected onto the grounds of the compound. David followed and joined her on the wet grass on the other side.

They scampered across the back parking lot to the rear door of the lab. David produced a magnetic card from the backpack. He paused and glanced at Tori. Her eyes darted back and forth as if expecting to be caught. Her hands were shaking. She realized David was staring at her and gave an approving nod. A rustling in the trees caused the pair to drop to their knees and spin toward the back wall they'd just scaled. David held his breath. The next few seconds lasted forever as he scanned the wall and listened. He could only see the outline of the trees protruding over the white wall. The back of his neck tingled and he felt someone was watching him. But seeing no other movement, he returned his attention to the card reader and prepared to insert the card Joe had stashed in the pack. Would the card work? Would they be immediately detected? Would an alarm sound? Were the cops already hiding inside, anticipating the move and ready to take these two murderers dead or alive? David took a deep breath and inserted the card.

The release of the magnetic lock allowed him to exhale and they slipped inside.


Two hundred yards away in the empty lobby of the administration building, a console held nine eight-inch video screens that monitored the activity around the compound. The security cameras were positioned strategically around the compound: one at the west gate, one at the south gate, two in the parking lots, two scanning the front and back entryways to the administration building, and four gazing at the four doors of the lab.

The tenth screen was seventeen inches and displayed an electronic schematic of the complex and showed the network of card readers in the complex. A red dot pulsated at the rear entry of the lab, and the banner on the right side of the screen displayed the information captured from the magnetic chip on the card.

*Carolyn Peters—Administration.*

Dressed in a gray security uniform, the guard at the console struggled to free his hand and feet to no avail. Bound to his chair with thick plastic pull ties, he wriggled and pulled until his face turned red. He knew the alarm meant trouble, and the fact that he was not reporting it meant certain death. A second red dot began flashing at the rear exit to the admin building as his assailant left to assist the intruders. The duct tape plastered across his mouth muffled his cursing. He knew the Long Beach warehouse had been connected to the console, and he knew they'd be coming.

David and Tori had maneuvered through the rear entrance to the lab and, scanning the darkness ahead, began to move cautiously up the stairs. David strained to open his eyes as wide as possible to let every speck of light into his field of vision. He could feel his heartbeat throbbing in his throat. Every neuron was telling him to run, to get the hell out of here. He knew they would be detected, if not immediately, soon after. They had two minutes at best before the system would automatically lock down each entrance and the building that focused on saving lives would become their tomb. They had to move quickly.

At the top of the second floor, David motioned to Tori to move past. The way was clear, and she could quickly move along the front hallway to the CGT lab. From his vantage point, David watched the administration building. There was still no movement. A few cars were scattered between the two buildings, and he scanned each one; still, he detected no movement. Tori's silhouette moved down the hallway and darted to the left into the CGT lab.

The alarm had been flashing for thirty seconds before the call was made from the Long Beach warehouse to the front desk. The phone rang for another fifteen seconds before it was clear that there was a breach.

"The front desk isn't responding, sir. We have a situation." The man pointed to the display in front of him.

Butch Donovan leaned in and examined the data. "It's them. They've used his secretary's entry card. How the hell did they get into the compound?"

"Don't know, sir. East and south gates report no entry or exit except for construction workers. They knocked off at midnight. Should we initiate lockdown?"

"Do it. They're trapped. And get our team in there. No cops. I'm on my way."

Donovan pulled a Glock from his shoulder holster, checked the clip, and ducked out the door, accompanied by a muscular man dressed in black.

Four successive clicks, only half a second apart, echoed sharply down the hallway. The sound ripped through David's body as if lightning had struck him.

*Lockdown!*

"Shit!" David said.

He rose from a squat to check the parking lot in time to see the armed guards from the west and south gates approaching in a trot. He ducked and yelled to Tori in a whisper. "We gotta get going, now!"

No response. David ran toward the northwest corner of the second floor. He scrambled past the office doors until he reached the CGT lab. This was where the secrets of the human genome had been unlocked and CGT had been born. It had occupied the entire north half of the building. As he reached the entrance to the lab, he remembered that computer stations and cubicles used to sit in front of the entrance to the clean room, where genetic material was handled and stored.

David reached the double doors marking the entrance to the CGT section and burst through. The cubicles were gone and the area was strewn with construction materials, tarps and paint. There was no sign of Tori. Panicking, David bolted to the clean room. A figure lurched in front of him, and he raised his fist.

"David, it's me," Tori shrieked.

"We gotta get out of here," David said.

"I can't find it. They've ripped out everything."

"Doesn't matter now. They're here. Let's go."

"No!" Tori bolted out the door and down the corridor.

"Damn it, Tori." David took off after her.

Outside, with weapons drawn, the security guards held their positions at the front and rear exits. Two dark sedans entered the compound and six men, all dressed identically in black and wearing balaclavas, raced to positions at each doorway. They joined with the security guards to form four teams, one at the front entrance to the lab, one at the rear, and two covering the two emergency exits at either end of the building. In unison, on signal from the lead, they entered the four doorways and began to systematically search the building.

David heard the clicks of the magnetic locks and froze. He stopped breathing and listened. Sweat beaded on his forehead. He heard the doors click shut, followed by footsteps too numerous to count. They were closing the noose. The sound of rattling glass came from the opposite corner of the building. If he could hear it, they could hear it, too.

He raced after Tori—she had gone through a doorway at the end of the corridor.

"This isn't part of CGT's lab," he said. "Let's go."

He grabbed her arm and dragged her along the corridor, retracing his steps. She seemed oblivious to the threat as she stuffed a few vials into the knapsack on his back. As they rounded the corner and headed along the corridor past the CGT lab and toward the stairs, David spotted the ruby-red pinpoint of a laser sight dancing along the wall. He froze and pinned Tori behind him with his arm. He heard the footsteps grow louder. He cut a quick glance at Tori. She'd obviously heard the same thing. The terror in her eyes frightened David.

He took a deep breath.

"This is it!"

He grabbed Tori by the arm and bolted into the lab, which was littered with construction material.

"They're in the lab!" a gruff voice yelled. "We got 'em."

As they ran toward the window, David looked back to see a dark figure appear in the doorway and point a weapon in their direction.

They were trapped. And if Joe wasn't ready, this was it—the end. Determination filled him—just when he had found his life's purpose, he wasn't going to let them snatch it from him. He turned to the window and spotted the construction chute that emptied into the dump truck below. He knew it would be better to jump than to take a bullet here. At least it would buy them a few more seconds.

At the window, a burst of muffled gunfire erupted and he pushed Tori to the left into the chute and out of the line of fire. Tori tumbled down the construction chute and landed with a thud on a pile of broken drywall. David tumbled out and landed facedown on top of her.

Within seconds, he heard the engine of the dump truck roar to life, and they were slammed against the tailgate as it lurched forward. Dazed, David wobbled into a sitting position in the pile of debris and heard a crash as the behemoth truck's engine roared and the west security gate shattered.

"*Semper fi*, assholes." The voice came from the cab.

# CHAPTER 39

THE LIGHTNING FLASHED through the window of the lab and revealed the deep scar on the left side of Butch Donovan's neck. Violence was his job, and he wore the scar as a warning. Surrounded by eight men, all dangerous in their own right, he assessed the damage with short, cutting questions and piercing glances as each man responded. He was certain the breach was caused by the incompetence of the security guard on the front desk, who quivered as Donovan made that point clear to all. Missing were several frozen blood samples from the clinical trials for CGT. The pair had searched a second office unrelated to CGT, and a drawer containing computer disks had been left open.

"Thanks to this asshole," Donovan said, nodding to the security guard standing just to his right, "they now have evidence. Evidence our client will not be happy about." Donovan's glare narrowed on the quivering guard. "If that were to happen, game over."

"Next steps, sir?" one of the six men in black said.

Ignoring him, Donovan pulled a Glock, shoved it within inches of the security guard's head and pulled the trigger. The blast, muffled by a silencer, sounded like a thud, as if he'd shot a melon. No one flinched and the guard collapsed to the floor of the lab.

Donovan spoke without emotion. "As you can see, Mr. Wellington is a dangerous and desperate man, desperate enough to kill his own security guard when he was confronted here tonight."

All but the remaining two security guards shared a chuckle.

"He and Miss Clarke are evil bastards trying to fabricate DNA evidence with the material they stole tonight in an effort to deny the world a cure for cancer and save their own selfish skins."

Each man stared at Donovan and awaited his next orders.

"Contact Waters at the Newport Beach Police Department and report this tragic death. Advise him of the theft and tell them to alert the FBI to a possible attempt to contact the FDA and present fabricated evidence."

"Yes, sir," the man to his left said.

"Tell them they're both armed and very dangerous, and unofficially they should shoot first and ask questions later."

"Got it," the man said and walked away with a phone to make the call.

Donovan turned his attention to the remaining four expressionless faces, whose eyes were still locked on his.

"Now, let's go over this scene one more time before the detective arrives. Time is running out, people. We have to eliminate the marks now. If we fail, we don't get paid." Donovan pointed to the dead guard lying in a pool of blood. "And when we don't get paid, I'm not happy."

# CHAPTER 40

THE BALBOA PENINSULA in Newport Beach had been a get-away for Southern Californians since the 1940s. The completion of the Santa Ana freeway in the 1950s solidified Balboa's reputation as a year-round destination. While the elite built their homes atop the sea cliffs, hillsides, and mesas, the Peninsula remained the seaside getaway for the common man.

The rental house was like every other one on the block: a beach-front stucco two-story wedged onto a fifty-foot lot with a shoe horn. Joe pulled the rented Ford Explorer out of the driving rain and into the double garage. He sprang from the car and opened the rear door where David was sitting. The bandages Joe and Tori had applied to his upper left arm at the transfer point had begun to show blood. David winced as Joe helped him from the car. Tori joined them at the door and guided David inside. David looked at the blood on Tori's blouse.

"You sure you're not hurt?" he said.

Tori looked down. "No, this is all from you."

David shifted his attention to Joe. "Are we safe here, Joe?" David asked as Tori eased him onto the sofa.

"Yeah, boss," Joe said. "This is a rental owned by my Marine buddy's wife's cousin. No one knows we're here." Joe dropped the black backpack next to the sofa and produced a medical kit. "A good marine is always prepared," Joe said and gave Tori a warm smile. "Don't worry, he'll be fine. The bullet passed through without hitting the bone. Besides, he's mean as hell."

David shook his head. "One of my best employees," he said to Tori, nodding in Joe's direction.

Joe began to redress the wound while Tori sat beside David on the edge of the sofa. David kept looking at her. Her smooth skin glowed in the dim light and her eyes were dark and soft. He felt her beauty as much as he saw it. She stroked his forearm with her long fingers, and her touch was soft and gentle. He could feel her concern: about her work, about finding the cure for the cancer that had taken her brother and for him. She'd risked her life for all of those things. They shared a common purpose in preventing approval of CGT and regaining control of its development, but they were sharing something else, something deeper. Something he'd never had before.

"Good as new, boss," Joe said.

Joe's proud exclamation broke David's trance. The rumble of the second major Pacific storm in two days signaled his return to reality. They were wanted for murder by the authorities. An entire team of assassins had been called in by someone who'd rather see them dead than in jail, and CGT approval was forty-eight hours away. Sheets of rain pecked at the sliding glass door, and another flash of lightning warned of the next clap of thunder.

"We almost didn't make it out," he said to Tori.

"I'm sorry, David. I feel terrible. If it wasn't for me, you wouldn't have been shot." She continued stroking his forearm. "But when I saw the CGT lab had been dismantled, I panicked. All of this for nothing. I couldn't leave empty-handed. I remembered where the blood samples were stored from the last clinical trial." Tori reached into the black knapsack and produced what looked like small silver thermoses. "So I grabbed them. We need to get them into the freezer."

She handed the container to Joe, who responded to David's nod toward the refrigerator in the kitchen.

David paused. Then his eyes flashed wide. "The DNA—we have the DNA in these blood samples."

Tori smiled proudly. "That's right. During my presentation to Mr. Brayton last Friday I'd given a copy to one of the techs down the hall, who was helping me with the PowerPoint graphics and transitions. He'd kept the copy and e-mailed me the final presentation, so I grabbed it. It contains the results of the microarrays I ran on some of the clinical samples."

David pushed himself up from the sofa, cupped Tori's face in his hands and kissed her.

"We've got the proof. You did it!"

Tori blushed, then smiled. David, surprised by his own show of emotions, dropped back onto the sofa. He'd never felt so alive. He could feel each breath fill his lungs. His senses had been awakened to the world around him, and for the first time he could remember, his heart was drawn to another.

Joe returned from the kitchen, interrupting their wordless communication. "I'd hate to be the spoilsport, but who do you take the evidence to? You two are wanted for murder by the authorities. And based on the beating I took at the hands of the guy flashing a detective badge at that warehouse, the cops are in on this thing, too."

David's heart sank like a helium balloon suffering from a pinprick. Joe was right. The authorities thought he and Tori were cold-blooded killers. On the trip to the beach house, Joe had described his encounter with the hired killer and a Newport Beach detective in a darkened Long Beach warehouse. Going to the authorities was not an option. The newspapers and media weren't an option either.

They'd already sensationalized the case and characterized David as a billion-dollar killer.

But, damn it, he wasn't beat yet. Not now—not when he had just discovered something even sweeter than discovering the cure for cancer.

"We've got two options as I see it."

Tori and Joe locked their gazes on David.

"Get to the FDA or to the Rexsen board."

As David heard himself say the words he realized the risks were extreme. A call to the FDA by the murderer of the founder's son would result in a call to the FBI, and any meeting could be used to apprehend David. David's credibility would be dismissed immediately. But he personally knew the division director of the Pacific Regional Laboratory Southwest, in Los Angeles. They'd attended Harvard together, and he just might trust David.

Getting to the board was even more problematic. Someone within the power structure of Rexsen was willing to kill to get CGT to market. While he suspected Brayton, he couldn't exclude someone else on the board. None of the directors would risk speaking to a murderer, and he wouldn't be receiving any invitations to the next board meeting. He wasn't the CEO anymore; he was a fugitive.

"I don't think either of those will work, boss," Joe said as if reading David's mind. "They're pinning everything on you two. The papers think you're the Bonnie and Clyde of the corporate world. And whoever is behind this must be spending a ton of money to see that you two are taken dead, not alive."

David sensed Tori flinch, although she remained quiet.

"Okay, Joe," he said, reaching for Tori's hand. "That's enough."

Joe looked at Tori. "I'm sorry Miss Clarke."

Tori waved off Joe's apology. "How can I help?"

Joe dropped into the chair to the right of the sofa, grabbed the TV remote, and turned on the TV. He flipped through the channels and stopped on the early morning news. The anchor summarized the weather and traffic and then excitedly began the news.

"In breaking news, we've received a report of another gruesome murder associated with the bizarre fall from grace of Rexsen Labs CEO David Wellington."

David and Tori perched on the edge of the sofa and leaned toward the TV.

"Reports are just coming in from the Rexsen Labs compound in Newport Beach, where authorities say David Wellington, the former CEO, who was dubbed the 'miracle man' after surviving a plane crash in the Pacific, apparently broke into the company's complex and stole genetic material in an effort to sabotage the approval of the company's blockbuster new treatment, CGT, the first gene therapy treatment for cancer. Detective Skip Waters of the Newport Beach Police Department had this to say moments ago."

A reporter in a tan trench coat and holding an umbrella stood in front of the Rexsen Labs headquarters. "I'm here with Detective Skip Waters of the Newport Beach police. Detective Waters, what's the situation inside?"

The camera shifted to Waters's face. "It's gruesome. One person, a security guard, is dead, apparently executed by the perpetrators."

"Can you identify the suspects?"

"The alleged suspects are David Wellington, former CEO of Rexsen Labs, and Tori Clarke, his accomplice and a researcher at Rexsen. They're already wanted for the murder of Prescott Rexsen and are considered armed and extremely dangerous."

"We have reports they were attempting to steal genetic evidence in an attempt to fabricate a story to exonerate themselves from the murder of Prescott Rexsen."

"I can't comment about an ongoing investigation. I just want to remind the public not to approach these suspects. If anyone sees them, call the Newport Beach police or the FBI immediately."

"We didn't kill anybody," Tori whispered. "We're not killers!"

The anchor moved on to the next story.

"Joe, turn that off, please," David said, holding Tori's hand hard.

Joe grabbed the remote from the arm of the La-Z-Boy rocker and the screen went black. They sat in silence. Tori leaned against David, and he could tell she was trying hard not to cry. He listened to the rain, driven by bursts of wind, pop against the sliding glass door. The surf pounded and added a constant roar to the storm. More than anything in the world, he longed to help this woman at his side. And, of course, Amy and all those other children who were dying of cancer.

"Is CGT really a bad thing?" Joe asked, breaking the silence.

"There's a prob—" David said.

"No," Tori said. "There's a problem but we have a solution."

David turned to her, his heart lifting with hope. "We *have* a solution?"

"Yes," she said. She picked up the disk. "It was in my presentation to Brayton. He never let me get to it. There is a problem with the base-pairing process, where the genes are transferred from the DNA to RNA, an intermediate molecule. It resulted in key proteins not being made correctly. The same new microarray process that allowed me to see the flaw also allowed me to isolate the problem. Like I said before, it's repairable, and now we have the proof."

David and Joe looked at each other. Joe shrugged and raised his hands to either side. David couldn't believe what he'd heard. CGT could work and Tori had the proof. FDA approval should be delayed, but after a rapid review by the National Institutes of Health and the FDA, clinical trials for terminal cases could begin almost immediately.

His thoughts turned immediately to Amy.

"Did you get any update on the girl in Cedars we met, Joe?"

Joe hesitated, as though carefully sorting through his choice of words.

"Not good news, boss. I called her mother. She said six to eight weeks."

David dropped his head. He remembered Amy's smile and her uplifting faith, then imagined her lying in a dark hospital room, clutching her Elmo doll, and wondering if the man she'd believed to be the miracle man had any miracles for her. He thought about his young son who'd died of a genetic imperfection while his hotshot biotech father stood by and watched. He glanced at Tori as flashes of lightning illuminated her face. He recalled her pain when she described the suffering of her nine-year-old brother. At that point he'd again witnessed, firsthand, the damage that cancer caused not just to the tissue but also to the hearts of anyone who cared.

*Not this time*, he promised. *Not this time.*

# CHAPTER 41

ROYCE BRAYTON FELT the long corridor on the fourth floor of the Rexsen Labs headquarters closing in. Although it stretched the entire length of the building, it only connected the office of the CEO to that of the chairman. He'd feared the walk when the old man had the helm, and he hated the walk when Prescott was in control. But this walk was a first: He was being summoned to what used to be the old man's office to give a status report to the woman he'd been sleeping with just days before. He stormed toward Priscilla's office, and he heard his steps echo down the wooden planks of the polished floor. His fingernails dug into his palms as he clenched his fists. With each step, the air grew thicker, his breathing grew stronger and more deliberate, and the thought of losing control of Rexsen Labs to a woman who'd turned the tables and used *him* pushed his composure to its limit. This would be a Thursday morning he'd never forget.

The trip to New York had turned into a nightmare. He'd been blackmailed into giving his underwriter a piece of the yet undisclosed merger. Priscilla had embarrassed him in front of Wall Street's most powerful banker when she claimed to be in control of the IPO as the head of the Rexsen trust. The final dagger was thrust into his ego when Priscilla rebuffed his sexual advance and retired alone in her suite at the Plaza. He'd spent the night fuming and concocting ways to put Priscilla in her place and envisioning the gruesome methods the Marcosa family would use to make an example of him, should something go wrong with the IPO.

Upon reaching the suite, he stormed past the secretary and sent the door to the chairman's office bouncing off the doorstop. He stopped and leaned across Priscilla's desk.

"Who in the hell do you think you are? I'm not some jackass flunky that you can order around. I'm the CEO of this company, and without me there'll be no IPO and no twelve billion for your polished ass!"

With her head down and her eyes focused on the letter in front of her, Priscilla remained still and unflustered. Brayton had always been able to make a woman cry. Once they were no longer a source of sexual satisfaction, he'd cut them off at the knees. It was cleaner that way. But Priscilla's indifference to his opening barrage unnerved him. He hesitated, and it was a mistake he immediately regretted.

Priscilla slowly raised her head, and her dark brown eyes appeared black and dead. For the first time, Brayton felt the primitive jolt of the fight-or-flight response programmed into the human genome through millions of years of mutations. He was in danger.

"It seems, Mr. Brayton"—Priscilla carefully measured each word—"it is you who has failed to recognize your place in this enterprise." She shifted in her chair and calmly folded her hands in front of her. "I am the head of the Rexsen Family Trust, and at the moment, I'm the sole owner of this company."

Priscilla regarded him calmly.

Brayton crossed his arms and scowled. "That may be true, but I run things here."

"At my pleasure you do." Priscilla wagged her finger in Brayton's face. "And you need to watch your step. You can be replaced. If you think being a pincushion for you will keep this bitch in line, think again.

I can make my twelve billion now or a year from now, I don't care. But know this: I can replace you with one call, you son of a bitch."

Brayton was stunned with the voracity of Priscilla's attack. He searched for a response, but none came. He examined the situation for his leverage here, but there was none. She'd beat him at his own game and Brayton knew he had no choice. His plan hadn't anticipated this about-face. He needed time to think—but most of all, he needed Priscilla to follow through with the IPO or he'd be dead in a week.

She owned the company and could throw him out any time she wanted. She already had a company worth $2 billion without CGT. Even if David Wellington was somehow able to survive and divorce her, she'd have a billion to last her until the next gene therapy treatment, Proteus, emerged from Rexsen's pipeline. Despite the problem with CGT, Rexsen was going public—if not Tuesday, then six months or a year from Tuesday. The company's trajectory was set.

Brayton tried not to cringe in front of her, but the image of his mutilated body being discovered in some public place forced him to swallow hard. He didn't have her flexibility. He needed the IPO to happen now.

"That's better," she said with a cunning grin. "Now, what about this problem last night at the lab?"

Brayton looked out the window. He'd give her the report, he decided, but not the satisfaction of looking at her.

"He broke in with the Clarke woman, killed a guard, and got away with the help of an accomplice. They got into the lab. Several vials of frozen blood from the CGT trials are missing."

Brayton stopped short of telling her of the problem with CGT. No one else needed to know. He would clean up that mess on his own.

Priscilla studied his face. He became self-conscious; he thought about his eye movements, his expression, and his breathing. Priscilla leaned back in her chair and grinned.

"What about the problem with CGT?"

Brayton froze. Was she fishing? Did she know? "What problem?"

"The problem that caused you to remodel the lab." Priscilla was still smiling, like a hunter certain of a kill.

Brayton shook his head. "We had to make some changes in the team. That bitch Clarke presented information to me that she'd uncovered some kind of new process that allowed us to see even more minute genetic imperfections. Said she'd run a test on a few of the DNA samples from the trials and identified a problem with the treatment. We checked it out with an outside lab. Her work was flawed. There's no problem with CGT."

Priscilla rested her elbow on the arm of her chair and cradled her chin. "Is that so?"

Brayton thought it safer not to respond.

"So that's why David and Clarke thought it was worth killing a guard to steal the DNA samples. Sounds like they think there *is* something wrong with CGT and uncovering that problem may get them off the hook."

Brayton wiped the sweat from his forehead. Still, he remained silent. Priscilla stared and waited for a reply. Brayton felt his breathing slow. The only noise in the room was the ticking of the grandfather clock. To Brayton, each tick seemed to be at least ten seconds apart. Finally Priscilla broke the silence.

"Well, it seems you don't have everything under control here. I suggest you solve the problem. If David even has a chance to sabotage this deal, he will. You need to solve that problem. Do you understand?"

Brayton was trying to read between the lines. Did she know about his debt with the Marcosa family? Was she saying it's either David or you, but one of you has to go? He was sure the possibility of losing half of $12 billion to Wellington in a divorce and proving her father wrong about not letting his little girl run the company were enough to motivate her to eliminate her husband. In less than forty-eight hours the FDA would approve CGT, and in four days Rexsen would go public in the most successful IPO since the dot-com bubble burst.

But Brayton knew if David Wellington prevailed, he would not see another Thursday, ever. He swallowed the lump of pride in his throat, and he choked out the words his ears couldn't believe his mouth said.

"I understand," he said.

At least he'd still have a throat.

# CHAPTER 42

IT WAS LUNCHTIME on a beautifully crisp Thursday afternoon, and David Wellington spotted Dr. Kyle Harmon as he sat under the shade of the olive trees in Maguire Gardens, adjacent to the Los Angeles Central Library. Built in 1926, the library's imposing architecture combined Byzantine, Egyptian, and Spanish styles. The massive stone figures sculpted into the library's facades seemed to warn the encroaching skyscrapers to keep their distance. The library had survived two horrendous fires, but the stone figures still stood as strong survivors. As David watched the courtyard, he hoped the library's luck would rub off.

Just as he did every Thursday, Dr. Harmon read the latest *New England Journal of Medicine* and enjoyed his trendy boxed lunch from the Café Pinot. Traffic noise bounced off the surrounding buildings and mixed with the chirps of birds perched in the greenery spread throughout McGuire Gardens. As the director of the Pacific Regional Laboratory of the Office of Regulatory Affairs arm of the FDA, Harmon and his team were often referred to as the eyes and ears of the FDA. They analyzed samples of regulated products to ensure compliance with applicable standards.

Today was different, though; David's eyes were on him.

David knew his plan was full of risks, but Dr. Harmon was his only chance. They'd graduated from Harvard together years ago, and David considered him a friend. With his contacts in the FDA, he could get the information to the director before the approval action letter would be released for CGT on Friday. Equipped with the information, David and Tori could get a fair investigation into the murder charges, and the conspiracy to cover up the genetic imperfections caused by CGT would be exposed. A long shot at best, but it seemed the only shot he had.

From his vantage point on the second level, David scanned the library's West Lawn. His eyes meticulously examined the plaza in grids, first following the central axis of the plaza and then moving in blocks to either side until his survey crossed Flower Street to the City National Plaza. Evergreens in all shapes and sizes stood behind the low walls and provided shade to the reddish walkways. At another time, David might have seen the lush courtyard as a respite for urban-bound Los Angelenos, but today he knew it could be his cemetery.

Olive trees, planted to create the setting for the outdoor café, screened his view of the lunch crowd. He'd have to get a close look. Every person was a potential problem: a fed, a detective, an assassin. He tugged on the bill of his blue Dodgers ball cap until it reached his sunglasses, and then he turned up the collar of his black microfiber jacket and left the library. Entering the open plaza, he felt the cool breeze left behind by last night's storm. With every neuron firing, he walked along the plaza toward the café. Behind his glasses, he eyeballed each person he encountered. A man in blue jeans and sweatshirt sat on the low wall reading the *L.A. Times*. Was he wired or really reading? A woman with eight teens in tow approached. No problem; just a tour. David turned right and entered the patio of the café. Now under the umbrella of the olives, he could clearly see the dozen or so diners spread among the white-clothed tables and umbrellas. He drew in a deep breath and moved toward Harmon.

Harmon was a pencil-thin man with short gray hair and round wire-rimmed glasses. Tucked away in the corner of the patio, he studied his magazine while aimlessly poking at his salad with a plastic fork. Six tables were occupied. Three tables sported digital cameras and maps and were immediately eliminated as a threat. The fourth table hosted two businessmen, dressed in $600 suits, probably executives from the Financial District. The table closest to Harmon was shared by a middle-aged man and an attractive young woman. Giggling, she slipped her foot from her black pump and rubbed the inside of her companion's leg. Adultery. David certainly knew what that looked like.

With one last glance over his shoulder, he jammed his hand into his jacket pocket. The cold steel of the gun felt strange, but it was time to take the liability of being a wanted killer and make it work for him. He walked to Harmon's table for two and took a seat.

"I beg your pardon, sir," Harmon said.

"Kyle," David said, "I hate to do this, but there's a gun pointed at your balls. You need to listen to me."

Harmon dropped his fork into the salad and froze. "You can have my wallet. Here." Harmon started to pull his hand off the table.

"Keep your hands on the table, Kyle."

It was then that Harmon realized this mugger knew his name. He stared at David.

"Oh, my God! It's you, David."

"Stay calm and quiet, Kyle."

"Shit, David, you killed those people." Harmon's eyes grew wide in fear.

"Listen, I didn't kill those people. There's someone else, someone who's covering up a flaw in CGT. It's gotta be someone inside Rexsen. I want you to get word to the director who's about to sign off on it to suspend the approval."

"Sure, David, whatever you want."

It was clear by his tone he didn't trust David. Harmon was his only hope, and if he didn't cooperate Tori and David were as good as dead. Any second, someone could spot David. He didn't have much time left. He had to get through to him.

"Don't patronize me! Just look at this."

David pulled a brown envelope from his pocket and tossed it onto the table.

"Okay, okay, David. I'll do it. Just don't shoot me."

David watched Harmon look over his shoulder. He glanced back and saw the two uniformed L.A. policemen walking along the plaza. His eyes froze on them for a second too long. He heard the chair shoot out from under Harmon, and David spun in time to see him dive to the ground.

"Help me! He's the killer! He's the killer!" Harmon yelled, pointing at David.

Suddenly all eyes locked on David. The policemen pivoted and immediately spotted him. One reached for the radio mike clipped to his shoulder. David flipped the table on top of Harmon and bolted across the patio, toppling umbrellas and tables, then jumped over the wall and sprinted across the lawn.

"He's got a gun," were the last words he heard from his so-called friend.

"Stop! Police officers," one of the two officers commanded as they sprinted behind him with guns now drawn.

He was across Flowers Street and in the middle of City National Plaza in seconds. One quick glance at the officers showed them fifty yards away and closing. A siren screamed down Flowers. *Just enough time.* He cut to the right around the corner of the massive skyscraper and sprinted to Fifth Street. The officers in pursuit cautiously approached the corner and cleared it. Sprinting to Fifth Street, they lost sight of the suspect. A patrol car raced toward them from the right, and the Harbor Freeway ramp gathered the building afternoon traffic to the left. No sign of David Wellington. They jawed among themselves for a few minutes, then shook their heads in disgust. They headed back to the café to interview the near-victim.

Just moments later several detectives and FBI agents arrived on the scene. After interviewing Harmon and reviewing the contents of the envelope, their conclusion was unanimous. Wellington and Clarke had broken into Rexsen Labs to conjure up some bullshit story in an attempt to save their asses. Under questioning from detectives, Harmon reported that the FDA had followed every step in the clinical trials. Each section of the FDA, including Biotechnology, had signed off on CGT. The FBI and a detective from Newport Beach had warned them this would be his next step.

Wellington was becoming predictable. They'd prevented another murder, they said. The FBI and the detectives spent the rest of the day patting themselves on the back and conducting media interviews. They had their slick sound bites, but still, there was a problem they couldn't hide.

The miracle man turned murderer had disappeared—again.

# CHAPTER 43

DUSK HAD PUSHED the last remnants of sunlight into the Pacific, and Royce Brayton jammed his red Ferrari into third gear and raced down the rain-wet street. He shot past home after home of his wealthy neighbors. Usually on his drives home, he'd spot visitors to Laguna Beach gawking at the cliff-side estates, basking in the glowing warmth of the Southern California sun and dreaming of writing that blockbuster, starring in the movie of the year, winning the lottery, or riding a skyrocketing career to the top. He'd gloat and ignore them as he passed. But Royce Brayton wasn't gloating this evening. He slammed the Ferrari into fourth and shook his head. He was at the top, the CEO of Rexsen Labs, and yet he was taking orders from a woman who'd spent the last six months underneath him—literally. Shit, he couldn't believe this was happening.

The storm had cleared out and left a chill in the air. Still, he drove with the top down. He needed the air. The pressure was suffocating him. FDA approval had to happen tomorrow. Priscilla had cut off the sex, the one weapon he could use to control her. She'd assumed an active role as the chairwoman, even though the board had not appointed her to that position. That, however, was only a formality.

She *was* Rexsen Labs. With Wellington on the run and wanted for murder, she was the sole trustee and beneficiary of the Rexsen Family Trust. Brayton's stomach ached as he pulled through the gates and parked in the driveway.

The dark hulk of the tri-level home, once the crown jewel of his possessions, now hung around his neck like a noose. He'd leveraged everything. He'd covered his margin calls, bought the Ferrari and this magnificent home with money from the only source left willing to take the promise of the IPO as the payoff. The old man still had connections, even in prison. He hated having to ask him, but he'd been tapped out. Now he'd mortgaged his life, and it hung precariously by a thread. If the FDA approval or the IPO failed, the Marcosa family would call in the note with a bullet.

Brayton opened the front door and a chill rattled his nerves. The dark floors and ebony furniture were invisible. He flipped the light switch in the entry. The loud click was followed by darkness, and he instinctively flipped it again. He stopped breathing and listened. The hum of the refrigerator was the only audible sound. He scanned the first floor. Shadows filled the room. Minuscule specks of light from a pair of ships at sea seeped through the back windows. They reflected off the polished surfaces of chrome and lacquer and appeared and disappeared as his glances chased them around the room.

Through the back windows he could see the cold, dark ocean, and he felt as if he were floating in the middle of it, unable to see the denizens lurking in the darkness. His legs became heavy, and the hair on his arms tingled. He moved slowly, by memory, toward the middle of the room, where he remembered a chrome lamp was stationed among two black leather chairs and a sofa. He reached out in the darkness ahead of him and probed for obstacles until he felt the cold metal hood of the lamp. He twisted the thin stem of the switch and heard a click. Nothing.

He knew it was not a blackout. Lights from the homes on either side had been visible as he pulled in. This was something else, something intentional.

Too late, he turned to run.

A meaty hand throttled his throat. He was pinned on the couch, and as he gasped for air, he felt the first blow of cold brass explode in pain on his cheekbone. He opened his eyes wider and gawked at his attacker. The pitch-black outline of a hulking monster raised its arm, and the brass knuckles caught another speck of light just before they slammed into his face again. Warm rivulets of blood ran down his cheek, and he began to feel nauseated and weak. The final blow was to his stomach, and every muscle in his body contracted into a ball around the pain. Bleeding and unable to breathe, he struggled to stay conscious.

"Just a taste of things to come, Mr. Brayton," the voice boomed. "Fix the problems. Pay your debt."

Brayton retched in pain, silently. The Marcosa family was sending a warning.

"You're losing control of the situation," the shadow said.

"No. No, I'll deliver," Brayton choked out.

"Not if Wellington succeeds. He went to the FDA today." Brayton felt the powerful hand tighten around his neck. "Fix the problem or die."

He didn't see the last one coming. The brass ripped into his jaw and sent his head spinning into darkness. His last conscious thought was a strange one. He wished that he'd never gotten into this mess and that he'd never heard of Rexsen Labs, CGT, Priscilla Wellington, and the Marcosa family. He could thank his father for the last one.

For the first time in his life he felt regret. He took responsibility for what he himself had done. Yes, he had gotten himself into this, and now he wasn't sure he could get himself out.

# CHAPTER 44

DAVID WELLINGTON LEANED over the rail of the upper deck of the Starship Express and scanned the Boat Terminal as the vessel docked in Avalon Harbor. The few boats moored in the harbor bobbed gently in the calm water, and the lights from the shops on Crescent Avenue danced across the dark harbor. At nine on a Thursday night, Catalina Island seemed deserted. Standing next to David, Tori shivered in the damp night chill. David shrugged off his black microfiber jacket and covered her shoulders.

He surveyed their disguises and chuckled. Tori was engulfed in an oversize multicolored cable knit sweater and baggy faded carpenter's jeans at least three sizes too large. A tattered straw cowboy hat topped a blonde wig to complete the look. Black boots, blue jeans ripped at the knees, a gray sweatshirt covered with an unbuttoned red and black checked lumberjack shirt, and a grease-smudged Chevy cap completed David's bubba look. David was confident they could easily pass for quirky local potheads returning from a raid on the mainland. The boat jerked to a stop and David completed his survey. He nodded toward the stairs.

"Stay close," he said as he took Tori's hand and led her down the stairs and out of the terminal.

Everyone was a threat now. They'd already decided not to speak unless absolutely necessary. Even their voices needed to be concealed. They maneuvered down the gangway and through the terminal, past the uniformed man at the end to the gangway, slipped by the lone patrolman flirting with a young woman at the end of the pier, and stepped around the three teenage smokers leaning on the worn wooden pile at the entrance to the dock where the Zodiac was moored. At each encounter, David felt Tori's grip tighten, and in response, he tightened his as if to say: *I've got you. You're safe with me.*

Of course *safe* was a relative term. He knew that the anticipation and hope Tori had held quickly turned to disappointment when David dived into the waiting Explorer on Fifth Street that afternoon. They'd been racing up the ramp to the southbound Harbor Freeway when David punched the back seat and said, "He didn't buy it."

He was still thankful the emergency escape plan had worked. He'd changed clothes in the Explorer while they raced to San Pedro. Concealed behind a warehouse on the wharf, David had described what had happened to Joe and Tori while they waited for the cover of evening to board the last express to Catalina. Joe had left in the Explorer to make arrangements for the final part of their plan.

Now in the Zodiac, the chill they'd felt onshore turned to a cutting cold on the water. With Tori huddled under a blanket in front of him, David maneuvered the light gray Zodiac out of the harbor. Hugging the coastline and moving north in the darkness, he stared ahead into the black water. He knew these waters well. They were among the richest in the world and teemed with sea life, probably darting through the thick kelp beds beneath them and dodging the nocturnal predators. David tried to bury his thoughts of the great whites that prowled these waters. Sufficiently disturbed by his own imagination, he breathed a sigh of relief as they circled the catamaran. It appeared to be just as they left it twenty-four hours ago.

David secured the Zodiac and unlocked the cabin. The small splinter of a toothpick was still in its hiding place, indicating that no one had attempted to enter. He fired the generator and the cabin came to life.

"I need to change," Tori said, still shivering. She disappeared into the stateroom below, and David felt the heater kick on. Closing the cabin door behind him, he stepped out onto the deck, leaned on the rail and listened to the water gently lapping against the hull. The same three boats were still moored in the cove. They were still undiscovered. He turned his gaze out to sea. A light, probably from a container ship, tracked slowly across the horizon as if a star had decided to sail the sea. David replayed the words that had been echoing in his head since the hospital.

*Remember His reason is not always obvious. Seek it. Listen to your heart; open it up to everything.*

David was certain of a few things. The young girl he met in the hospital was dying of a genetic imperfection called leukemia—fast. CGT could save her, but it would have to go back to clinical trials after Tori's revision, if she'd ever get that chance. He'd risked his life to get the information on CGT to the FDA but had failed. Now he was wanted for two murders and had dragged Tori into this mess with him. It was just a matter of time before they'd be captured, if they were lucky, or more likely killed. As thoughts of Amy and Tori filled his mind, sadness filled his heart.

The cold seeped into his body. He looked north, up the Santa Barbara Channel, and recalled the panic of the plane crash. The life he'd lived to that point had been worthless. As the plane went down, he'd concluded hell was his appropriate final destination. He hadn't pleaded with God for forgiveness or tried to make a deal with the devil; he'd simply accepted it. His son had died as he stood by helplessly; his marriage to Priscilla was a loveless sham. At the time, he thought he deserved to die a lonely death in the cold waters of the Pacific.

And then he'd met Amy.

"David, come inside where it's warm," Tori's voice called out.

And Tori. He turned away from the dark abyss and saw her smiling in the doorway. Her face glowed. Her hair fell gently across her shoulders. She'd found a soft white sweat suit that clung to the gentle contours of her figure. Their gazes locked on each other as David entered the door. Pulled together by a force stronger than either of them, their bodies seemed to become one. Passion ignited, and David was lost in her warmth. He'd never felt such raw emotion. Her lips were wet and sweet. The light scent of her perfume mixed with the fresh sea air. David recognized they both wanted this. Tonight, more than anything else, they wanted each other. David sensed Tori had resisted love in the past. Now she seemed freed, as if a weight had been taken off her heart. They were no longer two people struggling to find the truth. They were one and would remain as one for the rest of their lives, no matter how short. After living a life of selfishness, David Wellington had found love—on perhaps the last night of his life.

# CHAPTER 45

ROYCE BRAYTON SQUINTED in pain. The warm California sun he loved now attacked like an enemy. The daylight assaulted his eyes, and they painfully, reluctantly, fought back. The dried blood had caked on the swollen flesh of his upper cheekbones. It was the beating he'd been dreading, the worst of his life—even worse than the ones at the hands of his old man. He struggled to sit up on the sofa, and the pain stabbed deeper into his face.

At the kitchen sink, he gently washed his wounds with a terry-cloth towel. He decided not to use a mirror; visual proof of the damage would only intensify the pain. The blood swirled in the stainless-steel sink and disappeared. The dark red swirls faded each time he dabbed his face and rinsed the rag in the running water. He felt a little better; at least he'd survived. But he knew they'd be back; in four days they'd be back if Wellington wasn't stopped. And Wellington was getting too close.

He hated the idea of his fate being in the hands of anyone but himself. He was used to being in control.

Now Priscilla was calling the shots at Rexsen. And her soon-to-be ex-husband had made contact with the FDA. Had he succeeded in his attempt, Brayton knew he'd be dead instead of nursing his pulped, bloody face. He decided he'd do whatever it took to regain control. His life hung in the balance.

He wobbled to the edge of the counter and grabbed the phone. He pressed the numbers but stopped before hitting the "send" button. He despised having to make these calls. He didn't like dealing with the man. He was a python ready and willing to strike anyone for the right price. He knew the man didn't care about him. But today Brayton was desperate, just like every other time he'd called. It was getting expensive. He was running out of money but running out of time more quickly. He pressed the button, and the call went through.

"It's me. I need more help on the problem we discussed before," Brayton said.

"Serious help?"

"Yes. It's urgent. The matter requires immediate attention."

"All right. Our friend will be in contact." The phone went dead.

"What an asshole." Brayton slammed the phone on the dark granite counter. He walked to the sofa, lay down and passed out.

The ringing shattered Brayton's sleep. Sitting up on the sofa, he glanced at the digital readout on his watch. One p.m. The phone's ring seemed to pick up the pace as he cleared the cobwebs from his mind and shuffled to the counter.

"Brayton."

"Ah, it's a pleasure to hear your voice again."

"How much?" Brayton snapped.

"Well, aren't we grumpy for a Friday afternoon?"

"How much?"

"Same packages?"

"Yes, and they need to be sent overnight."

"That will be expensive, considering their location and condition."

Brayton knew it would be expensive. He didn't need to be reminded. The packages were both wanted for murder. But money was no object. With both packages delivered overnight, there would be no risk of the FDA's withdrawing its approval, and the IPO would be a go. He'd have nearly $900 million. This was chump change. If he paid the money and the postman failed, well, he'd be dead anyway.

"How much?" Brayton repeated.

"Five for each."

"That's ridiculous."

"Five. That's a good deal for you considering how much they're worth to you delivered overnight."

Brayton knew he was right. Ten million for both. A little more than 1 percent of his total take. No bad for shipping.

"Done," Brayton said.

"Same arrangements as before. You'll need to postmark by four today."

Brayton knew the arrangements. A messenger he'd never see would deliver the money to an address he'd never know by 4 p.m.

"Nice doing business with you. Enjoy your weekend."

"Overnight delivery!" Brayton ordered.

"Come rain or shine." The phone clicked dead.

Brayton tossed the phone onto the counter. He knew that the voice on the other end had never failed. Wellington and Clarke would be eliminated. Priscilla would get what she wanted, and he'd get what he needed. He felt sorry for David Wellington; anyone who remained married to Priscilla for all those years probably should be sainted, not murdered. He'd love to see Priscilla get hers instead of getting everything she wanted, but that would have to wait until another day. It was kill or be killed. He would live with his decision.

# CHAPTER 46

BUTCH DONOVAN BURST through the door of the make-shift control room. In unison, three pairs of eyes that had been focused on the glowing monitors snapped their attention to him. The aluminum frame of the warehouse thundered when he slammed the door shut. Donovan marched to the conference table covered with maps, papers, and police reports. He flicked on the fluorescent light suspended in the darkness over the table.

"Gentlemen," he announced, "our client is unhappy, and therefore we are unhappy. Red! On the double, now!"

A freckled man with swollen muscles bulging from a black T-shirt and sporting a red crew cut pivoted from his station and hustled to the table.

"Yes, sir."

"Update?"

"Yes, sir," Red said as he unrolled the detailed map of the Los Angeles area.

"We've marked Wellington's movements here. He disappeared here at the Newport Beach Marina at 12:30 a.m. Wednesday."

Donovan listened with his arms crossed. "A check of all public terminals, including commercial flights from John Wayne, LAX, and Burbank, were all negative. Private aircraft departures from the area were negative. Rental car records were checked and monitored by the authorities and turned up no clues. The authorities had eliminated bus and train exits from the area. Both the marks' vehicles remained in the marina parking lot. Surveillance by our team and the authorities turned up nothing on other boats in the marina."

Red pointed to the Rexsen Labs campus marked in red on the map.

"Wellington entered the lab at approximately 2 a.m. Thursday, here in Newport Beach." He pointed to the third red circle on the map that marked the Los Angeles Central Library. "Then at noon on Thursday he confronted the FDA lab director here, then disappeared, probably down the Harbor Freeway."

Donovan leaned in and studied the three circles. He picked up the red pen and connected the circles in a triangle and wrote the times at each point.

"We know the driver is helping them?" Donovan said, looking to Red for confirmation.

"Yes, sir. The interrogation didn't reveal anything, and we've lost him ever since he eliminated Lane."

"Damn jarhead!" The thought of losing his best man to a former special ops Marine gnawed at his gut. He'd selected the best, and he'd never been proved wrong, until now. "Which way on the Harbor?"

"We think south."

Donovan traced the Harbor Freeway south to the Pacific at San Pedro. "What about the other marinas along the coast?"

"Detective Waters had them checked from Marina Del Rey to Dana Point. The storm kept the departures to a minimum, still too many to track, but all boats moored in the marinas turned up nothing. Still a few vacant berths."

Donovan traced his finger south to Newport Beach. He loved the hunt almost as much as he liked the kill. It was a game. And in this game the winner got it all. Donovan looked at the times.

"Disappeared just after midnight here, then reappeared here at 2 a.m. Thursday," he said. He moved his finger to the red mark by the library. "Then here at noon Thursday again." He guided his finger along the Harbor Freeway to the Pacific. "Then disappeared here— again."

Donovan stood up straight and locked his black eyes on Red.

"You think he's on the water, sir?" Red said.

"Yes, I do."

"In what?"

"Get the schedules for the departures from San Pedro and the Newport Beach Balboa Terminal."

"Catalina!" Red said, nodding. He ordered the two men remaining at the terminals to pull up the schedules. In less than a minute he held the printout. "Departures and arrivals run from 7 a.m. to 7:20 p.m. from San Pedro." He shuffled the papers. "And only one departure at 9 a.m. and one arrival at 5:45 p.m. in Newport."

Donovan fixed his eyes on the map again and rubbed his square, ruddy face. "Who's covering those terminals?"

"Detective Waters had uniformed officers at both places. No reports of seeing Wellington."

Donovan pondered Red's response, then leaned with both hand on the map.

"You still think they're there?" Red said.

Donovan just stared at the map. He focused on Catalina. It was just a hunch, but he trusted his hunches; they had saved him time and time again. It was Friday, and the client had expected matters to be dealt with by now. Donovan knew his lush retirement hinged on this payoff; he'd take the money and head to his own South Pacific island and never be heard from again. But this deal had to be closed now. He'd trusted his instincts in the past, and something drew him to Catalina.

"Sir?"

"Catalina," he said, drilling his thick finger into the map. "What do you have there?"

"We can check the harbormaster's records there online through the Newport Beach Police computers."

"Do it. But forget Avalon. It's too busy there. Check all the other moorings around the island for arrivals between 2 a.m. Wednesday and the departure time for the Catalina Flyer that arrives at Newport at 5:45 p.m. Thursday."

Red disappeared into the darkness and dropped in front of the vacant terminal. Donovan began to pace like a lion stalking his prey. He could feel it. Trying to relieve the tension surging through his body, he clenched and released his fists several times. It seemed forever until Red returned with the information. He laid the printout on top of the map, and both men examined it together.

"Looks like the storm kept arrivals way down," Red said. "I count thirty arrivals over the time specified."

"Too many, Red. Let's limit our search to Wednesday until noon. That gets us down to seven. Trace those and try to make contact with the owners. Get me the mooring location for the boats where we can't get a response." Donovan stepped back from the table. "Get our team going to Catalina. Night approach. I want this one done clean. No noise, no bodies."

"Yes, sir."

Red returned to the terminal. Donovan strolled to the coffee pot, filled a Styrofoam cup and took a long slow sip. He knew they were closing in on the marks. The hair on the back of his neck tingled as it always did just before a kill. He only wished he'd be there to do it himself. He'd have to settle for listening to the team's progress, step by step, until the cold steel cut through flesh, and once again he'd feel the ultimate power of intentionally ending two lives. It would be a long but rewarding day.

# CHAPTER 47

DAVID STEPPED INTO the swirling gray mist that had muffled the morning and allowed them to sleep until nearly noon on Friday. After four days without it, he'd welcomed the deep sleep. He zipped the blue windbreaker to his neck and shook off the mist drizzling on his cheeks. The cold felt good. Stiff from a plane crash and being shot in the arm and thrown down a trash shoot, he limped to the edge of the deck and gripped the frigid rail that was covered with condensation. The pain in his joints was only surpassed by the nagging pain under his sternum. What did he expect after the abuse his body had taken?

The marine layer had settled in and engulfed the catamaran. With visibility near zero, it felt as if the boat had been lifted into the clouds. David squinted, and his eyes strained to see anything but the milky gray that surrounded them. Nothing. He looked at the waterline and could barely see the black water splashing gently against the hull. Cold and sufficiently frustrated, he returned to the main cabin.

Tori's soft voice welcomed him. "Did you see anything out there?"

She had donned jeans, a sweatshirt, and a pair of Sperry deck shoes. Her hair was pulled back into a ponytail that protruded from under a faded blue Nautica cap. Things were different between them now. He could feel the warmth of her heart. He wanted to stay in the fog forever. But the desperate hopelessness of their current situation demanded action.

"Not a damn thing."

He sat next to her at the lacquered pine table tucked into the corner of the cabin. She snuggled against him and they both stared at the fog outside.

"What are you thinking, David?"

He reached for the steaming coffee cup and sipped. The steam warmed his face. "I'm wondering who the hell put us in this mess."

"I've been asking myself the same thing," she said and continued to stare at the gray wall of fog.

"Whoever they are, they're hell-bent on killing us and anyone else who gets in the way." He took another sip from the coffee cup.

"I know," she said. "They don't want anyone to find the problem with CGT, and they don't care about the damage it will do to the cancer patients who receive it."

David clunked his coffee mug on the table and thought about Amy. She was probably smiling, still sporting her Angels cap to cover her bald head stripped by the chemicals that ravaged her body. He suspected she'd never see her eleventh birthday. Being wanted for multiple murders and chased by well-funded assassins, he knew he probably wouldn't see his forty-sixth birthday. Every angle he'd tried had failed. The FDA obviously gave him no credibility. He was a caged animal waiting for the hunter to return to the trap. His hands began to shake. He shattered his ceramic mug against the wall and jumped up from the table.

"Shit!"

He began to pace as Tori watched him. David could see she was startled and stopped in mid-stride.

"I just can't sit here and wait," he said.

Tori nodded.

He turned his back on her and kept pacing. "I know that asshole Brayton is behind this. But either way he was going to get a big payday with the IPO."

"That is until I told him CGT had a problem a week ago," Tori reminded him.

He continued to pace and he felt Tori's gaze following him. "That's right," he said. "The same day our plane went down. But your meeting was at 4 p.m. We were already in the air from San Francisco. There's no way he could have heard the news and then done something to the plane. And that crash was no accident. I'm sure of that now."

Tori cocked her head in a curious pose but continued to track David as he executed an about-turn and continued his pacing.

"Doesn't that leave your wife?"

David pivoted and looked sharply at Tori. She looked guilty, as though her comment had reminded her she'd slept with a married man.

"My soon-to-be ex-wife. I told her Saturday night in the hospital."

"Now, there's a motive," Tori pointed out.

David stared. Of course, she was right. With Adam and Prescott gone, Priscilla was the sole owner and trustee of the Rexsen Family Trust. With the divorce, she'd lose half of the estimated $12 billion to be generated for the trust by the IPO. He followed the string of logic until it reached its dangling dead end. Then he shook his head.

"She'd never kill her father and her brother. She's selfish, arrogant, and a great liar, but I can't see her doing that. Besides, her share of the trust would have been worth four to six billion. Her father was not in the best of health, and she and Prescott were the sole heirs. How many billions does a person need?"

David listened to the words tumble out his mouth. A week earlier, he would have thought that to be a stupid question. He would have answered it: *as much as they can get.* After all, it was how he used to keep score.

"Who else could it be?" Tori said.

"The only ones with a big stake are Brayton, Priscilla, and the underwriters and investors involved in the IPO."

"Well, for my money, I think Brayton is either behind it or he knows who is. Call it intuition or a hunch. He was so mad when I told him about the problem I didn't get the chance to tell him it could be fixed. He caught himself, and then he tried to act like nothing was wrong. The next Monday, he promotes me out of the group and cleans out the lab."

David stopped pacing. He had to agree; Brayton was the key. He had a lot riding on the IPO. It would be his redemption on Wall Street after the dot-com carnage he left behind. The only piece that didn't make sense was that everyone knew Rexsen would go public, if not now, a year from now. They had at least four treatments targeting cancer-causing genetic imperfections in the FDA pipeline. If CGT were delayed, it was no big deal. The IPO would be put off for a year and Brayton would still make his money. Probably more, if Rexsen's research pipeline continued to bear fruit. Even David may have agreed to reorganize the CGT team after its leader, Jeff Reese, had been killed in the plane crash. After all, they would be moving to the marketing and production phase; the trials were over.

But he *knew*, David reasoned, Brayton *knew* there was a problem with CGT, and it looked like he was covering up.

"Brayton?" David said, looking at Tori for confirmation.

She nodded. "Brayton."

David's original dislike for Royce Brayton quickly grew to hatred. He was certain Brayton had to be in on this. He somehow was involved in killing David's mentor and friend, Adam Rexsen. He was somehow involved with the death of Prescott and the attempts to kill Tori and him. And, in David's eyes, he'd be the one responsible for Amy's death.

He looked sharply at Tori and leaned on the table. "We're going after that bastard!"

Tori looked surprised. David was tired; tired of being the hunted; tired of being on defense. He was accused of being a cold-blooded killer, and it was time he acted like it. At least three lives hung the balance. He'd hunt him down and stop him—an eye for an eye.

David saw the fear seep into Tori's eyes. He could tell she was worried about heading back to the mainland again, right into harm's way. He sat beside her and held her hands in his. "I know. But it's the only option we have." He kissed the tear rolling down her cheek.

Tori took a deep breath and wiped her eyes. "I'm with you, David."

David hugged her. He loved her: for her bravery, for her selflessness, and for the love she gave back to him. He'd do whatever it took to protect her.

Suddenly David heard the distant hum of a marine diesel. He bolted to the sliding door and jerked it opened. He dashed to the rail and strained to see through the thick blanket of fog.

*They've found us!*

David turned to get the pistol from the console in the cabin, but the noise faded. A boater, moored somewhere in Hamilton Cove, had briefly fired his or her engines. The false alarm reminded David that as long as they were wanted and until they exposed those behind this conspiracy, they'd be targets. And the killers could come to end their lives at any time, in any place. They could be coming now.

Tori, now frozen in the doorway, stared back at David.

David shook his head side to side. "We leave tonight."

# CHAPTER 48

THE TWO-MAN TEAM was well-equipped: MK 23 handguns with silencers and laser-aiming modules, combat knifes with six-inch 1095 carbon steel blades, and LAR V Drager self-contained, closed-circuit breathing apparatus. The knife was the weapon of choice—a silent kill preferred. The handguns would only be used as a last resort. The mission was well-planned. The team had already slipped into the cold dark waters of Hamilton Cove. Using the LAR V, which recirculated the swimmer's exhaled air and prevented any bubbles from reaching the surface, ensured they'd be undetectable until it was too late. The team had reported optimal conditions; the marine layer was thickening again on a moonless night. The target had been located.

Butch Donovan checked the red numbers on the digital clock on the wall of the dark command center. It was 8:12 p.m.; they were right on schedule. The room's only light came from the four terminals that lined the wall. Two men monitored the surveillance information flowing in from more than twenty sources and monitored all police, FBI, and Coast Guard radio traffic. Donning lightweight headphones and a mike, Donavan sat between them. His hulking figure blocked the light emanating from the flat screen in front of him. He listened with pride as the team he'd handpicked and drilled himself moved through the water and approached the catamaran moored three hundred yards from the coastline.

Donavan shivered. He could almost feel the cold water. His adrenaline surged as if he were in the water, too. He closed his eyes and tried to visualize the mission. They'd entered the cold murky water and swum two hundred yards at the surface when he'd received their last report. Now submerged, they would surface at the bow between the craft's two hulls. After confirming the locations of the marks, they'd slip to the port side and silently board, concealed by the fog and darkness.

Donovan's heart pounded slow but hard. He instinctively slowed his heartbeat. He checked the clock: 8:25 p.m. They were close to the catamaran now, if not onboard. In less than a minute the ice-cold steel of the combat knives would slice through the two jugulars like butter; they would slump to the deck with air bubbles gurgling from their throats between the throbbing gushes of blood. They'd live a few seconds, long enough to see their attackers and know they were dying. Their bodies would quiver and go quiet. And the team would slip back into the water—undetected. Donovan loved the kill.

# CHAPTER 49

THE NAVIGATION DISPLAYS were tucked in the forward corner and filled the main cabin with an eerie glow. The shadows on Tori's face reminded David of his childhood friends sitting in darkness while they told horror stories with a flashlight held under their chins. His stomach knotted as it did back then. Without lights, the pair sat in silence and waited for their midnight departure, still nearly four hours away. David surveyed the cabin for the hundredth time. Paranoid after four attempts to kill him, he examined his surroundings, and escape scenarios raced through his mind.

David had carefully studied all sixty-two feet of the catamaran. With the main deck suspended five feet above the water between its twin seven-foot-tall hulls, it was clearly built for speed. The underside had been reinforced with Kevlar to protect against rupture, and the six watertight compartments spaced along each hull ensured safety and made the vessel nearly unsinkable. The main deck contained a great room that included the helm, the galley, a sofa, and a table. A navigation desk loaded with communication equipment, Raymarine integrated sonar and radar, and a sleek color monitor connected to an underwater camera at the bow was in the starboard corner. Its owner obviously loved to cruise the massive kelp beds in the area and amaze his companions with colorful underwater views of the teeming sea life. Outside, narrow decks surrounded the cabin, with a thin silver rail protecting the perimeter.

Each six-foot-wide hull was accessible from two narrow stairways on either side of the main cabin. The port hull was divided into forward and aft cabins elegantly designed to accommodate as many as four guests or crew. The starboard hull contained the owner's suite, which traversed the entire length of the hull. Behind a watertight door, a library, a vanity, and master suite with a queen bed justified the boat's price tag.

The rhythmic sound of the water gently kissing the hull was occasionally broken by a creak as the boat rocked ever so slowly in the tide. As David completed his sweep, the color display on the navigation desk changed and a soft but audible beep caused him to pivot and creep low to the display. He'd turned on the sonar and the radar as a precaution. Three alarms had proved to be fish, but as he watched the display, the fish kept a constant pace and depth on a bearing directly for the boat.

Still crouching below the windows that surrounded the cabin, he motioned for Tori to join him. Together they watched as the images closed. David glanced at Tori. Her eyes looked frozen in disbelief. He glanced back at the screen. His body grew rigid, and he tried to will the images away. But they kept coming. His muscles grew taut as he watched the colored blotches continue on a line directly for the bow: two hundred feet, one hundred and fifty feet, one hundred feet …

"Oh no, David," Tori sobbed in a whisper.

Taking her hand, he slowly grabbed the handle of the door leading to the forward work deck outside and pushed down. It squeaked and he winced. He opened the door and led Tori to the pitch-black corner of the deck. Just beyond the low chrome rail, the dark blue trampoline stretched between the hulls and disappeared into the darkness.

David and Tori huddled in the chilling dark on the working deck just forward of the main cabin and waited. David's heartbeats throbbed inside his ears and grew louder when he slowed his breathing to listen; timing here would be critical. Tori dug her fingers into his arm when he heard the water slosh underneath them. He held his breath; only the thin Kevlar skin of the hull separated David from the deadly predators as they stalked their prey and crept along the surface of the dark water between the hulls. David estimated they were close enough to touch. A click against one of the hulls sent his heart racing. He fought the invisible force trying to catapult him from his hiding place. Just a few more seconds, he thought, wait just a few more seconds.

The drips and muffled splashes tracked past them, then aft. He heard the water dripping from their bodies as they pulled themselves onboard onto the aft, port side hull steps and emerged from the waterline. Tori's hand, still gripping his arm, began to shake. He shared her fear. Who wouldn't be afraid? They were floating in the middle of a pitch-black deepwater cove with at least two killers onboard less than thirty feet away.

David pulled Tori forward and slipped over the rail to the trampoline. They had to move fast but make no noise. They wormed along the damp dark blue canvas to the edge, and he looked over into the inky water swirling less than five feet below. He nodded to Tori, and she swallowed hard, threw one leg over the side and rolled over the edge. David repeated the maneuver.

Clinging to a rope with his feet dangling just an inch or so off the water, David looked over at Tori. She was balled tightly around the rope. He couldn't tell if she was more afraid of the murky abyss below or the noise of shuffling feet that approached above them along the deck. For the second time in as many weeks, David closed his eyes and invoked God's help. His arms began to ache; they wouldn't last much longer. With his eyes still closed, David translated the sounds into a visual image.

At least two men moved along the deck on either side. Their footsteps stopped at the edge of the canvas on the forward working deck. This was it. If they detected David or Tori, they'd be dead in seconds, probably picked off in the water as they surfaced for air. David held his breath and prayed. The pain in his arms grew, worse in his right where he'd taken the gunshot days before. As he looked down the length of the underside of the canvas trampoline, he spotted two sooty shadows, their hulking outlines frozen except for their heads, which slowly swiveled, apparently listening intently as they scanned the tarp. He was sure Tori couldn't hold on much longer. Neither could he.

*Move, you bastards. Move!*

As if they heard his pleading, he saw the silhouettes retreat and heard the footsteps reenter the main cabin. He waited for the noise. It would indicate they'd moved below. The timing had to be perfect. He closed his eyes and stopped breathing and remembered the exact creaking of the steps. He'd memorized the sound when he had Tori move down the carbon stairs into the starboard hull while hanging in exactly the same spot on the first day here. Planning pays, he repeated to himself.

His muscles were beginning to go into lactic acidosis. Pain ripped through his biceps, and they began to shake. He glanced over just as Tori slipped down, then caught herself. Her shoes submerged in the cold seawater, and her panicked look said it all; she would drop any second.

Then he heard the soft creak of the carbon-fiber steps.

"Now!" he whispered and nodded topside. He strained to pull himself up. His muscles shook violently and he wanted to scream, but he couldn't. This was it. Push yourself. One more step. He reached over the edge of the trampoline and pulled himself up. He looked to the left. No sign of Tori. He couldn't help her. He was exposed. He sprinted along the trampoline to the working deck. The silence was broken when his foot stomped onto the hard surface of the deck.

He imagined the armed assassins looking up from inside the starboard hull and sprinting back to the watertight door. It was a footrace, and if he lost he'd take a bullet center mass. He vaulted through the door and pivoted to his left in the cabin. He heard them coming. They were closer to the door than he'd planned on. Lunging for the door, he saw their shadows. He slammed the door and jammed the steel rod across the bolt. Simultaneously, they hit the door hard. It bowed, and they hit it again.

*Tori! Where's Tori?*

David spun and looked to his right toward the bow. No Tori. He heard the Zodiac motor roar to life, and he snapped his head toward the stern. It had to be her. He harnessed the jolt of adrenaline surging through his body, stormed out of the cabin, and dropped off the port hull into the Zodiac. The Zodiac lurched forward, and he swore he saw Tori laugh. As the catamaran disappeared into the darkness behind them, David pulled out a cell phone, dialed a number and spoke.

"Omaha."

# CHAPTER 50

TORI AIMED THE small flashlight ahead of the Zodiac as it skipped along the coastline. David's eyes traced the beam that cut through the blanket of darkness and thickening mist and illuminated the water's dark surface. He knew that at this speed a partially a submerged rock would disintegrate the craft and result in an unplanned burial at sea. Keeping his main focus on the treacherous path ahead, he traced the silhouette of the rugged coastline to his left that towered over them. He estimated they'd reach the rendezvous point in ten minutes. But that presented a problem: they'd be early—too early.

The cold spray cut deep into his cheeks as the craft sliced through the waves. He cut a glance over his shoulder and checked for the pursuit he knew would eventually come. These people weren't common criminals. They were well-trained; they'd have contingency plans. He remembered Joe's Special Forces stories. In every case they achieved their objectives.

*Nothing but darkness—so far.*

He turned back into the mist, which was condensing on his cheeks and running down his face. The droplets burned, and he tasted the saltwater on his lips. He lowered his head slightly and pressed on. Holding the front of her windbreaker over her face with one hand,

Tori held the light steady with the other. She didn't look back. He wouldn't either. Looking at the coastline, he recognized the outline of Willow Cove. He'd snorkeled there several times, trying to impress voluptuous young women who'd filled the void left by his wife's adultery. He looked at Tori still battling the bow wake. Those days were over.

The Zodiac lurched and the spray slapped David from his daydream. Ten minutes to White's landing. The code name Omaha was Joe's idea. With the widest sand beach on the island, Joe had called the beach Omaha in homage to the World War II landing site. Now it wasn't such a good name; too many noble men had died there.

The plan was simple. Joe had come up with a high-speed powerboat and would meet them at White's Landing at midnight. He'd pick them up close to shore, then head to Newport Beach. From there, he'd arranged for a vehicle so David could launch his planned assault on Brayton.

David hoped Joe was now racing to the meeting point early, covering the twenty-two miles from Newport Beach to Catalina in less than forty minutes. The math was simple: Forty minutes until Joe could pick them off the island, but they'd be there in ten minutes. They'd be exposed and on their own for half an hour until Joe arrived. David knew that meant a confrontation, and the most committed would prevail. He dug deep and harnessed his anger. He wasn't just fighting for his life—he was fighting for the lives of Tori, Amy, and every child, mother, and father CGT could save.

He stole another look over his shoulder. "Shit!"

Tori spun and looked at David.

"They're coming," he said, nodding toward the light bobbing on the water behind him.

Tori leaned to look around David. Without a word, she returned her attention to lighting the water ahead. David willed the Zodiac to speed up. Checking over his shoulder in thirty-second intervals, he watched the approaching light cut the distance between them in half as they turned toward the beach at White's Landing. David cut the Zodiac's engine and it slid onto the beach. He could hear the deep-throated roar of the approaching speedboat. Tori jumped up, and David grabbed the black pack stuffed behind her. They sprinted across the beach and into the tree line. David looked back to the Zodiac. It was illuminated by the light from the approaching boat.

*Damn, they're close!*

The area was deserted; the storm and cold weather had kept the campers away.

"Kill the light," David said.

He took Tori's hand and began to ascend the steep slopes. The island scrub oaks and coastal sage thickened as they climbed. On one of the steepest slopes on Catalina, they'd climb nearly two thousand feet in elevation in less than a mile. While the heavier vegetation and the darkness provided cover, it also made it difficult to see. Reaching into the darkness, David cleared the invisible maze of branches and sage with one hand while he gripped Tori's hand and led her up the mountain with the other. The tug of her hand grew heavier, and David's legs grew fatigued. His breath was labored. He could hear Tori gasping, too. They couldn't keep this pace.

David stopped, and they both bent over and propped themselves up, hands on knees, and tried to catch their breath. David felt a crushing pain deep in his chest. Looking down the steep slope, he spotted a light bouncing rapidly toward them. He raised his hand and touched Tori on the shoulder, and then he pointed down the hill into the darkness. He could hear them now; the branches snapped and the dried brush crackled under their feet. They were running. They were in much better shape.

"We can't outrun them," he said, huffing and puffing.

"What then?"

"We split up here."

"No, David. I won't leave you."

David grabbed Tori by the shoulders and their eyes met. "Yes, you will. There's no time. You've got to get to Joe. Head to the right; go about a hundred yards and hide and wait for them to pass. I'll lead them up the hill and away from you."

"No!"

"Yes!" David shook Tori. "You hear that?" He pointed to the light still flickering through the darkness and closing fast. "They're coming. They'll catch us and kill us. We have no chance together. It's better if we split up. Promise me you'll get to Joe. I'll ditch these guys and meet you there. But if I don't show by eleven fifteen, Joe will know what to do."

"But ... David."

He heard the terror in her whisper. Leaving her now would be the hardest thing he had ever done. But he had to. It was *her* only chance to live.

"Go! Now!" David pushed Tori away. She lunged back and hugged him.

"I love you, David." She released him and disappeared into the dark brush.

The words rocked David for a moment.

"I love you too," he whispered to himself.

Run, he said to himself. *Lead them away from Tori.* He clutched his chest and stumbled into the darkness. The pain was crushing, but a bullet would hurt much worse. David knew they were less than two hundred yards away; their footsteps were rapid and heading directly for him. He could hear their breathing, and he was sure they could hear his now. He could not outrun them. He knew there were at least two well-trained assassins. Once they had him, he'd be no match for their strength and deadly training. They'd overtake him soon. He hoped they would be efficient and end his life quickly. His death would at least have a purpose now—and maybe the flames of hell wouldn't feel so hot. He prayed for the third time in a week. He prayed for forgiveness, and if not forgiveness, an idea.

# CHAPTER 51

TORI SHIVERED SILENTLY. She clung to the trunk of a scrub oak, and the rough bark dug into her palms. David's footsteps faded, but now the crackling footsteps racing up the mountainside grew louder and sounded like explosions. She closed her eyes as she used to as a child playing hide-and-seek. Maybe if she couldn't see them, they wouldn't spot her. She held her breath.

*Don't stop. Keep going.*

But the footsteps stopped. No noise; their breathing had stopped. They were listening. Tori felt her skin crawl. She could feel their gazes sweeping the forest and knew the despair of hopelessness. She didn't want to die at twenty-eight, but she didn't want the first man she'd ever loved to die either.

She gripped the tree tighter, and the bark popped softly. The sound stabbed through her heart. Did they hear that? A twig snapped. It was closer than where the men had stopped. Were they coming? Had they spotted evidence of her trail? She was paralyzed. She couldn't open her eyes, let alone run. She waited. The hair on her neck bristled. They were so close. Could they be standing next to her, just waiting for her to open her eyes? Would she feel anything? Her eyes sprang open at the sound of footsteps exploding in the brush up the hill, and she saw two silhouettes disappear into the night. The footsteps faded. She remained where she was for another minute. They wouldn't hear her departure now.

She had made many bike trips to this side of the island. She knew that nearly 90 percent of Catalina Island was under the control of the Santa Catalina Island Conservancy. With its mission to preserve the island's natural beauty for posterity, most of the windward side of the island remained pristine, with no permanent development. While this ensured limited human occupation, it also ensured that anyone huddled on a seaside mountain face around eleven on a Friday night was very much alone and exposed to whatever lurked in the darkness.

Quietly, she picked her way down the hillsides and retraced their path of ascent. She paused at the tree line and scanned the beach. A speedboat beached next to the Zodiac was unattended. She scanned the shoreline from right to left. Nothing but darkness as far as her eyes could see. Then she saw movement to the left. Her eyes strained, and she spotted the sleek silhouette of an offshore powerboat. Her heart leaped. Joe, she thought. She maneuvered along the tree line, parallel to the beach, until she was directly in front of the craft. She heard the idling engine. After a quick glance to either side, she raced across the open beach into the knee-deep water.

"Joe. It's me, Joe!"

Joe extended his arm and hauled her into the boat. Tori hugged him.

"Where's David?" he said.

"He's still up there. There are two men chasing him. He told me to find you, Joe. He said you'd know what to do. We've got to save him, Joe. How? What should we do?"

Joe looked away, not answering.

"What, Joe? Why don't you do something! Tell me what he told you!"

Joe spoke slowly, as though it was hard to get the words out. "He made me promise that if he had to sacrifice himself for you, I'd get you out of here … out of this mess." Joe checked his watch and gazed at the ominous dark outline of the seaside mountains.

"No, no! They'll kill him! Can't you go after them?"

"My job is to save your life, not his. Boss's orders." His voice was grim. "We're out of here."

Tori shook her head. "No."

"I'm afraid so."

"Wait, Joe! Wait. David said if he wasn't here at eleven fifteen, we had to leave without him. That means he'll try to meet us here."

Joe looked skeptical. "He really said that?"

"I swear it. Eleven fifteen."

"If he doesn't make it …"

"I know."

He checked his watch again. "Ten minutes, then."

Tori strained her eyes through the dark. *Come on, David! Come on!* She imagined him still racing up the mountain, through the thick underbrush, wounded and exhausted. And alone. The assassins were getting close by now; maybe they'd even caught him. Would she hear the single shot ring out, ending his life, or would David die silently, alone and afraid in the cold? Had he heard her last words to him? Would he die knowing she loved him?

She refused to cry. Not yet.

"Don't give up, Ms. Clarke. Never give up," Joe said, a cold stony expression on his face. "Mr. Wellington is smart. He told us to wait because he thought he had a chance. Otherwise he would have told us to take off as soon as you got here."

Tori joined Joe at the stern. They stared at the tree line. They didn't speak, just listened. Tori knew Joe was listening for any sign of the attackers as well as David. She knew he had a deadly side. He may have even trained with the men trying to kill her. But he was loyal, a man of his word. He'd already risked his life for David, and if David asked him to whisk her away to safety, he'd do it, no questions asked.

Joe checked his watch again. "Two minutes."

Tori felt a weight she'd never felt before. She'd never felt such love for a man; she wanted to spend the rest of her life with David, but now he'd be taken from her. God, please help him, she thought as she implored a higher power. Joe began to move around the open cockpit, preparing to leave. Slowly he pulled on the anchor rope, hand over hand, still staring at the tree line. With the anchor in hand, he made a final check of his watch.

"It's time."

Tori buried her face in Joe's shoulder and wept uncontrollably. After gently guiding her to the seat next to the helm, he pressed forward on the throttle and the boat began to pull away from the beach.

Tori wiped her tears away to take one last look at the island where her lover had died. It would be a place she would never forget.

Then she saw the miracle. A lone figure racing along the tree line toward them.

"Joe, look!" Tori couldn't believe her eyes.

Joe looked up sharply. Immediately, he reversed the engine and backed toward the beach. He reached under his coat and cocked the Glock in his hand.

"Ms. Clarke, take the helm, and when I say go, push the throttle all the way forward and head straight out to sea."

Tori nodded and took her position at the helm. The massive twin engines idled in neutral fifteen feet from shore. Joe leaned his elbows on the stern and targeted the figure, while it followed the same path Tori had taken. Now directly in front of the boat, the figure paused in a crouch. Tori heard the click of Joe's safety being released. The figure sprang from the darkness and charged the boat. Joe braced to fire. Tori waited for his order. Either David had made it or, more likely, a third man had found them. But she knew they had to be sure. Knowing the odds were against its being David, Tori grabbed the throttle.

Tori flinched, surprised by the sound of Joe releasing the hammer. She heard the splashes of footsteps in the water and turned. Joe extended his arm and David appeared from the darkness. His face bloodied and his jacket torn, he hit the deck with a thud. Joe's and Tori's stares fixed on him as he rolled over and looked at them.

He was smiling. He focused on Joe.

"*Semper fi*, assholes."

Joe chuckled and pointed at the helm.

"Go, Miss Clarke. Let's get the hell out of here."

# CHAPTER 52

BUTCH DONOVAN PACED like a caged tiger. He never tolerated failure and wasn't about to start now. Stopping at each station, he barked orders, cursed and scowled as the identically dressed men at the terminals reported his teams' movements and avoided eye contact at all costs. They were well aware of the fact that Donovan had the same look in his eyes he'd had before he executed their fellow team member at Rexsen Labs for his dereliction of duty. He snapped his wrist in front of his face and checked the time. It was nearly midnight. Team one had failed at the catamaran. They'd extricated themselves from below decks and reported their failure over an hour ago. The powerboat manned by the second team had tracked the Zodiac northwest to White's Landing, along the rugged windward coast. On foot, Wellington and Clarke should have been overtaken by now. He knew the kills should have been reported thirty minutes ago, but still no word. He'd resisted acknowledging what his experience told him was a certainty: they'd failed—again.

"Anything?" Donovan said.

"No, sir," Red said. "Team two has gone black."

Donovan crushed the Styrofoam coffee cup in his hand. "Shit. Call it off. They failed. Alert the rest of the team."

"Yes, sir."

Donovan knew they couldn't cover the entire coastline of Catalina. With his team down to eight, they could barely cover the harbors at Avalon, Dana Point, San Pedro, and Newport Beach. Wellington had gotten help again, and Donovan and his men had failed to deliver a second time. The client would not be happy. Hell, *he* wasn't happy. He'd never failed on a mission, legitimate or otherwise. Failure was never an option, and it wasn't an option now.

Standing at attention, as if preparing to give a report to his superior officer, he snapped up the black phone from the table and put it to his ear.

"It's me. We missed them."

"Again?" the synthesized voice said.

"It's only temporary, I assure you," Donovan said with deadly confidence. "I'll deal with them myself."

"Your failures have caused another problem."

"The one we discussed earlier?"

"Yes."

"I'll do that one for free."

"We're running out of time. They need to be dealt with within twenty-four hours or no deal."

"I know where they're headed. I'll have it done in twelve."

He pressed a button to end the call and tossed the phone onto the table.

"You know where they are, sir?" Red said.

Donovan shook his head. "I've got a hunch."

He grabbed his black leather jacket and marched to a steel door along the back wall, nearly beating the man dressed in black fumbling to produce a key. Donovan nodded, the door was opened and Donovan stepped into the makeshift armory. He ran his hand along the neatly displayed assault rifles, shotguns, semiautomatic handguns, ammunition, Kevlar vests, laser sights and silencers racked on the walls and stacked neatly in bins. He plucked an MK 23 from the wall. He stuffed several clips of ammo into his jacket pocket and slammed the door. All eyes were on him as he stomped through the command center and left without saying a word. He didn't have to. Everyone in the room knew that when Butch Donovan had a hunch, someone always died.

# CHAPTER 53

DAVID WELLINGTON WATCHED the first light of the day seep over the hills to the east and invade the thick coastal fog that hugged the seaside cliffs of Laguna Beach. Parked on the boulevard, he rubbed his tired eyes and refocused on the outline of the security gates that barred entry to Royce Brayton's exclusive neighborhood. Looking at his quivering hand, he knew his nerves were frayed. His entire body ached as well, and he hadn't slept much in a week. Still, his drive and resolve remained high. He'd get him if it was the last thing he did.

He was certain Brayton was behind the plane crash that had taken the life of his friend and mentor, Adam Rexsen. He'd killed an innocent father of four, Jeff Reese, in the process. He had Prescott Rexsen killed in order to frame David and Tori. And with the cover-up of the problems with CGT, he'd be responsible for the death of a ten-year-old girl and thousands like her. And if Brayton prevailed, he'd ultimately be responsible for David's death and the death of the only woman he'd ever loved. Yes, Royce Brayton would pay now, David promised himself.

He watched Tori while she slept in the passenger's seat of the white Explorer. Despite David's protest, she'd jumped into the front seat when he'd left Dana Point Harbor two hours earlier. The contours of her face were barely visible and looked delicate and frail. David gripped the steering wheel and his knuckles turned white at the thought of Tori's innocence; she'd done nothing to Brayton. She'd discovered the genetic imperfection in CGT and had identified a solution. She would save millions of lives with her discovery, and for that Brayton wanted her dead. David reached into his pocket and rubbed the cold steel of the pistol.

He turned away from Tori and peered through the driver's window to his left. A faint yellow glow began to grow in the gray mist. As it grew, the shadow of the vertical iron bars came into focus. Two headlights finally pierced through the fog and the gates creaked open. David started the car and yanked the wheel to the left, jolting Tori from her nap. The newspaper carrier pulled through and turned right, and David slipped the Explorer through the closing gates. Without the aid of headlights, David inched the car through the fog. He knew the way. While he'd always viewed Brayton as an ass, he'd made the obligatory appearances at dinner parties for customers, bankers, and suppliers at Brayton's house.

He pulled to the shoulder about thirty yards from Brayton's driveway. The gravel crunched beneath the tires and the SUV rolled to a gentle stop. Shielded by the thick landscape and the heavy fog, they moved into position undetected. David opened his window and listened. The only sound came from the rhythmic sloshes of the waves muffled by the cliffs and the heavy fog of the marine layer blanketing the coastline.

He reached into his jacket and gripped the pistol. With a click, he forced a bullet into the chamber and released the safety.

"Stay here," David said.

"No, I'm going." Tori zipped up the black jacket to her neck and reached for the door handle. David grabbed her wrist before she could open the door. He scolded her with a sharp stare.

"This is not your fight. You stay here. You promised. If you hear anything or see anyone but me approaching, take the car and head to the house on Balboa. Joe—"

"I know. Joe will know what to do."

Tori pulled her hand from the handle, and David released her wrist and gently covered Tori's hand with his on the seat between them. Tori's soft brown eyes locked on his. David couldn't look away.

"Come back to me safe, David."

"I will."

David turned, slowly pulled the door handle, and slipped out of the car. As he crossed the pavement, the water droplets chilled his face and hands, and he crept along the hedging toward Brayton's driveway. Reaching it, he crouched and listened. Still, the only audible sound was the distant hissing of the surf. Leading with the gun, he scampered to the corner next to the garage door and pressed his back against the wall. He slid to the corner and peeked around it, toward the entrance. Darkness was still winning its battle with dawn, and David could only see a few feet ahead of him. He turned the corner and halted. A shadow moved in the distance. He held his breath and listened. Nothing. He slipped past the entrance and hugged the wall, stopping just short of the utility room window. He slipped the gun back into his pocket and removed a glass cutter and two suction cups connected to a steel rod.

He prayed his memory had served him well. Brayton had the typical alarm system, equipped with transducers mounted in the window frames that would detect an attempt to open window. He'd didn't recall seeing the foil used in some systems that lined the windows and would detect any breakage. Under these conditions, though, he'd never be able to detect it from the outside. He softly pressed the cups against the center of the window and traced the perimeter with the cutter. He winced when he heard the soft grinding of the cutter against the glass. With a tug, the first pane was removed and placed in the bushes. No alarm. He wiped the sweat from his eyes. He repeated the process with the second pane and climbed through the four foot-by-four foot opening.

Inside and on his feet, he pulled the pistol from his jacket and began his hunt. It was much darker inside. His eyes strained to adjust. His body tingled as other senses tried to compensate for the darkness. The hair on his arms stood up and his skin rippled with electricity and he tried to detect any hint of Brayton's presence. He gently opened the utility room door and entered the short hallway that led to the first floor.

One step at a time, he advanced, scanned, listened, and advanced again. He stopped at the entrance to the great room on the first floor. He detected no motion. His gaze drifted from left to right, and he identified and cleared each outline and shadow he saw. His eyes locked on the stairway across the room. He quickly plotted the course to the stairs and continued his step-by-step approach along the room's perimeter.

At the base of the stairs, he stopped and listened. He lifted his foot to take the first stair but froze when he heard a creak from above. He held his breath and aimed the pistol up the steps. Another creak snapped his attention farther down the second floor. Brayton was moving. He'd either heard the break-in or just got up to take a leak. Suddenly, David realized this wasn't a hunt. This prey could be armed and waiting. He'd already proved he would kill, and he had practice. David hadn't killed a man before.

He wanted Brayton dead more than anything, but if it came to a battle of wills, would he prevail? Would he be the most committed? David took the next step. His legs felt heavier and stiffened with each stair. He heard no other sounds as he approached the top. He was now crawling up the steps. At the top of the steps, he stopped and listened again. Peeking over the last stair, he could see the three doorways opening onto the hallway. To his right, the double doors of the master suite were open about two feet and a little light leaked out. The doors to the left were open; he remembered one was the guestroom and one was Brayton's home office. The noises had come from the left side of the second floor.

He quickly weighed his options. Moving down the hall to the left would keep the perceived danger in front of him. But if he were wrong and Brayton awoke, he could attack David from behind. On the other hand, moving to the bedroom would put the noises, and therefore the threat, behind him. Choosing the lesser of two evils, David crept to the left and down the hallway toward the first open door.

With his back against the opposite wall and his gun pointed at the doorway, he moved to a position just short of the opening and froze. Gripping the gun with both hands, he calmed his nerves with a deep breath and thrust the gun into the doorway. A quick sweep of the guest bedroom detected no movement.

One door remained at the end of the hallway. The diffuse light of a foggy morning had grown brighter. The office was tucked at the end of the second floor and overlooked the rocky coastal bluffs. David remembered a large desk sat in the center of the room, facing the window. While losing the cover of darkness, he'd have the advantage of surprise if Brayton had simply gotten up to clean out his e-mail. Suddenly, a click followed by a rush of air behind him jammed his heart into his throat. He spun and saw that the double doors of the bedroom were moving, and he nearly fired. The familiar dry stuffy smell of incinerated dust filled his nostrils. The heater, he thought. The soft sound of the airflow through the vents confirmed his assessment. Remembering the threat at the end of the hall, he pivoted back and slid down the opposite wall, splitting his attention between the office to his left and the still wobbling bedroom doors to his right.

Raising his gun in his hands in front of him, he paused and then stepped into the doorway. Sitting in the chair with his back to David, Brayton stared at the glowing monitor on the desk. David's finger pressed against the trigger. Kill the bastard right now, he told himself.

He had the advantage, and he certainly was justified. The high-caliber bullet would blow the back of his damn head off and his body would slump forward. Maybe just a few dying twitches and David would have his revenge.

But an uncontrollable force inside him paralyzed his finger. A murderer; that's what he would be, a cold-blooded killer. His purpose in life wasn't to kill another man, his conscience argued. He stepped closer, and Brayton snapped his head around. Brayton's eyes flashed wide open and his jaw dropped. He braced himself on the armrests of the chair, pushed back hard, closed his eyes and flinched, apparently expecting the bullet he deserved. Filled with rage, David locked both hands on the gun, narrowed his eyes and took aim at Brayton's forehead. Brayton reached for the top drawer of the desk.

"Freeze, you bastard," David ordered.

Brayton froze, then dropped his hand into his lap.

"Turn around."

Brayton sank into the tan leather chair and raised his hands. "Please, David. Please don't kill me."

He'd never seen Brayton beg, but David remained silent. He was face-to-face with his tormentor; the man who'd stolen his company; the man who'd killed his mentor and friend; the man who, if given the chance, would kill David and Tori in a heartbeat.

David stepped closer and thrust the gun against the center of Brayton's forehead, now beaded with sweat. He began to pull the trigger. He felt the guilt already growing deep inside his heart, and he felt whatever redemption his soul had gained in the past week dying away. He couldn't do it. He wouldn't do it.

"Why did you do it? Why kill Adam?" David said, pressing the gun barrel harder against Brayton's head.

Brayton still held his hands in the air, but they were shaking now. "You've got to believe me, David. I had nothing to do with that."

David shoved Brayton's head backward with the gun.

"I didn't do it. Please, David."

"You did it to hide the problem with CGT. You knew Adam and I wouldn't have gone forward with the IPO, had we found out."

"No! Think about it. Yes, I covered up the problem with CGT, but I found out from that Clarke woman at four that afternoon. Your plane was already in the air."

David's certainty wavered, but he kept the gun pressed against Brayton's head. "What about Prescott?"

"Prescott?" Brayton said. "You killed Prescott."

A chill rippled through David's body. Brayton's eyes said he wasn't lying.

"Didn't you?" Brayton said.

David kept his mind clear in spite of the doubt that was beginning to seep through him. Was Brayton telling the truth? If he didn't kill Adam and Prescott, who did? Who else stood to benefit the most? A sickening feeling accompanied his conclusion: Priscilla.

David heard a shuffling in the hallway. Bolting behind Brayton, he grabbed Brayton's neck and pressed the gun barrel against his temple.

Then he practically crumpled with shock when he saw Tori in the doorway. She was shoved inside the room, imprisoned in the choke-hold of a massive chunk of a man with a ruddy face and a scar on his neck.

"I'm sorry, David," she sobbed. There was an ugly gash on the side of her lovely face.

The man who held her stabbed the barrel of a revolver into her side and glared at David. "Drop it."

David's heart sank in despair greater than he'd ever experienced. As he met Tori's terrified eyes, he wanted to die. He'd committed to protecting her, and he had failed. Now they'd both be killed. He removed the pistol from Brayton's head, and his arms went limp at his sides.

"Now," the man growled, "throw it over here."

He tossed his gun, and it hit the floor with a thud and skidded to the stranger's feet.

Shoved roughly into the room from behind, Tori fell at David's feet. David helped her up and wrapped his arms tightly around her. They clung to each other, not speaking.

"You three have made it easy for me," the stranger chuckled. "Which one wants to go first?"

*"You three?"* David glanced at Brayton. He could see from the look in his eyes he didn't know this man.

Then who was he?

He raised his black semiautomatic and pointed it at Brayton. "My client thinks you should have been thinking with your other head." He smiled. "I think I'll start with you."

"Priscilla, that bitch!" Brayton shouted.

Expecting a blast from the gun, David locked his arms around Tori and closed his eyes. The shot wasn't as loud as he'd expected. He opened his eyes. The hulking man, dressed in a black cap and turtleneck sweater, had opened his eyes wide in surprise and collapsed to the floor.

All three stared in shock. Then they heard footsteps walking toward the open door.

Hearing the last step before the killer would be revealed, David invoked God's help for the fourth time. Joe's familiar smile lit up the doorway, and then he looked at the man lying dead on the floor.

*"Semper fi,* asshole," Joe said.

"It's sure good to see you haven't lost your sense of timing," David said, smiling.

Brayton started to rise from the chair, but Joe took aim and he stopped.

"We gotta get out of here," Brayton said. "There's another."

Joe and David locked eyes.

"Another what?" David scowled, shoving Brayton hard into the chair.

Brayton hesitated and looked away. His face became pale.

"Another what?" David repeated as Joe stepped over the body and jammed the pistol in Brayton's face.

"I hired someone to kill you two." Brayton seemed disappointed, as if he'd made a grave mistake.

"You son of a bitch." David's fist smashed into Brayton's face and knocked him to the floor. David picked up the 9 mm from the floor. Standing over Brayton, he wished he'd finished the job he started. Tori and Joe froze, and Brayton just stared at the floor. David cocked the hammer and took aim at Brayton's head.

"He's done, boss," Joe said. "Leave it to the feds."

Tori tugged on his arm. "He's right, David. You're no killer."

"Who's coming?" David said.

"I don't know. I hired someone through one of my father's contacts. I had to."

"You had to?" David roared.

"They're going to kill me if I don't pay what I owe them, and I can't pay unless the IPO goes forward, and the problem with CGT will kill the IPO."

Tori looked at David and then kicked Brayton in the ribs.

"You asshole. CGT can be fixed. You just never let me finish my presentation."

David couldn't tell which hurt worse, the kick in the ribs or the fact that Brayton realized he'd be charged with conspiracy to commit two murders he never needed to arrange.

"Look," Brayton said in a surrendering tone, "I'll call him off, but it's not safe here now. There are people who will kill all three of us if they find out you two are still alive."

"Who would that be?" David said.

"A particular family that I borrowed millions from. Now I can't pay them back, and I'm a dead man anyway. There's nothing I can do."

David pitied the broken heap of a man lying before him. He was a victim of his own greed. They also shared a common enemy: Priscilla Wellington. She had killed her father and brother and would kill everyone in the room if she weren't stopped. If she succeeded, CGT's imperfections would be buried in unsuspecting patients' DNA until it killed them, too. David released the hammer of the gun, reached down and helped Brayton to his feet.

"There is one thing you can do."

Brayton gave David a puzzled look. Tori glanced at Joe, and Joe shrugged. David had another plan.

# CHAPTER 54

THE FRESH SUNLIGHT glowed through the eggshell sheers that fluttered between the dark velvet drapes. Although her head ached from the Champagne and her body ached from the sex, Priscilla absorbed the elegance of the room and the sweet scent of her own cologne mingling with that of her handsome bedmate. Priscilla knew she now had money to burn. She'd chartered a NetJet and offered to pick up her underwriter in New York, and Jeff Thomas had eagerly accepted the invitation. The party started in California when the jet left for the cross-country flight with Priscilla, Brit Rodgers, her party girlfriend, and Hollywood bad boy Danny Flynn. It continued for the entire trip. Six thousand miles and fifteen hours of Champagne, sex, and rock and roll had ended just a few hours ago.

The exclusive villa was nestled among the thick tropical gardens of the Peninsula Hotel in Beverly Hills. Italian linens covered the soft luxurious bed. An electronic bedside panel provided control for every imaginable effect. Priscilla carefully slipped from under the thick comforter and into a soft white robe. She floated across the room and checked her makeup in the mirror. The huge bathrooms glistened with white Italian marble and decadently embraced the oversize Jacuzzi bathtub Priscilla and Jeff had proved was big enough for two playful adults. Then she tiptoed to the bedroom door and left her latest prop snoring.

The bedroom opened to the living area accented with expensive antiques, artworks and window treatments that covered the white-trimmed French doors. Priscilla soaked up the elegance. After all, she deserved it. She'd proved herself to be better than all of them: her chauvinistic father, who refused to let her into the business, her weasel of a brother, who'd been favored simply because he had a penis, her big-shot husband, and that prick Royce Brayton. She wondered if he'd begged for his life. She smiled when she thought about David and that goody-two-shoes lab rat getting it together. She needed men for one thing and one thing alone.

She tiptoed to the other bedroom door, gently knocked, and inched the door open.

"Brit? You up?" she whispered.

She saw Brit's blond mop pop up from the mountain of covers. Priscilla watched with more than a passing interest as Brit left the bed, naked, and slinked to the bathroom and retrieved her robe.

Brit slipped through the crack in the door and joined Priscilla on the sofa in the living room. She rubbed her puffy bloodshot eyes.

"You look awfully happy, Pris."

"Life's good."

"Duh?" Brit said, cocking her head and raising her hands in the air. "You're, like, the richest woman I know."

"I'll be richer in two days." Priscilla smiled.

"How's that?"

"I got a call yesterday from our regulatory affairs person. The FDA is releasing its approval letter for CGT Monday." Priscilla nodded toward her bedroom. "And lover boy in there says we're a go for the IPO on Tuesday."

"How much?" Priscilla now had Brit's attention.

"What?"

"How much you gonna be worth, Pris?"

Priscilla nodded toward the bedroom again. "He says over $12 billion."

"Awesome! I've never had a friend worth that much money." Brit thought for a moment and tilted her head in curiosity. "Don't you have to split that with David?"

Priscilla slammed her hand on the sofa. "I don't have to share it with anyone!"

"You think the cops will kill him because he's murdered those people?"

Priscilla remained silent. She wanted to tell someone how successfully her plan had gone, but she also knew Brit was a magpie; she'd spill her guts or brag to anyone. She wouldn't risk the electric chair for her need for approval. The phone rang and startled Priscilla. She reached to the end table, grabbed the silver cordless phone, glanced at the caller ID display and answered.

"Yes?"

"It's me, Royce."

"Royce?" The name ripped through her. It couldn't be. He was supposed to dead by now. Her newfound euphoria faded.

"We need to meet at the office. I have something you have to see. It's regarding CGT."

Priscilla listened closely for any changes or strange inflections in his voice. He sounded as cold and calculating as ever. Still, he should have been killed.

"What is it?"

"Not on the phone."

"All right, Royce. When?"

"Four o'clock, your office."

"Okay. I'll be there."

She slammed the phone on the table and peered at the floor.

"You okay, Pris?" Brit said.

She continued staring at the floor. What was this about? Had he found out? Had he found some way to escape and now he'd want revenge? Or had Donovan decided the timing wasn't right? Maybe someone had been with Brayton all night. That's probably it, she convinced herself. She wondered if Brayton might have found his conscience. He knew there was a problem with CGT, but Pris thought that problem would die along with the three people standing between her and $12 billion.

"Pris?" Brit said.

"Oh. I'm fine. I just have to get to the office."

"Gonna meet with Roycie-pooh?" Brit raised her eyebrows, implying another tryst.

Priscilla didn't answer, and Brit shrugged, left the sofa and disappeared into the second bedroom. Priscilla checked her watch. It was noon. She had four hours to get ready. Maybe Donovan would get him on the way to the office. He'd said he'd take care of it himself; she'd counted on Donovan doing his job, not just with Brayton but with all of them. He'd delivered on her father and her brother, and he'd explained it was just a matter of time before he got Wellington and the girl. While he'd missed them twice, she was confident he wouldn't miss a third time. Brayton, he bragged, he'd do for free. By the time 4 p.m. rolled around, everyone standing between her and her $12 billion would be gone and she'd get more money and power than her father, brother, or that cockroach of a husband ever had, combined. She planned on Brayton's not showing, but just in case, she decided to bring along a little insurance.

# CHAPTER 55

THE EXECUTIVE GARAGE of Rexsen Labs was buried deep
below the basement of the four-story administration building. It was
Saturday afternoon, and David stepped from the white Explorer and
shivered. He'd been here hundreds of times before but had never noticed how the thick concrete held a chill. The echo of three doors slamming shut bounced through the empty underground garage, and David
led Brayton and Tori to the elevator.

As they rose to the fourth floor, all three remained silent. David
stood between Tori and Brayton and eyeballed Brayton, who hung his
head and looked down. David could see he was ashamed and defeated.
He looked for any weakness in Brayton's commitment to help, but he
saw none. He'd help and then surrender to the authorities. He assumed
Brayton knew he'd be a little safer in custody, but not much.

The doors opened, and they began their walk down the long mahogany corridor toward the suite once occupied by Adam Rexsen.
David listened to their footsteps thumping on the wood-plank floor.
He eyed the priceless antiques, expensive artwork, and rich marble and
shook his head. The lavish surroundings he had insisted on meant
nothing anymore.

Back then, the fourth floor felt like a castle—his castle, and he was the king. Now the place felt more like a tomb, hollow and empty. He'd helped Adam Rexsen build it from the ground up. Adam's last lecture about knowing life's purpose haunted him. He thought about Amy. If they didn't succeed this afternoon, he might as well have put a gun to her head. He wondered how many kids like her he could have helped if he had listened to Adam earlier and lived his life with purpose.

They reached the entrance to the suite tucked in the northwest corner of the building and stopped. Brayton raised his palm and signaled Tori and David to wait in the hallway. He disappeared around the corner. Tori leaned in and hugged David. After a moment, David tried to release her, but she didn't let go.

David knew this might be the last time they'd see each other—ever. The plan was risky, but with time running out, it was the only option left. In less than an hour they'd be dead, on their way to jail, or perhaps free—free to live out their lives together. Brayton returned, and Tori reluctantly released David.

"It's clear, but we'll have to hurry. There's not much time, and Priscilla will be here soon."

Led by Brayton, the three entered Priscilla's office. David stopped just inside the door. It was the first time he'd been in Adam Rexsen's office since his death. He scanned the room. Adam's favorite paintings still hung on the paneled walls. His gaze was drawn to a limited edition by G. Harvey, centered on the wall to the left. Sadness tugged at his heart when he read the title engraved on a gold plate at the base of the ornate frame. *The Warmth of Friendship* depicted several cowboys, obviously friends, shrugging off a snowy winter night while they stood close and shared a conversation.

Tori headed directly to the computer sitting on the credenza, behind the desk. The monitor faced the room and flickered to life, and Tori's thin fingers flitted over the keyboard. After a few clicks of the mouse, she stood up, reached behind the monitor and yanked its power cord from the socket.

"Done," she said. "I've activated the webcast, and the webcam will broadcast the whole thing. Just don't let her turn on the monitor."

Brayton, apparently enjoying his last look at freedom, gazed out the window behind the credenza at the sails floating over the water, just off Newport Harbor.

He shook his head. "She never uses that thing."

David nodded. "You're on, Royce."

David listened to his words. The man he was ready to kill just hours ago was now his ally. He knew Royce Brayton might be guilty of covering up the problem with CGT, but compared with Priscilla's trail of murders, that was just a misdemeanor. David had actually felt some sympathy for Royce as he sat in his office at home, with Donovan still bleeding on his floor, and described his money troubles. His father's help from prison had only put him further in debt with the Marcosa family, and it was either be killed or cover up CGT's genetic imperfections and get to the big payday from the IPO.

Tori had shown much less mercy for Brayton. As he attempted to apologize, she slapped his face and called him a selfish, arrogant bastard. She finished the scolding by telling him that had he listened to her full presentation a week ago, he would have known there was a solution. Brayton appeared stunned at her revelation. Tears welled in Brayton's eyes when Tori described how his selfishness would deny young children, like her brother and Amy, the right to live.

Now David watched Brayton circle Priscilla's desk. Expressionless, he picked up the phone and began to place the calls as promised. One at a time, he reached each of the board members and instructed them to click into the webcast Tori had just initiated and wait. David checked his watch—three thirty. The last call would be made from the office down the hall.

Brayton rose from the desk and looked at Tori. "We need to get out of here."

Tori gave Brayton a nasty look, then walked up to David and kissed him. "Come back to me, okay?"

"Don't worry, I will." David kissed her. "You just bring the cavalry."

He watched Brayton leave the room, followed by Tori. She stopped at the door as if to take one last look, just in case. Then she disappeared. Left alone, David moved to the chair behind the desk. After checking the angle of the webcam mounted atop the computer screen behind him, he dropped into the chair and waited for his wife.

# CHAPTER 56

PRISCILLA ENTERED THE office and flipped on the lights. David spun in the high-back office chair to face her. With a gasp, she halted in mid-stride.

"Hello, Priscilla."

"David? What are you doing here?" Priscilla took a step sideways away from the door and, without taking her eyes from David, closed it. She slipped her Coach shoulder bag off and propped it up on the back of the wingback chair next to her.

"I thought I'd check out your spoils," he said.

"My spoils?"

David knew the last call had been made the moment Priscilla entered the fourth-floor elevator lobby, halfway down the hall. As planned, Brayton had invited the FBI to click into the webcast. They'd identify the location as the Rexsen headquarters immediately and swarm the building in minutes. He had to work fast.

"Yes, Priscilla, the spoils from all your hard work."

She scanned the room, as if wondering if someone else was nearby. "If I were you, David, I'd be worried about saving my own ass."

"Based on the meeting I had this morning with your associate, I'd say you have that backwards," he said.

Apparently satisfied they were alone, Priscilla fixed her stare on David. He'd never seen this look before: cold, calculating, and deadly.

"You have no idea what you are doing, you pompous ass," Priscilla scoffed. "You're just like the rest of them."

"The rest of them?"

"Yes, you asshole. My father, Prescott, Brayton—you all think you're so much better than I am."

David rose slowly and moved to the right of the desk with his back to the wall.

"Your father knew exactly who you are. He told me, just before you killed him." David knew the words would cut deep. He moved along the wall and closer to the door. Priscilla remained focused on him and held her ground next to the door.

"My father was a chauvinistic pig who got what he deserved! Now I'm calling the shots—not you, not him, and not that snot-nosed brother of mine. He never thought I was smart enough to run this company. He favored Prescott and he favored you. But I'm smarter than all of you put together."

"So you had your own father killed, you ungrateful bitch?" David tried to drift a little closer to the door, but Priscilla jammed her hand into her bag and pointed a black revolver at David.

"Stop right there, David."

David froze. He knew she'd pull the trigger. He hoped not too soon.

"You killed your father, didn't you?"

"You're damn right I did. I deserve this company. I put up with his shit all my life. I even married your sorry ass just to make him happy. What did I get in return? I'll tell you what—nothing! So I just took what I deserved."

Her eyes narrowed on David. "And now I'm going to end our marriage the way it deserves to be ended—permanently. Pretty good for a woman, huh?"

David felt his anger shifting to fear. He knew the plan was working from his end, but Brayton had to come through soon.

Priscilla stepped closer to David and blocked the door. "You were supposed to die in the crash, you little cockroach. If I hear that 'miracle man' crap one more time, I'll puke. I'm going to kill you myself."

"Just like you killed your brother?"

Priscilla chuckled. "I'd like to take full credit for that one, but I had a little help. That weasel got what was coming to him. He was weak. I had him wrapped around my little finger. That is until my father died and he became head of the family trust. He was actually buying into that having-a-*purpose* shit, after I'd just gotten rid of my father. He was going to turn to a life of service like his dear old daddy. But this is about what's mine. My father made him trustee in the will just because he had a penis. So I had you framed for his murder—kind of a two-for-one deal. Who says I can't watch the bottom line?" Priscilla grinned and cocked the gun.

"How are you going to explain this murder, in your own office?"

Priscilla smiled. "You know you're wanted for two murders. I just had to shoot you because you attacked me."

She reached down and ripped her white blouse with her free hand. She moved another step closer. David could smell her soft, sweet cologne now.

David saw Priscilla's look dart to the window. Red lights flashed and danced in the refection on the window, and he heard the screeching tires of several unmarked FBI cars coming to a halt at the front entrance.

David nodded toward the window. "You might want to reconsider."

Priscilla's glare bolted back to David. "You son of a bitch." She closed her eyes and squeezed the trigger.

The office door burst open, and Brayton lunged at Priscilla as she fired. David hit the floor hard. He saw Brayton crumple to the floor, and he ended up face-to-face with him. Brayton just stared at David and then slowly closed his eyes.

David sprang to his feet as Priscilla took aim again. Scrambling out the door, he heard another shot ring out. Splinters dug into his face as the door frame shattered next to his head. On a dead run, he raced down the hallway toward the elevators. As he approached the corner leading to the dead-ended elevator lobby, another shot exploded in his ear and ripped through the mahogany paneling. *If the elevators aren't open, I'm a dead man.* He couldn't believe his eyes. Four black-jacketed FBI agents leaped from the opening elevator and four weapons took aim at his chest.

"Freeze!"

David hit the floor. Looking behind him, down the corridor, he saw Priscilla pop into view and prepare to fire. She didn't seem to notice the agents until it was too late.

"You cockroach," she screamed.

She finally spotted the armed agents taking aim, and her jaw dropped, but still she targeted David and closed her eyes, anticipating the blast from her gun. The deafening roar of four Glocks firing in unison just above his head ripped through his ears. He felt the ejected shells pepper his back.

Priscilla recoiled like a bloody rag doll and landed on her back as all four bullets hit center mass. The agents advanced, checked her body and headed down the hallway. Two other agents stepped out of the second elevator, and David felt himself being cuffed. He let out a deep breath and dropped his head on the floor.

It was over. Priscilla was dead, and the FBI and the board had the evidence needed to clear him.

He was pulled to his feet and escorted to the first-floor lobby. Police, FBI agents and paramedics scrambled around in organized chaos. With his hands cuffed behind him, David was led to a circle of five men standing around the reception desk. A tall potbellied man with gray hair held a radio and gave orders.

"David."

He heard Tori's voice echo across the ebony polished floor. He struggled to turn, but the agents pushed him forward to the man apparently in charge. He lowered the radio from his ear and scowled at David.

"You're a hard man to find. You cost me a lot of sleep."

*Did they get the broadcast? Did something go wrong? Am I being led away a murderer?*

David felt the sweat begin to drip from his face.

"Uncuff him."

The agents gave the man a puzzled look.

"Uncuff him. He's not the killer. She's upstairs, dead."

The man smiled, and David felt the cuffs snap off. He pivoted and weaved through the crowded lobby to Tori as she stood on her tip-toes and tracked him with her eyes. She met him halfway, and they embraced. He never wanted anything more than this moment. Tori buried her head in his shoulder. He stroked her hair.

"We did it," David whispered. "We made it. It's okay, it's okay now."

David held her and didn't want to let her go, ever. They'd done it. She'd gotten the cavalry here just in time, and now they'd have each other for the rest of their lives. They'd saved more than each other's lives; they'd saved each other's hearts and souls. Priscilla and Prescott were dead, the result of genetic imperfections science had not yet, and might never, be able to control: greed and jealousy. The last remaining imperfection was in CGT. He'd have his company back, and he'd send CGT back into the pipeline. Suddenly, Adam Rexsen's purpose became his own. He pulled back and looked into Tori's eyes.

"We're not done yet," he said. "We have one more stop to make."

Tori wiped her eyes and read the look on his face; his eyes held the final clue. As if she'd received a silent message, a determined smile grew across Tori's face. She nodded and took his hand. They both knew who they needed to see.

# CHAPTER 57

IT WAS CHRISTMAS Eve, and David Wellington leaned back on the rail and grinned at the excitement on the ten-year-old's face. At the helm of the fifty-six-foot Manhattan luxury yacht, Amy Carlton pushed the throttle forward and the sleek craft skimmed across the open water. David tugged down on the bill of his cap as his brightly colored Tommy Bahama shirt flapped in the wind. Tori leaned against him and wrapped her arms around him. He saw Amy's eyes glance in his direction, and he nodded, giving approval for more speed. Her high-pitched giggles were drowned out by the deep-throated rumbling of the accelerating engines.

Two months after Priscilla's demise, David and Tori were living a dream. David would easily trade the last two months for the forty-five years he'd lived before. Tori was the love of his life. They'd been together every day. She'd stood at his side as the board unanimously voted to return him to the post of chief executive officer of Rexsen Labs. She'd sat in the mahogany offices of Adam Rexsen's law firm while the executor of Adam Rexsen's estate read the trust documents that named David as the sole heir of the Rexsen fortune. More important, she'd taken him to her parents' ranch in Los Osos, on the central California coast, and introduced him as the man she would wed.

Amy glanced at David again, and he stepped behind her at the helm. Together, they pulled back on the throttle and the boat slowed to a stop just outside Newport Harbor. Joe took the helm and began to guide the boat into the channel that led to the Eagle's Nest Marina.

"That was awesome!" she said as she turned and hugged David. Then she skipped across the deck to Tori and hugged her. "This is the best Christmas vacation ever, Miss Clarke."

David had to agree. They had come together to celebrate Amy's miraculous recovery. Thanks to Tori's discoveries, Rexsen had persuaded the FDA to allow an accelerated development and review of the revised CGT treatment. She'd convinced them it had met both of the special circumstances under which such approval was granted. Under her leadership, the Rexsen team demonstrated that by using their unique combination of nanoscale molecules called detrimers, a virus delivery system, and genetic recombination through base pairing, they could accurately deliver gene patches to every affected cell and repair the cancer-causing genetic imperfections. They were back in the clinical trial phase for CGT. The FDA had agreed to permit CGT to be used under their Investigational New Drug rule, which allows terminal patients facing certain death to receive new treatments before the general marketing is approved, and Amy had met the criteria; none of her physicians had expected her to see Christmas.

Amy's mother, Faith, joined the celebration on deck.

"My three favorite ladies, all in one place—that's the only present I need this year," David said.

Faith Carlton smiled and tears filled her eyes. "I'll never be able to repay you for what you've done for Amy."

"Yeah, thanks for the great medicine," Amy chimed in. "All the bugs are almost gone."

"You're very welcome, young lady." He touched the bill of her ball cap. "What's that I see under that Angels cap?"

"It's kinda cool. My mom says in a month or so my hair will be back completely."

"I'll warn all the fifth-grade boys your heart is already taken," he said.

Amy chuckled. "I can't think of anyone who deserves it more, but it was Miss Clarke's hard work that made it all possible."

The smile on Amy's face healed David's heart. Years ago, he couldn't help his young son, but he'd risked everything, including his life, for CGT, and the payoff stood before him beaming with joy. And there would soon be thousands more just like her. David wished he could meet every one of them. Amy hugged Tori.

"Thanks, Tori, for everything," Faith said.

David walked up to Amy and bent down to look her in the eyes. Amy put her hand on David's shoulder.

"I knew you'd do it ever since we met in the hospital," she said. "I knew you were the miracle man."

"Or maybe you were my miracle. Ever since I met you I've felt special but didn't know why, until now. Maybe we're both right, and like a friend told me, all things happen for His reason. It's just not always obvious."

Amy's eyes grew wide and a tear streamed down her face. David had hit a nerve.

David looked at Faith for help, but she just covered her mouth and stared at him. He returned his attention to Amy.

"What's wrong, honey? I didn't mean to make you sad."

Amy continued to gaze at David in disbelief. Tears were running down both sides of her face now and her lips were shaking. Finally she found the words.

"That's what my daddy said to me when he was in the hospital, just before we said good-bye."

Amy's words ran straight through his heart. David stroked her head.

"David, everything okay?" Tori said, bending down to join them. David didn't hear her question. He was too focused on asking the next question.

"Amy, I've never seen a picture of your father. Do you have one?"

Amy, appearing confused by David's question, wiped her eyes with the back of her hand, slipped the small brown purse from her shoulder and reached inside, never taking her eyes from David's. She pulled out a folded photo and held it up to David's face. The photo was a little creased, but David clearly saw Amy with her arms wrapped around a young man. The Pacific surf pounded in the background. Amy was grinning ear to ear; David recognized her smile, even in a picture taken five or six years ago. The man, dressed in a pair of jams, knelt on one knee, and Amy sat on the other.

"Can you hold it a little closer, Amy?"

Amy carefully guided the photo closer to David. He closed his eyes and smiled, then looked to the heavens. The deep blue eyes, the curly tight-cropped brown hair, and *that smile*—he should have recognized *that smile*. It was the mysterious orderly who visited David after the crash. Amy's father *was* the orderly!

David felt his eyes well with tears as he was overwhelmed with joy. His throat tightened while he forced his words out. "Your dad was a very special man and he loves you very much."

He wrapped both arms around Amy and hugged her. Tori looked at him while Faith stepped closer and smiled.

Tori reached out and softly touched David's arm. "David?"

David felt a wholeness he never knew in his forty-five years on earth. He released Amy, looked her in the eyes and started to laugh as the tears rolled down his cheeks. Unsure of his reaction, she hesitated, studied his face and then started to laugh, too. He stood up and pulled Tori in for a hug. Over her shoulder, he waved Joe and Faith into the celebration. They all hugged, smiling and laughing and enjoying the moment. David Wellington looked to the bright blue sky and thought about Connor, and for the first time he felt him smiling down on him. He finally knew the reason he'd survived. He was indeed the miracle man.

# THE END

If you enjoyed *Genetic Imperfections*, leaving a review will let other readers know how much you loved it and would be greatly appreciated.

To learn more about new books and exclusive content, sign up for my author mailing list and receive *The Sunset Conspiracy* free:

http://stevehadden.com

Keep reading for a riveting excerpt from my thriller, *The Dark Side of Angels* ...

# THE DARK SIDE OF ANGELS

by

Steve Hadden

**TELEMACHUS PRESS**

# CHAPTER 1

KAYLA COVINGTON HAD been here before, but this time she was determined no one would die. She examined the prefilled syringe in its refrigerated case and admired her life's work. Ten years after her twelve-year-old son died, she'd have another chance to regain her family. And this was the key.

She picked up her son's picture from the corner of her desk and let the flood of love and guilt engulf her. She couldn't feel one without the other. But it was a tradeoff she'd always accepted. It had been her decision. One any mother would have made for a chance to save her son. Even if it only gave them a few more months together. If she'd only had this technology back then, things might be different now.

She looked up and scanned the lab through the plate-glass window. After assembling the prefilled syringes for the first human trials, her team had stayed late to celebrate. Dressed in pale blue lab coats, they stood at their workstations in full personal protective equipment among the microscopes, computer stations and sparkling glassware and toasted the most remarkable breakthrough in the history of medicine.

Despite the public's concerns, she knew it would work. The primate trials had gone perfectly and soon the world would have a gene-editing therapy that would save millions and change the destiny of the human species. But this dose was for patient number one. The only person who'd supported her all along. She'd snatch her father from the relentless grip of Parkinson's disease, and maybe, just maybe, her daughter would finally forgive her.

Startled by a thud, she looked up from the case containing the syringe. Then the window to the lab exploded. Glass shards sliced into her face and the blast slammed her into the wall behind her. When she awoke, her skin felt on fire. Her ears rang and throbbed with pain. She wanted to rip them from her head. She thought her eyes were open, but she saw nothing but bright white light. The smell of tar mixed with the thick blanket of burning aromatics choked her. She pressed to a seated position and her sight returned slowly, as if she were peering through an evaporating fog.

Then she spotted them. They looked like aliens, with elongated snouts and large round eyes, roaming through the smoke and flames. She started to stand but dropped back to the floor when she saw the automatic rifles and recognized the gas masks and fire suits. The attackers systematically crept through the lab. The first attacker stopped, took aim at one of her team members on the floor and fired once, then grabbed their laptop computer from the debris. The others repeated the process equidistantly spread out across the flaming lab. An acidic bomb exploded in her stomach when she realized they were exterminating her crippled team.

She searched for her desk phone and found the shattered device against the back wall. She lunged for handset, pressed the talk button, and put it to her ear. Nothing. Tossing it aside, she glanced back toward the attackers who were still executing the last of her team. Catalyzed by the need to stop them and the panic detonating in her body, she stood and yelled, "Leave them alone! I'm right here!" Now the killers all headed directly for her.

Knowing they'd be on her in seconds, she forced her rebooting body to respond and scrambled onto her hands and knees, sweeping the floor ahead with both hands. Fighting off the numbing shock, she implored her stunned limbs to work faster as she searched under the debris for the only remaining scrap of her life's work. As the curtain of thick, acrid smoke filled her office, her right hand hit something, and she skittered her fingers atop the syringe. It felt intact. She snatched it up. While she crawled toward the shattered window leading outside, she moved her left hand back and forth along the floor hoping to snag her backpack, which held her phone and wallet. Her pinky hooked the strap and she shrugged it onto her shoulder.

Squatting behind her desk, she checked the lab one last time. The smoke screened her view and burned her eyes. She listened for her team, but all she heard was breaking glass and the growl of the fire. She sprang up and leapt through the shattered window.

She hit the gravel hard but kept her grip on the syringe. She picked herself up and sprinted away from the building. Her mind raced. *Who were these people? Why were they killing her team and destroying her work? When would help arrive?*

Cover around the building was sparse, other than the late January darkness, so she dashed around the side of the building and across the parking lot. They'd spot her quickly and have a clear shot. She expected a bullet to pierce her skull at any moment. She checked over her shoulder and saw the smoke billowing out of the broken windows of the lab.

As she neared Torrey Pines Drive, she glanced back again and saw two figures facing the front entrance of the building. When she read the yellow letters on their jackets, she skidded to a stop behind the trunk of a thick eucalyptus tree. *FBI. Were they responding?* They turned and targeted her with their rifles.

As she caught her breath, her body vibrated with terror and disbelief. She'd battled the government to get the trial approved and tolerated their restrictions and security requirements, but she'd complied. Now they were trying to kill her.

The crack of two slugs hitting the tree trunk jolted her. She ducked and bolted across the empty northbound lanes and hurdled the guardrail in the median. Another shot rang out against the guardrail. She realized she'd never heard the rifles fire. Just like the killers inside the lab, they were using suppressors. She wanted to look back but she didn't have time.

Ahead, she saw the dim security lights on the corner of the maintenance building for Torrey Pines Golf Course. Stuffing the syringe into her front pants pocket, she jumped and clung to the chain-link fence. She scrambled over it, but her backpack snagged on the rough ends atop the fence and pinned her body against it. Another shot buzzed past her head and she could see the two FBI agents advancing, still targeting her with their rifles.

She yanked herself out of the straps of the pack just as a pair of headlights appeared in the southbound lanes. She heard sirens in the distance and raced around the corner of the building.

In an instant, Kayla was into the thick darkness of the golf course. Guided by the feel of concrete under her feet, she followed the cart path until it ended. Then she entered the prickly brush marking the start of Torrey Pines State Reserve. The din of the city had faded, and she could hear the ocean clawing against the shoreline. The smell of coastal sagebrush was strong, and she stopped and listened.

Other than the noise from a passing car, she heard nothing. They'd either given up due to the first responders' arrival or they were far better at concealment than she was. She worked her way down the arroyo to the shoreline cliff and sat on a sandstone rock at its edge. Her heart raced as she caught her breath. The pain began to rise. Her entire body ached, and her face burned from the cuts.

Her thoughts began to emerge from the fog of panic. She had to get somewhere safe. But with the authorities possibly involved, she'd have to rely on someone she could trust. The attackers clearly wanted her dead. And something inside said they wouldn't give up easily.

THE DARK SIDE OF ANGELS 259

With no money and no phone, her options were limited. While it was usually called out as a liability, she thanked God for her obsession with staying in shape. Tonight, it had saved her life. But only for tonight. She needed a plan, and that plan would require a five-mile run and the mercy of someone she'd shown little mercy the last time they'd been together.

Her lab had been destroyed and all the other prefilled syringes that contained the synthetic vectors outfitted with CRISPR components had been stolen. The genetic instructions they carried unlocked the secret of *Turritopsis*, the only immortal animal in the world, and translated it to work in the human genome. The prefilled syringes that stopped the process before it went too far were gone as well.

She pulled the syringe from her jeans. It was the last sample on Earth, and it wouldn't last the night without refrigeration. Her life's work would be lost, along with the only chance to regain her family.

As she looked out across the ocean glimmering in the moonlight and thought about the millions of people her work would save, she knew what she had to do. She pulled down her jeans and uncovered the needle. Stretching the flesh taut on her thigh, she pressed the needle into it and pushed the plunger. She felt the sting and watched the syringe empty. The Cas9 protein and the guide RNA entered her bloodstream, and soon the CRISPR process would cut out sections of her DNA and paste the modified DNA letters in exactly the right order. The process she'd called RGR—rapid genetic reversal—would begin, and her body would grow younger.

Her cells would store the genetic code—but without the injection that stopped the process, she'd die in less than a week. To survive, she had to stop the process now operating in every cell in her body.

She looked back up the hill into the darkness and saw no indication they were coming for her. She almost wished they were. She'd been so close, and now her path seemed hopeless. Death, not her redemption, had come—and two words echoed in her head.

*Not again.*

# CHAPTER 2

NEVILLE LEWIS KNEW in his heart these killings would help him. He hated that part of himself. He absorbed the warmth of his five-year-old son, Darrin, asleep against his side, as if the boy were recharging his soul with innocence. He knew he'd need it.

His eyes scoured every word of the breaking news as it appeared on the crawler on the muted flat-screen TV. *An explosion has destroyed a building just outside San Diego.* The unedited film from the scene looked horrific. Fire crews poured water into the flaming building and police cars and ambulances hovered around the perimeter. Empty stretchers were slowly placed into the waiting ambulances whose drivers were in no hurry to leave. *Many unconfirmed casualties feared.*

The collateral damage was far worse than he'd hoped. But he'd done the calculation and the loss of life was worth it. There would probably be more, but eventually they'd all be revered as heroes by generations to come. Still, this act went against everything he'd stood for. He'd saved lives, millions of them. His foundation was one of the most successful philanthropic organizations in the world. He'd battled malaria, HIV, cholera and starvation. He'd delivered clean water to more people than the largest utilities in the country. His goal was to be counted among the world greatest philanthropists, like Carnegie,

Mellon and Gates. But now, one of the world's greatest philanthropists had embraced killing for the greater good.

Darrin snuggled closer and Neville shielded him from the truth with his hug. Neville heard his wife's footfalls from the darkness of their expansive kitchen. Without looking away from the TV, he felt around the soft sofa for the remote and changed the channel.

Lying to Charlotte was never an option. Her short, thick brown hair was tousled, and her eyes foretold that her own bedtime was imminent. Her appearance was the result of her nighttime ritual for Penelope: pajamas, toothbrushing and bedtime story, softly told while sharing a pillow with her Merrythought teddy bear, Chester.

Charlotte stopped between Neville and the TV. "You ready for me to take him up?"

"You mind?"

Charlotte leaned in and extended both hands. "Not at all. I've been reviewing the team's work on the robotic application of SZENSOR. We're close, but I'm wiped out. I'll take Darrin to bed with me."

SZENSOR had made them rich beyond all definition of the word through an exclusive deal with the US government that kept the technology out of the hands of the public and in the hands of the US intelligence agencies. It was also the reason he never lied to Charlotte. The technology used behavioral biomarkers to read people's minds. Minute shifts in facial muscles, changes in tone and word choice, length of smiles or frowns and fluctuations in the eyes all gave away humans' closest secrets. It was more accurate than a lie detector but still considered inadmissible in court. Offshoots of the technology were available in hundreds of other applications, ranging from attraction ratings in dating apps to helping robots assess humans' dispositions.

She was the behavioral scientist who'd helped him design the algorithms. They'd met after a lecture he'd given on the UW campus.

She was a smart and attractive Chinese American professor there. Her mother and father were from Beijing but had homes in Seattle and Vancouver. Her father ran an import/export business with offices in Seattle, Vancouver and Shanghai. Neville was immediately smitten. They were married the same year.

Neville scooped up Darrin. He swore he weighed twice as much when he was asleep. He slipped Darrin into her arms and she cradled him against her body with his head draped over her shoulder.

"See you up there." Charlotte shuffled quietly across the cherrywood floor to the staircase and disappeared into the shadows.

He turned off the TV and walked down the long hallway and across the covered footbridge to his office. He stood at the floor-to-ceiling windows, looking across Lake Sammamish toward Mount Baker. From a thousand feet above the lake, the reflected light danced on the water like fireflies. A knock on the door leading to the private entrance to his office interrupted his momentary meditation.

Max Wagner, head of his security team, entered. "I have some information."

"Okay. But we have to be careful. I don't want to know the details."

Wagner's silence and raised thick eyebrows said otherwise. Neville suspected it was a tactic he'd learned working in the intelligence community. He'd been with Neville since the second venture round, when Neville's net worth surpassed the one-billion-dollar mark. Recommended by one of the venture capitalists, his résumé was short: thirty years with the Central Intelligence Agency. Nothing else. But judgment and discretion were paramount for Neville.

Neville had to *ask* for more details since they'd both previously agreed on maintaining Neville's plausible deniability in all sensitive matters due to SZENSOR. "What is it?"

"They missed her."

"What? How in the hell could that happen? It looks like they blew up the building and killed everyone inside."

Wagner deadpanned. "She got out through a window."

"If she's still out there, she can make it again."

Wagner narrowed his eyes on Neville. "The word I get is that the FBI had an agent in there. She'll be gone by tomorrow."

"You're pretty certain." Neville knew that the longer Kayla Covington was out there, the greater the risk that she'd re-create this threat to mankind. "Did you at least get the new data?"

"Got all of it yesterday. On the lab computers, in the cloud, all of it."

"When will we have it?"

"Soon."

"Let me know as soon as it's secured."

Wagner nodded in agreement and moved back to the door.

"Hang on," Neville said. "You and I need to talk about the problem in Equatorial Guinea."

"Now?"

Neville just waited for Wagner to catch up.

"Right. We can't lie to her," Wagner said.

They headed to the side chairs overlooking the Cascades and talked about the logistics and security problems with the new water system going in at Malabo. Then Wagner left Neville alone.

Neville walked to the hand-carved mantel above the fireplace across from the windows. He gently placed his hand against the side of the gold urn. He turned and walked to the doorway to the footbridge. As he turned off the light, he softly said, "Good night, Mother."

If you enjoyed the excerpt, you can buy your copy of *The Dark Side of Angels* here:

http://stevehadden.com

# About the Author

Steve Hadden is the author of *The Sunset Conspiracy*, *Genetic Imperfections*, *The Swimming Monkeys Trilogy*, *The Victim of the System* and *The Dark Side of Angels*. Steve believes powerful thrillers lie at the intersection of intriguing stories and intelligent characters in search of dramatic revelations with global human impact. Visit his website at http://www.stevehadden.com